The Breedling & the Shepherdess

The Element Odysseys: Book Three

BY

Kimberlee Ann Bastian

WISE Ink
CREATIVE • PUBLISHING

ISBN 13: 978-1-63489-218-6

First Printing: 2019

Cover and interior design by Steven Meyer-Rassow.

Wise Ink Creative Publishing
807 Broadway St. NE, Suite 46
Minneapolis, MN 55413
www.wiseink.com

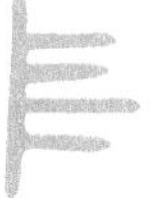

Coyote's Debt

Eden: Midwest, 1934

The coyote watched from a distance as the young man traveled across the dusty field toward a small grove of trees. It kept its distance, crouched low to the ground, pale yellow eyes transfixed by its prey. Studying the uncertainty in the young man's stride, the coyote was surprised his legs were even able to carry his weight, but even more surprised by the increasing lightness of his footfalls. The young man carried a rifle at his side, his posture ready to surrender, but jaded instinct told the coyote it was merely sorrow's mask—that given the right situation, the mortal would not hesitate to defend himself.

"Is this what you brought me here to see?" asked the coyote finally.

"It is," replied the tabby cat, sitting on the coyote's left.

The coyote snorted and turned away to sniff the air as though bored. It gingerly stood as the young man passed into the seclusion of the trees.

"Wait!" objected the tabby cat as it maneuvered in front of the coyote, halting its escape.

"Get out of my way, Euxian," growled the coyote as it leaped over the feline and took off across the field, toward the remnants of an abandoned shed. It kept its gait swift in order to outrun the tabby, but to its disappointment, the pink-eyed feline was already waiting on the single windowsill of the dilapidated structure, twitching its whiskers.

"I see your skills are as keen as ever, Master Chameleon," grumbled the coyote.

The tabby cat bowed slightly in acknowledgment of the praise but did not waste a moment to gloat.

"Oh, spare me your chivalry, Euxian," the coyote barked.

"As you wish, Prin . . ."

"Bite your tongue, spy!" the coyote snapped and lifted its head high, perking its ears. It waited, listening for the slightest whisper, then sniffed the air for the scent of an enemy. When neither produced a hint of concern, the coyote looked up at the cat and crinkled its nose. "I do not need my name on the back of the wind, Master Chameleon, nor do I need your utter folly revealing my secret."

"Many pardons, Master Walker." The tabby cat bowed apologetically. "But if I may, it is a secret that will not last."

The coyote appreciated neither the Euxian's input nor its condescending informal address. So, in response, it sprang into yet another sprint. This time it raced across the barren field to the opposite end, not necessarily to outrun the Fates' spy, but to test the feline—if the Euxian was serious about gaining its assistance, then a game of chase would hardly deter the creature.

The coyote came upon the wired fence post and sat panting in the corner of the plotted field under the protection of a single cottonwood. The tree's shade was cool, even with the lack of wind, and at the base of its trunk, rare moisture rested on blades of grass. The coyote idled a moment to catch its breath, its eyes scanning for the red tint of the tabby's fur. There was no sign of the cat in any direction, but though the coyote was certain of this, it could smell the feline. It lifted its nose, detecting a scent overhead.

"Are you truly willing to chase me to the ends of the earth?" The coyote looked over its shoulder, its eyes climbing the tree to the low-hanging branch.

The tabby cat narrowed its eyes and batted its tail. It clawed at the tree, inching its paws forward, dragging its belly along the bark.

"You try my patience, Master Chameleon."

"Your emotion is not lost on me, Child of Sea," remarked the tabby cat. "But as a creature with nothing but time on its hands, you will hear me out." Batting its tail, it continued. "And to answer your question, yes; yes, I would follow you to the ends of Eden and back, but as this is a matter of urgency, I will simply remind you of your debt."

The coyote sprang on its hind legs and reached for the low branch. It missed by an inch or so, its claws barely tagging the bark. It began to pace below the tabby, waiting for an opportune moment to catch the feline off guard.

"The years of isolation have not been kind to you, my friend," sympathized the cat.

The coyote whined. "I be no friend of yours, Euxian."

"As you say, brother."

"I do, now leave me be."

"If only, Master Walker—but my sender has asked me to relay a message and remind you of your debt. Saving your kindred Sweetwater was not something the Apothecary had to do, nor should he have meddled in the affairs of the Children of the Sea, but out of respect, he saved what is left of your court. With gracious heart you swore to serve should the need ever arise. I am honor bound to summon you into such action."

"Then speak quickly, spy," grumbled the coyote, sitting back on its hind legs. "I will hear your words but will promise nothing."

"Then listen with care, for the rumors are true. Bartholomew, the Fates' most beloved Breedling, has broken his chains of obedience and fallen from the grace of Euxinus. His escape has created something unforeseen, an enigma. The mortal who walks within those trees is the reason why I am here."

"Well, you can tell the Apothecary, I want nothing to do with the Son of Clay. He may ask of me anything else and I shall pay it gladly without complaint."

"Be that as it may, Master Charles . . ."

"Master?" said the coyote, flattening its ears. "Master Chameleon, no mortal claims such distinction in Eden."

The tabby cat's eyes gleamed with a smile. "While your words were once true, now they are as false as Hades' claim to sovereignty over Eden."

"Do not speak of the Scarlet Phoenix," snapped the coyote, the fur on its back bristling with anger.

"It is an inevitable evil, Master Walker," said the tabby, "for it is because of Hades the Apothecary has called you into service."

"And if I refuse?"

"You have no choice, Son of Sea. You forfeited that right with your promise."

"Mind your words, Euxian. I am beholden to no creature."

"No, you merely wander without purpose alone with your anger and regret," challenged the Chameleon. "Your Creator . . ."

"My Creator is dead!" cried the coyote. "Mortals destroyed what remained of the Black Tortoise. He is gone because of them, because he thought he could stop his siblings from stealing their souls, but with his limited strength all he could manage was to deter them for seven years until there was nothing left of his divinity."

"Surely you cannot believe that, Master Walker? You must still possess some hope?"

"My hope died long ago, and with it my father's mandate to protect the mortals of this realm," said the coyote, and shied its head away shamefully, catching a glimpse of the clump of trees on the horizon.

The tabby cat jumped out of the tree, landing next to the coyote's front paws. It sat regally on its hind legs. "For your ears alone," said the Chameleon. "The Apothecary knows of your plight, Coyote Moon." It paused for a moment; when the coyote did not respond, it continued. "Ever since the disappearance of the Black Tortoise, the Apothecary set in motion a plot for the return of the Lost Creators. He groomed the Breedling Bartholomew for his fall, and besides him has gathered a power of six to support him in his endeavor. You, Master Walker, are one of those six. You, along with the Fallen Valkyrie angel Lady Vala and four others, whose identities I cannot unveil, will at some point come together and restore the Lost Creators."

"Do not toy with me," snarled the coyote, pulling itself out of its moment of melancholy. "We cannot restore what is lost."

"But you can restore what is found," challenged the Chameleon.

"Your tongue speaks nonsense, Euxian."

"Well then, I say this unto you, Master Walker. At this very moment, the Breedling Bartholomew is on his way to Euxinus with the fabled Eden Wanderer, who will stand as witness for the Shepherdess, who, as rumor has it, knows the whereabouts of one of the Lost Creators."

The coyote pulled into an intimidating crouch, at the ready to attack the tabby cat. Its yellow eyes stared into the feline's pink spheres, searching for the lie.

"What you wish to be false you will not find," said the Chameleon. "What I have said is the truth. Eden's Rule of Seven has been decided, and you are a part of it, no matter how much you choose to deny it."

"And the mortal?" asked the coyote, not letting up on its stance.

"A piece of eight."

The coyote rose immediately, dumbfounded by the Chameleon's words, and took a step back as though the creature had landed a powerful blow. Turning its gaze toward the cluster of trees, it honed its senses, judging the strength of the mortal's aura. At first, it felt merely the meager pulse of a typical mortal, but as the wind swept across the open field, it rustled the energy in the air, revealing something with far greater potential.

"The energy you sense is the untapped reserve residing in Master Charles," said the Chameleon. "It is not yet consistent because the mortal is still holding onto the veil, refusing to acknowledge what he has seen."

"And what has he seen?"

"Enough," the Chameleon replied. "When Bartholomew died, he emerged here in Eden amongst the flames of an orphanage. Too weak to save himself, it was Charles Reese who rescued the Breedling from the inferno, and in doing so forged an unprecedented bond between them. At first, we thought it only temporary; however, our oversight proved Charles Reese to be much more. The mortal showed his mettle against Hades, beating the fiery deity at his own game, and though he was the true victor, he did not leave the confrontation unscathed. He now bears the mark of the Scarlet Phoenix. The important thing to consider, Master Walker, is the bond. For with his words Charles Reese can command the Breedling, asserting himself as Bartholomew's new master."

"And what is it the Apothecary wishes of me?" asked the coyote, trying not to acknowledge the newfound spark of hope buried deep within its heart.

"Your charge is to protect Master Charles from the agents of Hades and the watchful eyes of Heaven."

"Protect?" The coyote refocused on the trees and sniffed. Despair—despair and death were what lingered most. "What is there to protect? The mortal seeks a place to die."

"It saddens me to hear this, Master Walker, for the Apothecary thought you, most of all, would be able to sympathize with the mortal."

"Do not speak of things you do not understand, Master Chameleon."

"As you wish, but my utterance remains the same, though I do not possess the feeling to express it. And regardless, the charge stands." The tabby cat stood on all fours before continuing. "Go with caution, Coyote Moon, for it is unknown what abilities, if any, Master Charles may manifest. Use your healing waters to tame the curse of the Scarlet Phoenix; your wisdom to keep him balanced. Preserve the veil as long as you are able, and when it becomes a hindrance, encourage him to lift it. Protect the mortal at all costs, even if you have to protect him from himself."

The coyote's eyes glistened in the setting sun as the cat performed one final bow. It watched the feline sprint across the field toward an unknown destination until it was out of sight. It then turned back to the distant trees, its creator's final words burning in its ears.

"I know you do not agree with me, my child. I can see it in your eyes, but also, I can feel it here." The Black Tortoise pressed

against the coyote's heart. "Your concern is commendable, but your anxiety is ill-placed. Do not fear what is to come. All things now must pass with time, even the image of divinity, but upon this I swear to you: I shall return, even if it is not as I am. Be brave, Child of Sea, and carry on without me. Protect the mortals of this enchanted land and be mindful of the threat my siblings pose."

The coyote threw back its head and cried in solemn tribute, its voice casting a chill across the field.

"I shall obey, Father Sea, upon your mercy I swear," it had replied.

"Until we meet again, my son."

"I shall carry the hope of your return with me."

The coyote cried a second time, its mourning wail forcing the sun to retreat further from the sky. For far too long, its broken heart had blamed the mortals for the disappearance of its creator and had let the demon seed of its hatred for them fester. As time had given way to time, the seed grew, suffocating what little hope remained; and when it was gone, the coyote had abandoned its mission.

The coyote cried a third time, its voice cracking in the now painted sky. "Upon this I swear, Father Sea," proclaimed the coyote. "If protecting this mortal is my part to bring about your return, then it is a price I will gladly pay."

Element III: Euxinus

Awake

Jack's breath hitched as a thunderous crash resonated through the darkness with the force of waves colliding against a shoreline. He slowly spun to gauge every direction, looking for the source of the sound, but there was none. As he listened for further sounds, the stale air fell quiet and the only thing he heard was the nervous puffs of his own breath, his fear of inescapable darkness churning in his gut. He considered assembling his turnip lantern, but without knowing what awaited him in the pitch black, he thought better on it. Instead, he allowed his vision to adjust, testing his limited patience. Slowly, a faint hue of blue light appeared, bringing shape to the unknown world.

He stood in the middle of a deserted street as a silhouetted row of buildings appeared. There was a slumbering presence about them, and yet he felt a sense of foreboding; something eerie only the dead would understand. The one directly in front of him had three stories made with polished tourmaline crystal. He panned his gaze to the left, following a seemingly endless row, which reminded him of a particular stretch of terrace houses along Forty-Third Street in Chicago's Irish neighborhood of Canaryville—although, in this case, the structures were not the same height. Instead, the buildings appeared to ascend from one to ten before repeating the pattern. Nowhere along the quiet street was there any sign of life—upon this realization, Jack scanned for Buck.

"Buck," he said into the darkness, his voice barely above a whisper. He turned around to inspect the other side of the street but found no sign of the Breedling. Instead, he noticed a faint light ahead.

It came from an open door. Oddly enough, as he walked toward it, Jack noticed all the doors were open. He stood in the spotlight of the glow just outside the single-story building as the heavy smell of sulfur began to wreak havoc on his sinuses. He pinched his nose quickly to stifle a sneeze—he did not want whatever was on the other side to know he was present until he was ready to reveal himself.

"Are you all right, love?" came the worried sound of a strong feminine voice.

Pressing his shoulder against the doorframe, Jack positioned himself to eavesdrop.

"I am not sure," replied another female voice, her tone a little more fragile—or was it just lighter, stressed maybe? It was hard for Jack to decide. "I . . . I feel strange."

"It means he is here," replied the stronger voice.

"You are certain?"

When Jack did not hear a response, he inched his face around the doorframe to catch a glimpse of who was inside. He took a quick breath as he peered inside and found a woman standing in the candlelit room. Or at least what appeared to be a woman.

She was scantily dressed with braided leather sandals on her feet. Wrappings covered her bust and hips, leaving the rest of her dark skin exposed, though it practically blended in with the black, lava stone walls of the room. It gave her appearance a certain amount of camouflage, although the unnatural fluorescent blue hues of her bushy, curled hair made her stand out. She was staring at something Jack could not quite make out. Curious of the other voice, he peered further around the corner, but there was no one else present.

"Do you think he will come here?" asked the woman.

"Stingy Jack will not be able to resist," came the other voice. "Power calls to power, and being a Child of Sea, he will be drawn to me."

At the mention of his name, Jack stepped through the door. He did not appreciate being talked about as though his actions were not his own. And yet, once inside the rectangular-shaped room, it became apparent he was like a moth to flame.

"Who calls me by name as though ye know me?" Jack spoke, expecting the woman to give a prompt response. Instead, she remained still, her muscles tensing.

Jack felt an odd level of foreboding spread through the room. He kept his distance, trusting there was enough space between them to be able to outmaneuver any of her defenses. Shuffling his feet, he tried to get a better look at her face, but in doing so, his movements exposed him to an attack.

Before Jack knew what was happening, he was flat on his back with the wind locked in his chest and a large dagger pressed at his throat.

"How did you get in here, Son of Clay?" demanded the woman, the fragile tone in her voice replaced with ferocity. She pressed her blade harshly against his skin.

"Son of Clay?"

"You announced yourself as the one who claims the name Stingy Jack, did you not?"

"Well, I . . ."

"Then you are a Son of Clay. Mortal males are known by such distinction in Euxinus," explained the woman. "Now, answer me, Stingy Jack. How did you get in here? Do you not have any courtesy to knock before entering a residence?"

"The door was open," said Jack as he stared at her, his eyes captured by the intensity of her gaze.

The woman turned her head. Her expression changed in an instant, a sense of bewilderment taking hold of her. She swiftly stepped out of her power stance over him and ran out the door.

Jack gasped and reached for his neck to check for blood. His flesh felt clammy, but it appeared the woman had not broken the skin. After a few more breaths, he lifted himself and noticed the rug roped around his feet. He untangled himself, while at the same time admiring the ancient weave—Moroccan, if he was correct. Jack gained his feet, prepared to venture back to the street and resume his search for Buck, but the woman returned in a flustered fury.

"What have you done?" she shouted at him.

Jack blinked, somewhat at a loss for words.

"Do not make me ask you again."

"I . . . I don't know what ye are talking about," said Jack, resisting the urge to step back. He did not want to corner himself in the room.

The woman marched toward him and grabbed the collar of his tattered coat. She dragged him out of the building and into the street to a sight he was unprepared to see.

Jack squinted against the brightness of torchlight now illuminating the once dark street. Tall lampposts with caged balls of scarlet flame danced joyfully, happy to be awake. The street itself was flooded with a mass of creatures the likes of which Jack had never seen. There were giants as tall as the ten-story buildings, behemoths, dragons, packs of great wolves and a strange creature he could not name, only describe. It had the body of a horse, the head of a stag with a single horn on its forehead, the feet of an elephant and the tail of a wild boar. Jack had heard of such a creature from a story long ago—a monocero, if memory served. It was as though a circus had suddenly released all the animals from their cages, except in this case, these creatures merely stood at a loss.

Amongst these large beasts, there were clusters of children gathered together, their voices buzzing with confusion. They looked to be about the same age as Buck, and a part of Jack's brain wondered if they were more of the Breedling's kin.

Jack's mouth gaped open in awe at the wonderment before him. He took a step forward, his curiosity nudging him to interact with the creatures, but he felt another tug on his collar. Within a few seconds, he was back inside the rectangular room and released with a forceful toss. He stumbled over his feet, nearly losing this balance, but managed to right himself.

"Explain yourself," said the woman.

"Me?" said Jack defensively. "What about ye? What gives ye the right to . . ."

"You are Stingy Jack, are you not?" asked the woman.

"Yes."

"The famed Eden Wanderer said to be blessed by Earth and Sea?"

"Wait, what?"

There was a growl of frustration as Jack once again found himself flat on his back with a dagger against his throat.

"Listen," he said. "I don't know who ye are, or what ye want from me, but all I want to do is find Buck."

"Who?"

"It is the name Bartholomew was given by his mortal master, Charles Reese," came the return of the disembodied feminine voice.

Jack rolled his eyes about the room to see if he could find the voice's owner, but like before, he and the woman were the only two in the room. His gaze drifted back to her face before dropping down to his chest. The blade was dangerously close to his skin, and out of the corner of his eye, he saw her hand shaking. Was she nervous? Jack lifted an eyebrow, intrigued by the sudden insecurity. He was not sure if it was wise to unleash the Trickster with such an impending threat, but better try than risk a slit throat. Such an injury would take a great deal of time to heal, and remembering what Buck had said, there was not much time before Iona's trial. Curling his lips, Jack relinquished his control.

"Come on, doll, there is no need for such dramatics," he said. "We can do this without the blade to the throat."

"Do not listen to him," came the disembodied voice. "His words drip with venom."

"But they sound so sweet," said the woman, the tremor in her hand increasing. "Something is wrong. I . . .."

"It's all right, kitten," said Jack, the Trickster teasing his words. "Just put down the blade and . . ."

In response, the woman pressed the blade roughly against his skin.

Jack's Adam's apple bobbed. "Honestly, love, this is not necessary."

"Hold your tongue, Trickster," said the woman. "Now tell me, how did you open all the doors?"

"The doors were open when I arrived."

"Liar," said the woman, leaning forward, but she stopped

short. Her expression distorted. She took a deep breath, falling back slightly, the blade coming with her.

Jack seized the moment and grabbed the woman's dagger hand, his other hand taking hold of the blade. He thought it would be easier to subdue her, but her strength was surprisingly Amazonian. Her hand was still shaking, even more so now that he was holding her. He slid his hand down to her wrist to get a better purchase. In doing so, a kinetic spark passed between their skins, instantly stopping the tremor. Jack heard the woman's breath catch. Her dark pupils dilated, the whites of her eyes glistening. There was a moment of panic on her face. Jack tried to push her off, but the subtle moment made her snap.

The woman wrenched her hand away, the dagger slicing Jack's hand. He let out an uncomfortable groan, pain burning at the onslaught. Slithering on his back, he pushed his body along the floor with his shoulders and heels. He curled his fingers into his palm, pressing his arm against his chest.

"Jack!"

Jack's ears rang, the sound of Buck's voice calling him from somewhere outside. He wanted to respond, but the woman, who was now breathing heavily, palms and knees pressed into the floor, released a terrifying wail.

It was louder than any siren he had ever heard, its intensity heightened by the reverberation of the sound waves bouncing off the stone walls. Jack covered his ears, but it merely muffled the sound. With a curious intensity, he watched as the woman pounded her fists into the floor. It was an image Jack knew all too well—the woman was fighting with herself, something inside her trying to give way. Her tantrum continued, and as it did, Jack watched a fluorescent blue butterfly flutter from the safety of its camouflaged perch within her hair.

"That is enough!" shouted the insect.

It took a moment, but the woman responded to the command of the silvery blue butterfly. She quieted, her cries giving way to labored breaths. Her balled fists sat still on the floor with no signs of superficial injuries, but Jack was certain that underneath that black skin were bruises. The butterfly landed on the woman's hand, its presence completely undoing her. She calmed, steadying her breaths as she sat back against her heels. Her arms dangling, she positioned her hands into her lap; after a moment, she lifted her head.

Jack saw her eyes return to normal, her gaze focused on him. It appeared she wanted to tell him something, but the words seemed to be stuck in her throat, still too exhausted to do much of anything.

"Jack!" came Buck's voice again, this time much closer than before.

"Buck, I'm in here!" he managed, not taking his eyes off the woman.

The woman took a deep breath and with her exhale managed a few words. "Thank you," she said and presented a low bow, pressing her head to the floor.

Jack's face warmed but did not blush. His mouth gaped open, ready to ask the woman what she meant, but Buck stormed in through the door.

"Jack," said Buck as he crossed the room to him. "Jack, where have you been?!"

"I've pretty much been right here, mate," said Jack, a tad annoyed. He did not care for the scolding tone in the Breedling's voice. "I walked through the scar like ye told me, there was a loud crash and then I was in the street. It was dark, but then I saw a light on in here . . . oh, I don't have to explain myself, I was curious. Where the hell were ye?"

"Looking for you," said Buck, taking hold of him under his arm and helping him to his feet.

"Bartholomew?"

Jack's ears tickled from the soft mew of the woman, having nearly forgotten about her after Buck's entrance. He looked back to the center of the room to find her standing, the butterfly no longer visible. Jack glanced over at Buck—the Breedling still held his arm, his expression stupefied.

"Annaliese?"

Annaliese? The name sounded familiar to him. In the mounting silence, he thought about where he had heard it before.

"It is good to see you," said the woman. "You look well."

"I—" Buck let go of Jack's arm. "Annaliese, it has been . . ."

"Ages, I suspect," the woman said, chuckling.

Jack ripped a strip of cloth from his tattered coat and began to wrap it around his injured hand, before the realization washed over him. "Wait," he blurted, gaining the attention of the other two. "Annaliese . . . you mean the Breedling from your story. The one who tried to stop the Scar of Mankato."

"The same," said Buck with a smile, looking over his shoulder at the Trickster.

There was a brief pause between the three of them, the chattering voices from out in the street growing louder in volume.

"Bartholomew!" shouted the woman anxiously, her eyes suddenly wide. "You have to leave."

"What? Oh, yes," said Bartholomew, his tone slightly cavalier for their current timetable.

"No, you don't understand. The cut . . ."

"Not to worry," interrupted Jack, ignoring the uneasy sensation under his skin. "This, it's just a scratch. I've had much worse, believe me. It'll heal rather quickly. Probably won't even leave a scar."

"No, Bartholomew, you must listen . . ." said Annaliese, her voice pinched.

A rising howl cut her short, rolling through the air and dissipating without so much as an echo. And shortly thereafter, the stone beneath their feet began to vibrate with the intensity of a runaway freight train accompanied by the sound of clopping hooves.

"Buck, what's happening?"

"Coymorphs," said Annaliese, hopping straight to her feet and running outside.

"She means the watchdogs, right?" said Jack, as he and Buck followed her, recalling the Breedling's mention of them while they had waited in the confines of the canning truck in Le Sueur.

Together they stood directly in front of the door, staying as far from the pandemonium in the street as they could. The aforementioned creatures Jack had seen just moments ago were running in every direction, their internal instincts finally taking hold. However, Jack did notice one thing rather odd about the change of behavior—none of the creatures were retreating into the buildings. Instead, they ran every other way, all of them disappearing *between* buildings.

"Why don't they just go back inside?" shouted Jack, his voice nearly getting lost in the frantic noise.

"They cannot," shouted Annaliese. "You both saw to that when you arrived."

"Annaliese, what do you mean?" shouted Buck.

"You brought freedom to Euxinus, Bartholomew. Your combined presence has sent a tremor through the street, commanding revolution. It goes against everything the Fates have built here. And for my part . . .” Her voice drifted. “There is no time for that now,” she shouted, twirling the dagger in her hand. She stepped out into the center of the street as the number of creatures began to thin, running away from the stampeding sound of hooves.

“Annaliese!” shouted Buck.

“I’ll hold the creatures off,” she shouted. “Lead the Eden Wanderer to the artery two rows up. It’ll take you straight to the center of the valley.”

“Annaliese!”

“Go now!” she commanded. “The Lady Iona cannot afford for you to be captured and sent to the Reformatory. Run, cousin!”

Jack felt Buck grab his wrist and pull him along into a sprint. He did not object to the urgency but could not help but look back over his shoulder as the clopping hooves came to a halt.

He saw how tiny the woman became in the presence of the mammoth creature. A foul stench of decay struck his nose, which attacked him far worse than the sulfur. The creature cried the eerie scream of a woman once more as it reached for Annaliese, but her swiftness defied the bulky movement of the creature. Jack’s stomach tightened, nervous for her, but it was clear she could hold her own.

As they got farther away, the lampposts began to dim, save for the spotlights around the fight. Jack’s eyes were not ready for the entry into darkness, and he suddenly felt a fever begin to spread through him.

The creature let out another cry, except this time Jack noticed a hint of pain in it—the woman must have made her mark.

He felt Buck change direction, and not familiar with the darkened surroundings, he lost sight of the woman’s battle. He focused on the faint silhouette of Buck’s short frame as they slipped off the street through a thin alley—he was blind as they ran through, letting Buck be his eyes. He felt claustrophobic, but the adrenaline and the fever pumping through him kept this from mounting to a panic attack.

They came out on the other side and quickly crossed another street before sneaking once again through another alley, and then another and then another, until they had managed to pass seven streets. Cries rang out through the air as the sound of hooves vibrated through every street they crossed.

Jack's eyes finally adjusted, the blue light illuminating the shadows. His lungs began to burn, his brow perpetrated with small beads of sweat, and he felt his muscles begin to ache—he needed to stop.

"Buck, how much farther?" he managed through puffed breaths. "Buck."

"Not now, Jack."

"Buck, I need to stop."

"Jack, if we stop, we risk another Coymorph cutting us off from our destination."

"Buck, please," said Jack as his stride became sloppy. "I need . . ."

Jack collapsed in the middle of the next street, forcing Buck into a jolted retreat. The Breedling did not let go of his wrist, rather using his momentum to drag him into the next alley. Once to safety, the Breedling propped Jack up against the wall. "Sorry, mate," he mumbled through his panting breaths.

"Do not apologize, Jack," said Buck. "I should have considered you might need some time to adjust to Euxinus. You may be immortal, but your body still has mortal needs, and I am sure breathing in this sulfur air is taxing."

"Something like that," answered Jack, although he was certain there was something more to his rapidly rising fever. "So talk to me, let me catch me breath. Tell me more about where we are—Annaliese mentioned a valley."

"We are in what is called Cemetery Valley." Buck lowered himself to the ground, sliding his back down the opposite wall. "When you arrived, I'm sure you noticed it was completely dark and the street deserted."

"It wasn't hard to miss," quipped Jack with a chuckle.

"I guess that was probably too obvious." Buck laughed in response. "But Cemetery Valley is as it is because, a long time ago, during the War of Wind and Flame, many of the great warriors, like the ones you saw in the street earlier, deflected their loyalties to Hades or Everlyse, an unforeseen consequence of blessing them with autonomy. To combat this, the Fates created the Coymorphs to topple the uprising of their creations. After the rebellion was contained, the Fates never again gave another of their creations an ounce of free will, and forbade any creature from leaving the confines of their coffins, unless decreed by their authority or summoned by the council. Euxians only elude the roaming watchdogs if they are crafty enough, but even the smartest of us can find ourselves caught within their grasp. I have had a few near misses."

"What do they look like?" asked Jack. He closed his eyes and focused on taking deep breaths while listening attentively to Buck. The Breedling described the watchdogs as half-breeds, which had something to do with disagreements between the Fates. Their appendages and torso were similar to a horse, but their heads resembled a coyote. When they captured violators, they would rise on their hind legs and their front hooves would morph into bearlike paws to give them the tactile ability to grip their victims. Their bright yellow eyes shone intensely in the light of the flames, but the intensity was a ruse, for the creatures were blind.

"Blind?"

"Yes," said Buck. "I cannot really say why—maybe in their arguing the Fates just forgot to give them sight." He shrugged. "It is why the streets are aligned with the lanterns. Coymorphs may not be able to *see*, but they are able to make out shadows in concentrated light. What they lack in sight they make up for in hearing, and despite the overpowering odor of sulfur in the air, they have an impeccable sense of smell."

"So, moral of the story, don't get captured." Jack chuckled again, his breath beginning to even out, though the fever still persisted.

"Truly," agreed Buck. "Although it is not the worst that can happen here. There are many dangers in Euxinus. The inside of a Reformatory cell would make one of your Eden prison cells feel homey."

Jack laughed as he opened his eyes. "Don't kid yourself, Breedling, I've seen the inside of many cells, there is nothing homey about any of them."

The ghost of a smile formed on Buck's face. "Be that as it may, the real threat is the not knowing if you will be paired with a cellmate. The Euxian prison houses the most despicable creatures. I'm sure you could argue your Eden cells host similar threats, but here the most deadly creature is not Euxian."

"Ye made mention of them before, didn't ye?" Jack paused, trying to find the word in his head but not recalling it. "What are they, again?"

"Wickers," said Buck, "the most detestable and damned creatures of any realm; mortal souls cursed with the misfortune of claiming Cain as their direct ancestor. They were once plentiful in Eden, but have since dwindled in numbers, many of them having taken residence in the Reformatory."

Buck's voice trailed off as a chain of cries rang out one by one. Jack started to count, making it to thirty before he gave up. The Breedling rose from his spot and quickly dashed to the opposite end of the alley. Jack watched him, his corporeal figure giving way to shadow the farther away he got. He could make out a mere outline of the Breedling before he came back into full view.

"Can you stand?" he asked, reaching a hand out for him to take.

Jack was not confident he could, but with Buck's help, he managed to get to his feet. Moving, however, was a different story entirely.

"I know this is not ideal and I can see you are exhausted, but we have to keep moving. The Coymorphs have alerted each other, and once they realize we are on the fastest path to the center of the valley, they will cut us off."

"Well, it doesn't seem like this is up for debate," teased Jack, his tongue suddenly sharpening. "By all means, lead the way."

Buck did not move right away, but whatever the Breedling was thinking, he must have considered it better to keep the words to himself. Jack followed him down the alley, once again feeling a slight case of claustrophobia, but knew there was more to it. He felt warmth rising under his skin.

"Is it clear?" he whispered.

"Shhh."

"Buck . . ."

The Breedling ignored him this time and with ample trust darted across the street.

Jack huffed a few quick breaths and ran after him, his peripheral vision catching sight of the approaching scarlet flames. He did his best to keep up, but like Buck had said, he was exhausted and in that exhaustion he began to feel irritable. He managed to follow the Breedling into the cover of the next several alleys, moving swiftly and unchallenged by the Fates' watchdogs. But by the seventh or eighth, a Coymorph blocked their way.

Cemetery Valley

The Coymorph's call debilitated Buck and Jack, forcing them to press the heels of their hands against their ears. The gesture did little to block the sound as the intensity of the vibrations cut into their bones and forced them to the ground in submission. Buck kept his eyes on Jack, noticing the Trickster was having a difficult time. In the full light from the street, the Breedling became aware of the darkening veins on Jack's neck. His head was down, his face distorted, and his mouth gaped in a silent scream. Something was wrong with him, more than just a matter of getting used to the new surroundings. Jack was in pain.

Buck caught sight of the strip of fabric wrapped around Jack's injured hand and wondered if maybe Annaliese had been trying to tell him her blade was poisoned. The thought hit him hard as the Coymorph ceased screaming, only for the void to fill with an answering scream from miles away. The watchdog quickly left, its hooves thundering out of earshot.

Buck lowered his hands, his ears ringing despite his attempt to protect them. Inching closer to Jack, he cautiously placed a hand on his shoulder. Buck could feel the tremor running through him, but he did not flinch. He used what was left of the remaining light to further inspect the coloration of the Trickster's veins; their thickness bulged a dark blue, almost black. It was a familiar sight, but without knowing the poison's origin, there were a few dozen possible causes for this particular side effect, the worst of which the pair could not afford. Buck slid his hand around Jack's neck, the warmth of the Trickster's skin stinging against the cooling sensation of his touch.

Jack sighed deeply, his shoulders rising. After a moment, he leaned his back and head against the building. He had his eyes closed as his lungs worked hard to combat whatever was wreaking havoc internally. Beads of sweat glistened in the dying light crowning his brow. Buck studied his face carefully, making sure none of the dark veins reached his cheeks.

"Buck, I'm so hot," breathed Jack. "I—"

"Maybe its best you keep still, Jack," Buck offered. "We can rest here for a spell. The Coymorph has moved, so we should be in the clear for now."

Jack coughed before making an uncomfortable face. "So much for getting to the center quickly. Blimey, Buck, I haven't felt this warm since . . ." He paused.

Buck gathered that he was trying to remember a time back when he was mortal, but whatever memory he was attempting to reach, it was unattainable at the moment.

"Talk to me, Buck. Distract me. I can't take the silence."

"What do you want me to say?"

"Anything—tell me about the valley."

Buck released Jack, his hand having little effect against the growing warmth of the Trickster's skin. He positioned himself next to his companion, not wanting to chance any distance between them if he had to take more drastic measures, although he was uncertain what he would do if the situation arose. Crossing his legs, he hunched forward just enough for his fingers to reach the ground, drawing on the stone. His strokes left a trail of silver paint as he created a map of the valley. He drew a straight line with a partial triangle on either end; in the center he fashioned a circle, and outwardly drew several line marks on either side. From his peripheral vision, he saw Jack shift, opening his eyes and resting his chin upon his chest.

"Here it is, Jack, Cemetery Valley in all its monotonous splendor," he said, pointing to the partial triangle to his left. "This is Genesis Peak, the true origin of Euxinus. On its top, the Palace of Neutrality, where the Fates reside."

Jack huffed a snort of discontent.

"I share your sentiment. The Fates are far from neutral in their actions, or rather the actions of their creations." He raised his head to give a small smile. "You know the blue hue that shines overhead?"

Jack nodded with a slight wince.

"Well, that comes from the palace. Think of it as the Euxian version of the moon." Buck looked back at his drawing and pointed to the center of the partial triangle. "Beneath the palace, within a labyrinth of dark corridors, is the Reformatory, the Euxian prison. As I have said before, this is the only thing you truly have to fear about this place."

"Besides poison, I suppose. Maybe next time I shouldn't interrupt the lady when she is trying to explain a life-and-death issue," said Jack with a dark chuckle, giving his ailment a name. He leaned back to offset the increasing weight of his head. "Keep going, Buck, tell me more."

"Jack, it is not that important to tell you about these things now," said Buck. He shifted to gain his feet, but Jack grabbed his wrist.

"Give me a few more breaths, mate. I'm sure the unease will pass soon."

Buck bit his lip. He knew they should not linger, but there was no way he could drag Jack across the valley, not in this condition. "All right, Jack, I will tell you a bit more, but just enough to get the lay of the land."

"Fair enough," said Jack. "Tell me about the line."

"That is the Equadria, or the center artery of Euxinus. It runs from Genesis Peak to Hollow Mountain, the only street in Cemetery Valley where the Coymorphs do not patrol. This is why it is imperative we reach it."

"And why Cemetery Valley? I mean, next yer gonna tell me these buildings are coffins." Jack smirked, pleased by his own wit.

"You are not wrong," said Buck. He waited for Jack to say something more, but when he did not, the Breedling cleared his throat and spoke as if reciting from a book. "For it is written in the histories kept by the Tales Teller, that any creature of Euxinus who is not in the service of its masters is as good as dead, for to serve is life. If not in service, no creature has the right to leave the confines of their coffins until such time as they are summoned."

Silence settled between them, with only the sound of Jack's heavy breaths and the roaming pound of hooves thundering all across the valley.

"And what lies atop Hollow Mountain?" spoke Jack, breaking the stillness.

"Squabbles Hollow, the trial chamber."

Jack took a deep breath. "And the heart of the valley?"

Buck hesitated a moment before answering. He began to feel warmth radiating from Jack with all the intensity of fire, and placed his hand once more against the Trickster's skin—his fever getting worse. Hoping to stifle the building heat, he began to mutter the Apothecary's healing spell under his breath.

"Buck . . ." Jack's breath hitched.

Buck felt the cool pulses burst from his palm and was grateful to see them bring Jack some relief, the swelling of his veins dwindling.

"The center, tell me about the center."

"It is home to the oldest Euxian creations, the Coffins of Seven, or the Council of Elders, as they are best known. My former mentor, the Apothecary, is among them. We can find sanctuary in his coffin and he can fix whatever this is."

"That'll be a relief," sighed Jack, his breath steadying. "Although, ye seem to be handy enough with the healing yerself, Breedling."

"Yes, well," said Buck a little flustered. He removed his hand, thankful to see smooth skin. "What I did is more than likely only temporary. The poison will have to be cured on the inside."

"Well, then, we should be going."

Buck got to his feet before assisting Jack from the ground. Upright, the Trickster wobbled on weakened legs and leaned on him and the wall for support. Buck gave him a moment to get his bearings as the last of the street lamps extinguished in the absence of the Coymorph. The cry of the watchdog was far in the distance, as were the others, all searching for the confused Euxian creatures running amok in the valley. Buck had not had time to think about how it all happened, but Annaliese had spoken about their presence here. It made him wonder—was the sensation of freedom the escaped Euxian creatures were experiencing finite? Buck shook away his thoughts, unable to dwell on the idea now. He needed to get Jack to the Apothecary's coffin before he became worse.

Buck cautiously inched to the mouth of the alley and peered around the edge of the coffin into the returned darkness. In the distance, he saw the torches flickering, the Coymorph idling miles away. Buck gazed at the sky, welcoming the haze of blue light. His eyes readjusted to allow him to see better; the path in front of him became clear in the dimness. Turning once more toward Jack, he placed a cool hand over the Trickster's mouth to prevent him from speaking. He pressed his pointer finger to his lips and shook his head. At first he was not sure if Jack could even see him in the dark, but then the Trickster blinked in recognition. Buck removed his hand and started making animated actions in order to convey the plan. This time Jack nodded in compliance.

Tiptoeing back to the mouth of the alley again, Buck peeked around the corner. The Coymorph was still in position. Buck glanced over his shoulder, taking note of Jack's close proximity; his balance still was not fully desirable, but it would have to do.

Buck took one last look up the street and dashed across, making it to the confines of the alley and thrusting his back against the wall. He inspected the street again, then frantically signaled Jack. The Trickster sprang off the balls of his feet with a burst of energy and darted toward him. In his weakened state, however, he ran awkwardly and his hand tangled in his coat, dislodging the silver cross from his pocket. It fell onto the glossy black stone with a serene chime like a droplet falling into a pool of water.

Jack abruptly stopped when he heard the noise. The ring lingered as the sounds of creaking doors began to open along each side of the street.

Buck scanned the immediate vicinity, anticipating several creatures to evacuate their coffins like before, but all remained still, even the Trickster, who appeared momentarily frozen. The Breedling watched Jack turn slowly before heading back to retrieve the cross. Buck peered around the corner to gaze up the street—just as he had feared, the disturbance was enough to alert the Coymorph, its hooves already moving with malicious intent.

The street erupted with a red glow as Jack reached down for the cross. The Trickster did not even get his fingers clasped around it properly before the large shadow of the Coymorph fell over him.

"JACK!"

Buck slapped a hand over his mouth as the Coymorph shot an immediate glance toward the alley. He retreated into the shadows, making sure to stay out of the light. The creature rose on its hind legs, its chestnut coat bristling as its straw-like tail swatted from side to side. Its front hooves morphed into large paws and collected Jack by his neck. The Coymorph hoisted him off the ground, his legs dangling beneath him.

"Buck . . ." The word escaped Jack's lips scarcely in a whisper, the Coymorph's chokehold rendering him helpless. Buck watched him put up a valiant struggle as the air in his lungs dissipated. He saw the discomfort on Jack's face, the sensation no doubt unpleasant. His eyes rolled back into his head.

The Coymorph pulled Jack closer to its gray muzzle and sniffed. It perked its large black-tipped ears and liberated a disgruntled growl, unfamiliar with the scent of its prey. As it breathed in another whiff, Jack's body went limp. Pleased with the submission, the watchdog pivoted on its hind legs and twisted its head toward the alley for one last inspection.

Buck held his breath.

The Coymorph sniffed the stale air and let out a triumphant howl.

Buck covered his ears this time and bit his lip to force back a groan. His teeth dug into the soft flesh of his lip. He tried to remain calm as the blood trickled down his throat, the taste of roots and bark filling his mouth. Buck's eyes watered and his nose twitched. The Coymorph narrowed its limited sight, staring right at him. Buck felt a chill crawl down his spine, fear gripping him.

After a thorough scan, the Coymorph stuffed Jack's ragdoll of a body in its mouth and made its way toward Genesis Peak.

Buck relaxed and hung his head, his eyes staring into his lap. He loosened his teeth from his lower lip and swallowed hard. A large batch of blood mixed with his saliva, and he gagged on the earthy taste, surprised anything could burn worse than the liquor Charlie had forced upon him or even his own vomit. Buck wiped away the blood with the inside of his jacket sleeve, then sucked on his lip to stop the bleeding. He gagged once again from the lingering grit on his tongue, then closed his eyes to help them adjust to the returned darkness. Muffled footfalls reached him, but his ears were still ringing, so he paid little attention to the noise. He pressed his lids tight and then opened them, adjusting to the blue hue filtering around him. He needed to go after Jack, but first he needed to retrieve the cross.

Hauling himself to his feet, Buck entered the street, unafraid of the Coymorph's return, for the creature had its prize. He grabbed the cross, noticing the fissure in the black stone below as if the weight of the sacred relic of Sea had caused the crack. He ran his thumb across the smooth surface as it winked, and oddly enough, it felt heavy in his hands. It was one of only three remaining gifts the Black Tortoise had left before his disappearance, and Buck could not help but wonder how such a divine gift had ended up in the hands of Stingy Jack. Even if he had gotten it from his mother before she died, it was still mysterious enough to wonder how it had come to be in her possession.

"Bartholomew."

Buck lifted his head to find Annaliese standing in front of him. Her physique, as always, blended in with the darkness, her fluorescent hair standing out. He watched the silvery blue butterfly flutter out of her hair and land over the crack in the street. Upon contact, a tremor shook through the ground, forcing Buck to stumble back. The butterfly lifted its wings, lightly touching them together as water began to bubble and pool. Upon contact, the butterfly pulsed with more colors, its wings adding a streak of purple. Water continued to seep, covering the street with a thin sheet of liquid.

Buck was lost in thought, awed by the miracle before him—the physical sight of Sea had been absent from Euxinus since the creation of Breedlings, if not before. The scent of salt water tickled his noise, granting a reprieve from the burning sulfur in the air. His gaze remained fixed on the butterfly as it continued to drink from the elixir, its wings continually changing colors. It was then that he realized the butterfly was no ordinary Animalia, and he followed its movement as it took flight and landed on Annaliese's shoulder.

"Is that . . ."

"This is Zarna," began Annaliese. "She is . . ."

"An Animawalker. How, I mean, were you, are you . . ." He was having a hard time finding the words, unable to comprehend another Breedling working against the Fates.

"If by your mumbling you mean to ask if I am blessed, no, I am not like you, Bartholomew. None of our kin is like you."

"But Annaliese is unique," interjected the butterfly.

"Not now, Zarna," said Annaliese, her tone matching the stern expression on her face.

"But, how . . ."

Annaliese sighed, clearly agitated by the inquiry. "Zarna has been my confidant since my first charge as a Scar Healer. Ever since then, she has not left my side."

"Nor will I," the butterfly interjected once again, its tone holding an enduring sweetness.

"Bartholomew, where is Stingy Jack?" asked Annaliese, shifting the attention from herself and back to the matter at hand.

"The Coymorph took him."

"What?" The woman gripped his arms forcefully, her voice suddenly stressed. "There is little time to waste, then—you must retrieve him immediately and take him to the Apothecary. My blade, it is poisoned with Wicker blood. If you do not get to him, he could . . ."

Buck's eyes widened as her words took hold. What he had hoped not to be true was true. He had so many questions dancing on the tip of his tongue, hungry for some sort of explanation.

"Why is your blade stained with Wicker blood?"

"That is a question that warrants an explanation, but the short end of it is that after your imprisonment, the Fates charged your sister Miriam to retrieve them, and me to be their executioner."

"My sister," said Buck, taken aback.

"Bartholomew, you have been distant from Euxian matters for too long, and you will soon learn things that may upset you or make you second-guess your defiance. What happened to your sister was contingent upon you, but Miriam received punishment because of what she did at your trial. She acted without thought in defense of you, against the natural order, and for that the Fates punished her. But, we cannot discuss this now, you must go. The Eden Wanderer needs you."

"But what about you?" asked Buck, suddenly concerned about her well-being.

"Your worry is only lost on me, cousin." She gave him a soft smile before releasing him. "I shall be fine. Thanks to you and the Eden Wanderer, free will has returned to Euxinus. That is why the coffins opened and the Euxian creatures left them. That is why the stone cries. Granted, you have only brought this gift, and it is another thing for it to actually take hold. Only I have been affected profoundly, because . . ."

"You are unique." Buck gave his cousin a knowing smile, although he was curious to know more about the Scar Healer's story.

Annaliese let out a chuckle.

"Where will you go? Surely, being free, you cannot stay here."

"Stay I will not. There is a charge of my own I must bear, but I do hope to see you again, cousin." Annaliese presented a bow before darting off back into the confines of the dark alley.

Buck watched her until he could no longer see the fluorescence of her hair, before putting the relic in his jacket pocket next to Charlie's harmonica and Maddie's ribbon. As he started to run, his feet splashed through the extended puddle that seemed to have grown the length of the street. He went deep into the darkness, using his tether with Jack to guide him toward Genesis Peak.

From the Library of the Tales Teller

Sentencing

"*Master Breedling, you will be wise to answer the question,*" *boomed the Apothecary. His deep voice resonated up to the domed ceiling of the throne room, the quartz absorbing the vibrations.*

Bartholomew stood like a statue in the center of the palace atrium, though how he was able to was beyond him at this point. His body was exhausted. The paralyzing grasp of the Retrievers still lingered, but also, he ached from what he had witnessed. The smooth lava stone beneath his bare feet was warm and assisted in thawing the chill of the wet Ireland mud still sticking to his skin and the broken hem of his patchwork trousers. It presented little comfort, but comfort all the same.

The stone walls of the palace emitted the cool azure of wind, shining not unlike a blue moon. The brightness stung his eyes, despite the subtle vibrancy of the glow. He kept his head down, eyes on the floor, not willing to look at his mentor standing in front of him on the bottom step before the Fates. Nor could he bear the sight of his masters sitting on their granite thrones. On either side of him, the long shadows of the Retrievers guarded him like a prisoner, none of them realizing what he would shortly become. Behind him, he sensed questioning eyes, the highest members of his kin waiting for him to speak, to report his charge. He tried to reassure them through his thoughts but was unable to reach any of them, his connection to them severed.

"Master Serkan, if you would," said the Apothecary in a commanding voice.

Bartholomew balled his hands and prepared himself for the lash of the Retriever's wing, but it hovered in delay. Something was wrong. The Retrievers never failed to carry out an order.

"Master Apothecary, I do not see . . ." Serkan felt a firm grip steal him away. He looked at his beloved companion, Jardina, and knew she was saving him from making a grave mistake. It was no secret the Retrievers, as well as the other members of the council, had the ability to question the orders given to them, but the dark eyes of his mate warned this was not the time. He turned his head to look at her, her stance shielded by the elastic cloak of her bat-like wings. Chagrin stirred within him, but he knew she was right.

"As the Fates command," he said, bowing as strands of his wavy hair fell around his pale face. Serkan took a step back, and his shadow disappeared from Bartholomew's view. He opened his great wings; their translucent lace shimmered. Standing askew, with delicate precision, he commanded his wing to strike the Breedling's back.

The lash did not break through the fabric of Bartholomew's damp coat, the Retriever holding back his strength. Serkan had no intention of bleeding the Breedling, but he had to tread carefully and make sure the punishment had ample ferocity. He increased the velocity of the strikes.

"Bartholomew, you must scream," whispered Jardina.

Bartholomew distorted his face, but did not scream. He refused to give his masters the satisfaction of his pain. Instead, he stole away his thoughts, protecting his conscious self from the brutality and concentrating on the numbness still present in his body.

"Again," boomed the Apothecary's staff.

Five more sharp lashes followed—before the sixth could strike, Bartholomew fell to his knees.

The Breedlings behind him gasped collectively, but no one dared raise a voice in objection, not that he expected them to interject on his behalf. But in the sudden stillness of the atrium, soft sobs arose. The focus of the palace shifted as the group of Breedlings parted their ranks, distancing themselves from the sorrow amongst them. Their fanning revealed a girl with russet skin and long violet hair. Her fingers gripped the cloth of her gray robe, forcing her knuckles to burn white, and her lavender eyes stared ahead at the unnerving sight, lost in a grief none before had ever had the ability to convey. The Breedlings began to whisper, their voices hushed and nervous, their collective minds uncertain if this Breedling's display was yet another act of defiance.

"Master Breedling," thundered the Apothecary. "The Court of the Fates shall not ask you a fourth time. Did you or did you not discover the whereabouts of the Golden Faun or the Black Tortoise, as you were so charged to do? Did you find the one they call the Eden Wanderer?" The Apothecary's bronze face remained stern for appearance's sake, but inside, he was genuinely concerned for the Breedling. Maybe even a little scared. In all his scheming, he had been unsuccessful in preparing for this moment. He knew Bartholomew would have to break his bonds in order to fulfill the role he had planned for him, but he had not considered the threat it would be to his very existence.

The Apothecary tightened his fingers around his staff. Bartholomew remained hunched over, his ratty hair dripping water on the epicedian tiles. The Apothecary's fear magnified as

Bartholomew maintained his silence. What awful thing could have happened to him? Did he find the Eden Wanderer? Did the creature steal away his voice? Did he discover the Creators? Did they do this to him?

Bartholomew kept still and bit down on his tongue to keep the ripe truth from spilling out of his mouth.

"Master Breedling, if you do not answer, the Fates will sentence you to meet a punishment suited for those who disobey."

"No!" objected the violet-haired girl as she rushed to Bartholomew's side with no regard for reprimand. The Breedlings' whispers increased, her name—Miriam—on their lips.

Miriam's actions caught the whole palace off guard, especially the Retrievers, who, out of astonishment, stepped away from the unprecedented display of affection. She knelt down in front of Bartholomew, the impulse to protect him stronger than any command the Fates had ever given her.

Bartholomew felt a tender hand brush his arm and he lifted his head to meet tear-ridden eyes. He had not expected the sight of his sister. Not like this.

"Please, Bartholomew, tell our masters what you know." Her voice was urgent and pinched, her plea sincere and real.

Bartholomew lifted an unsteady hand to his sister's face, unable to do more than stare at her with pain in his eyes. Her skin felt smooth and radiated with the grace of the Fates. There was something more, however, a piece he could not place but knew it to be for him alone. He brushed his thumb along her cheek, wanting nothing more than to do as she asked, to spare himself the sentence he was about to receive.

He sighed. The secret he now shared with the ill-fated Iona Covington was paramount knowledge to the whereabouts of the Golden Faun. He could not betray her, not even to save himself.

As she burrowed against his touch, Miriam began to cry. "Bartholomew." She held her voice in a whisper to conceal it in the shock around them. "What happened to you?" Keeping her eyes on him, she searched his aura for any signs of poison or a curse. Any explanation as to why he was so unwilling to obey. But none of the usual tells marked him. No scars created by Hades and his demons nor Everlyse and her angels. All Miriam could grasp was that he had changed.

Bartholomew widened his gaze. She had asked the right question, one even he could not answer, at least not in that moment. He struggled to listen for her thoughts and talk to her as they had always done when they wanted to keep prying ears from listening, but he could not reach her. Bartholomew opened his mouth, unsure if he could even speak her name, but before he could, the Retrievers dragged her away.

"No—let me go! Please—Bartholomew!"

His hand fell to the floor, her cry flooding him with foreign emotions he was not equipped to handle. He closed his eyes to hide himself, but it only brought about the presence of phantom rain. He felt it hitting his tired body, his knees drowning in Irish mud. The Shepherdess' voice pleaded with him. Bartholomew balled his fists against his knees. Her voice continued, fragments of her final moments cycling through his head—"I shall gladly take his place . . ."

"Please leave him be . . ." cried Miriam, her voice mixing with Iona's words in his head.

The palace atrium fell silent as Bartholomew lifted his gaze. He expected to see his sister, but instead he saw Iona's hazel eyes pleading with him. The sorrow and distress on her face were so foreign to him, her love stronger than any mortal will. He could feel her small hands grasp his shirt, her body trembling; the air *around them grew thicker with a presence he could not place, even though it was familiar. Her eyes, there was something in her eyes.*

"How could I have let you die?" he mumbled under his breath. His ears began to ring with the eerie pain of Iona's scream.

"Master Breedling," began the Apothecary.

"No, I should not have let you die," Bartholomew mumbled, his focus still warped.

"Dearest Brother, do not say such things—I am right here, your sister is here," said Miriam.

The sound of Miriam's voice pulled him back, the chill and scream lifting from his thoughts. He blinked, the vision of his sister's face coming into view. His face distorted, his muddled thoughts trying to separate Iona and his sister.

"Please, oh benevolent trinity, my brother is unwell," spoke Miriam. "Something is wrong with him, his aura, it . . ."

The thunder of the Apothecary's staff resonated through the atrium.

Bartholomew felt the vibration pulse through him, terror gripping him. Miriam was saying too much, and if she were not careful, the Fates would turn on her. He could not allow her to take any brunt of punishment, for this was his burden. Gathering his strength, he rose to his feet. He looked at the Apothecary, the Retrievers, his sister, and then to the Fates who sat unsettled on their ornate thrones above the height of seven steps.

"What is it you wish to ask?" said Bartholomew, directing his attention directly toward the trinity he called master. He tried to keep his eyes from wandering, but his peripheral vision caught the sight of etched words inscribed in the rounded wall—to his left, obedientia; *to his right,* neutralitatis.

The Fates sprang from their thrones at the Breedling's lack of respect. "Speak of where—where are the Golden Faun and the Black Tortoise? What message did the Eden Wanderer bear?"

The assembly gasped in disbelief at the Fates' reaction. Never before had a Breedling been so belligerent or had the gall to address the Fates so directly, nor had the Fates themselves responded with their own voices.

Bartholomew returned his eyes to the center, not at the Fates, rather above them. The back wall of the palace showed a magnificent mosaic of Euxinus in its infancy: a high, volcanic mountain with slopes of rich earth surrounded by a vast sea and guarded by gusts of wind. For the first time, Bartholomew saw the beauty in the carved strokes as well as his masters' great sin. The evil they had committed. He felt a pinch in his chest, overwhelmed by the sudden realization. He did not have the words to describe it. Lowering his gaze to meet the furious expressions of his masters, he folded his hands in front of him.

"Speak, Breedling!" they shouted, their collective voices shaking the foundation of the palace.

The Apothecary tightened his fingers on his staff, his hope burning in his gut. He had to believe that his words of condemnation would put Bartholomew on his true course, the one he had so masterfully planned. He stood up straighter and lifted his chin, his gray eyes fixed on the Breedling.

"Very well, Master Breedling—as you refuse to speak, you are hereby sentenced to the confines of a Reformatory cell, where you shall remain until time has loosened your tongue."

Bartholomew stood unmoved by his sentence. He stared at his mentor for a moment, unsure of his expression. There was something he was trying to convey—a standing order of some kind—but he did not understand. Bartholomew felt his body tingle at the sudden paralyzing sting of Serkan's grasp. His body went instantly limp.

"*Bartholomew, please, just tell them,*" screamed Miriam, beginning to squirm as the male Retriever escorted him out of the palace. She started to cry, the tears reddening her eyes. She watched as the crowd of Breedlings parted, her brother moving across the floor involuntarily. She searched their faces until she locked eyes with Annaliese, her cousin's expression ghosting a hint of—sympathy? But just as quickly as the emotion crested on the Scar Healer's face, it dissipated.

"*Miriam, you must stop now,*" whispered Jardina, relaxing her hold to give the Breedling some relief. "*There is nothing we can do for him. If you keep this up, the Fates will pass judgment on you.*"

"*I care not,*" replied Miriam with a resounding spark of defiance. She winced instantly against the phantom pain that thrummed through her.

"*You will do better to keep such venom from your tongue, Mistress Breedling.*"

"*I . . .*" Miriam began, cut short by the return of paralysis. She felt her legs weaken under the strain, but did not allow herself to fall and kept watch until her brother was no longer in sight.

Mistress Bitter

Miriam heard the cell door open but did not bother lifting her head to see who was entering. There was a minor sound of something dragging across the floor, before a hefty thud and a yowl from the creature present. It sounded similar to a mountain lion from Eden, but the *Felis Caudaglobosa* was more than just a mere Animalia. The fearsome Euxian creature was one of thousands of its kind that guarded the prisoners of the Reformatory, their instincts and reflexes even sharper than the valley's watchdogs. Often, she heard the pounding noise of their balled-tails as they wandered the dimly lit passageways.

Miriam listened carefully as the ball-tailed cat exited, its voice vocalizing displeasure. The door shut with a forceful slam, the sound pounding in her ears. She tried to muffle the bang with her palms, but the brunt of it had already shaken her eardrums. Groaning from the discomfort, she waited for the vibrations to dissipate.

Silence returned, but the previous emptiness was no more.

It had been some time since she had had to share a cell. Her last fellow occupant had been the Wicker she had retrieved from Eden. It had been one of the most dreadful charges since the Fates had handed down their punishment upon her. The creature had been severely grotesque in its deformation, and its wickedness had far exceeded any of the others previous. It had been so obstinate, strengthened by such a surprising amount of free will that she had had to chain the creature with a special collared leash. Unfortunately, that is what had gotten her into trouble upon her return to Euxinus—the damned creature had caused enough ruckus for a Coymorphs to scoop them up.

Sharing the cell had been the worst of it; the creature's cries were earsplitting, and its venomous negative energy drained her of all happiness—what little she had left. She had grown increasingly weak due to their close proximity, so by the time Annaliese had come to dispatch the Wicker, it was hard for her to even lift her head. But once the creature was gone, she finally had some semblance of peace. Her elder cousin had even offered to fetch the Apothecary or have her Animawalker restore some of her energy, but Miriam had declined the generosity, unable to openly accept it.

Groaning, Miriam pulled her knees into her chest. How badly she wished she could have said yes. *Damn the Fates*, she mouthed. She dared not speak such blasphemous words aloud, not after that time in the palace atrium. If it had not been for the paralyzing hold of Jardina, the pain might have undone her. It still surprised her that she was even able to mouth them. Her grievance was not yet comprehensible in her mind. All she knew was that something in her had changed. She was broken, her heart in pieces since her brother's harsh sentencing. A piece of herself was missing, but she could not put a name to it. She took a deep breath to steady her wild thoughts and finally gave herself a chance to breathe. It helped her relax, still holding up the appearance she was asleep. She had no idea what type of creature the *Felis Caudaglobosa* had left with her, so she remained guarded, centering herself and reaching out for the energy in the room to get a read on her unknown cellmate.

At first, she sensed nothing, which was extremely odd, but when the creature began to stir, a mass of energy emanated from it. The heat wave pressed against her to the point of burning her skin. It was a strong indication that the creature was indeed a subject of Hades, perhaps a lesser demon. It was not entirely unheard of for demons to take residence in the Euxian jail, but once the intensity of the aura waned, Miriam sensed a layer beneath—a mortal one. She shifted slightly in panic, convinced the creature was a Wicker.

"Hello?" announced the creature, its voice expressing its penchant for trickery. "Hello."

Miriam braced herself. There was a click, a spark, and then suddenly light cast back the shadows. The soft glow illuminated the space above her with a small crescent ring before increasing in vibrancy.

"Put it out," she screeched, shocking herself with how dejected her voice sounded. "Please put it out, it hurts."

The light vanished with a sharp snap, allowing the darkness to recapture the confined space.

The glow had hardly hurt, but Miriam's words came from a place of fear, her tired mind second-guessing her ability to read auras. Was it possible the creature in her cell was, in fact, a demon? She could not suffer through another go around with a Wicker. Plus, for a Wicker to have the ability to conjure flame was a torment she would not be able to survive.

As a softer glow appeared, she lifted her eyes, sighed, and slowly shifted her weight. There was no use prolonging a confrontation, not in such tight quarters. After all, she had nowhere to hide. Miriam sat up with her back to the creature and then stood. She brushed her hands along her paper rags, pressing the cloth against her skin. She combed her fingers through her lengthy hair, until they ended up knotted amongst the strands. Then, taking a final deep breath, she tried once more to read her cellmate.

It was very faint, but hiding underneath the fiery energy she discovered the mark of a tether—a charge.

Miriam took a few steps backward, still not trusting the creature enough to reveal itself. "Would the Master of this charge come forth and identify himself?" Her voice rang with a cordial radiance.

Silence.

"I ask again, to the Master of this charge . . . you have nothing to fear from me, cousin. I am Miriam, Breedling of the Second Grade, and I ask you reveal yourself."

"He's not here," came the creature's response.

Miriam's ears tickled. There was a hint of caution in the male's tone, the words well spoken. "Not here?" she pressed for a better answer.

"As I said, he's not here."

"Your words ring true, but her tongue plays tricks," she said.

"I . . ."

Miriam cut the creature off as she turned with a swift elegance through the halo of faint light. She approached to get a better look, the flame in the creature's hand spotlighting the mortal face of a young man. His cerulean blue eyes stared at her, no doubt taking in her dismal features—her unhealthy hourglass figure, the emptiness in her lavender eyes, the paling of russet skin. She found his pasty face hard to read, the sweat on his brow giving her a moment of pause.

"Where is your Breedling?" she asked. "And do not play games with me. I shall know if you are lying."

"We were separated in the valley. I dropped something and . . ."

"Psst, that is not possible." Miriam wrapped her arms around her chest, a ghost of unease present in her stance that she wished were not there. "No Breedling can separate from their charge, especially not a low-class creature. Those who are caught are caught together."

"But it's true," reiterated the creature. "I was careless and ended up getting snatched by the watchdog. Buck had already made it across the street and . . ."

"Buck?" Miriam crinkled her nose. "There is no Breedling by such a name."

The young man shrugged. "Then it must be his nickname."

"Breedlings do not have nicknames."

"Well, that is the name he gave me. Ye can ask him to clarify why he changed it."

Miriam heard the distinct growl in the male's voice, frustration behind it. She kept her arms barred around her chest for security as a precaution, but there was something about her new cellmate that was incredibly off-putting. She needed to know more.

"What is your name, creature?"

"Jack."

"And who is your master, Jack?"

"Master?" There was confusion on the male's face. "I have no master."

Tightening her hold around herself, Miriam subconsciously retreated a step, the male noticing. He lowered his hand, unrestricting the flame he had been shielding in order to keep her in full view. There was a slight frown in his expression; it caught her by surprise, confusing her.

"Listen, I don't know what ye might have heard about me, but I ain't gonna hurt ye."

"Lie," said Miriam. "Your voice drips with trickery, Wicker,

I will not be fouled by your scarlet tongue."

"Wicker?" Again there was confusion on the male's face. "I'm no Wicker. Damned, yes, but I don't share . . ."

"Do not riddle me with more lies," ordered Miriam as she dropped her arms and did her best to take a commanding step forward. She was not going to let the creature trap her in its mind game. "You are a mortal of flesh, yes, which means you cannot be a Spirit. You may have no life in you anymore, but that does not exempt you from being a Wicker, for no living mortal, Wicker or not, could ever travel to Euxinus and survive. So there is nothing else you can be, not with all those scars on your soul."

The male immediately dropped his gaze as though trying to see what she meant.

"Make no mistake, I am not a fool," she continued. "You are a Wicker, Jack, a cursed mortal marked with the original scar of Hades."

"Ye will get no argument from me. As I have already said I am cursed."

Miriam let out a triumphant huff.

"But I ain't what ye say," continued the male.

Miriam squinted, making sure to project her skepticism, but behind her expression, she heard the truth. The creature was not lying. But that was impossible. There was simply no other creature he could be, unless—she felt her breath hitch. The possibility gave her hope, too much hope. Her mind began to reel and her feet moved without command. She paced, paying no direct attention to Jack. There was something else he could be, if the rumors were true. But he had said his Breedling went by the name Buck. She shook her head. What were the Fates playing at? She was the only one meant to retrieve the Wickers. Had they forgotten about her? Left her here to rot?

Miriam stopped and looked at the creature. "Tell me, Jack. How is it you came to be in the charge of this Buck you mention?"

"Of that I am not entirely sure," replied Jack. "He told me it started with the breaking of his bonds with yer masters the Fates and there was this lad Charlie who helped him . . ."

"I said no lies," snapped Miriam. "No Breedling has ever been able to break ties with the Fates; our obedience will not allow it." She stamped her foot, sending a slight vibration through the ground. It disturbed the flame, which she had not noticed until now sat inside in a turnip lantern. As she glared at the twisted face present on the root vegetable, the image jogged her memory. She knew this totem. She lifted her gaze again to meet Jack's eyes. "Tell me, Jack—" She paused, hesitant to ask, the tightness in her chest constricting her lungs. "Tell me about Buck; describe him to me."

"Buck? Well, he's a resilient lad—erm Breedling. A little shorter than ye in stature, I'd reckon. He bears a wisp of short brown hair and has the most annoyingly truthful pair of emerald eyes. His skin is creamy, though it never seems to flush. He has a way with words, a voice that holds truth within every syllable."

Miriam's eyes widened. "Lies," she whispered more to herself than to Jack, unable to believe her ears. Was it possible? Had her beloved brother truly escaped? No—of course not. The Fates must have let him go.

"If that's how ye feel, I don't think I can say anything ye will believe . . ."

"Miriam," she managed, offering the creature a word of address. She pressed her hand against her chest, her thoughts cloudy and her head dizzy. She wanted her heart to be right, but her mind kept pushing doubt.

"Miriam."

She heard Jack say her name, shocked by the hint of concern in his tone—or was it twisted pleasure? She could not tell. But he was right, there was nothing he could say she would honestly believe. All his words were laced with wickedness. She tried to read his aura again, but this time it only confused her more, a complicated web of scarlet and . . . Her eyes closed before she could manage to get herself safely to the ground and, instead, felt herself falling. She anticipated the hard impact, but what met her was the radiance of fire.

"Miriam?"

She heard him say her name, but she could not bring herself to answer, her body engulfed by the onslaught of heat. She had grown more empathetic to the effects auras had on her since Bartholomew's imprisonment—she felt the fire's rage, its malice, its intent to harm, but its intended victim was not her. Opening her eyes, she let out a gasp, unprepared for the humanistic potency of his stare.

Jack held her in his gaze, his eyes partly concerned and partly assessing. There was a distinct duality in him, a battle the likes of which she had not seen in a mortal soul. She watched the two sides vying for dominance, neither able to get a foothold over the other, at least not at first. It was only when a pulse of warmth from his embrace attacked her that the scale tipped.

Miriam squirmed, and after a moment he released his chivalrous hold on her.

"A thank ye would be nice," hissed Jack.

Miriam rolled out of the trickster's grasp, sliding across the floor to put space between them. Though she tried to gain her feet, her head was too heavy, his rising energy keeping her subdued.

"You have shown your true colors then, Wicker," she managed in a puffed breath, her hope dying in the rise of Jack's wicked smirk.

"As I said before," he said with a sly calm. "I'm not a Wicker. Those cursed mortals can't hold a candle to the Master of Tricksters." He pounded a fist against his chest. "My feats of trickery are legendary. The only thing I share with those damned descendants of Cain are scars from the Devil."

"You mean Hades," corrected Miriam, finding the term odd and wondered if Jack even knew the truth about the Scarlet Phoenix.

Jack began to laugh, his haunting tone filling the cell with an eerie madness.

Miriam shifted her body in order to position herself against the wall. Panic gripped her chest as the scarlet aura around Jack began to thicken and bend. She fixed her eyes on him, wary of his nature, but in the cast of the candlelight, she finally noticed the dark, thickening lines on his neck and the sweat saturating his brow.

"Jack," she whispered cautiously.

"Me name is Stingy Jack," snarled the young man. As he made an attempt to step forward, pain ignited across his sickly face, freezing him in place. "Miriam—" His voice was a whisper, his expression softening. "I—I," Jack crumbled to his knees.

Without a second thought, Miriam prepared herself for the outburst. The wail out of Jack's mouth was sharp and haunting, riddled with torment—nothing like the shrill, demonic sound of a Wicker. Miriam cringed, but felt mostly shock from his transformation. Something was wrong with him.

Eventually, the trickster ran out of breath and collapsed to the ground. His body knocked over the turnip lantern, the candle tumbling onto the clammy black stone. The flame danced violently, but the wick remained lit. Jack's chest panted in staccato spurts, his clothes saturated with sweat.

Miriam lowered her hands to the sound of mumbling.

"Please, Buck, please."

It was one of the most pitiful pleas Miriam had ever heard. There was so much anguish behind it.

"BUCK!" Jack shouted.

"JACK!"

Miriam lifted her gaze to the cell door, the voice coming from the passageway. She felt her breath hitch again, her senses brimming with a flurry of hope once more.

"JACK!" repeated the distinct voice from beyond the door. She knew that voice.

Turning her attention back to Jack, Miriam saw the trickster's eyes rolling into the back of his head, the cast of candlelight illuminating his empty face. He was telling the truth, she mused in disbelief.

"JACK, answer me!" The sound of jiggling keys followed.

The door opened, and there, just beyond the halo of light, stood the silhouette of one with a shorter stature than her.

REUNION

Buck stepped into the cell, his eyes first falling on Jack's candle, its flame flickering angrily. He bent over to pick it up and held it in his palm. Flickering gingerly in thanks for the assist, the flame cast a soft glow on his face. It brought out the tint of brown in his hair and the cream color in his skin. He lifted his gaze from the candle and out toward the bundle coiled on the ground.

"Jack." The word left his mouth in a delicate whisper full of anxiety, and he rushed to the Trickster's side. Kneeling on the ground, he put the wax back into the turnip and set it close to him. He gently brushed his hand across Jack's face, the Trickster's skin much too warm for his dead mortal flesh to produce. Buck lifted an eyelid, the sight of cerulean blue staring blankly at him. He gently shut the eye and resumed his examination. Pulling back the Trickster's collar to check the skin on his neck, he saw the black veins were once again present. He untucked his shirt to reveal the numerous scars on Jack's chest and absentmindedly started to count them, but stopped around fifteen. Instead, Buck's eyes shifted to the number of black snakes slithering underneath his skin.

He laid the shirt back down before taking hold of Jack's bandaged hand. Buck unraveled the wrap, the cut an angry crusting of dry blood and charred skin, then pulled back the sleeve, the Trickster's skin almost too hot to touch. The veins in his forearm were bulging, thick, and black. Buck felt a surge of panic at the sight; his healing magic would not be able to combat the Wicker's poison, not at this stage. He opened his mouth to at least try to extend any relief he could provide, but before he spoke a word, a soft coo whispered his name.

"Bartholomew?"

Buck looked up and saw a female Breedling hovering over him. His eyes widened when he met the familiar pale lavender of her eyes. There were tears already swelling in them, emphasizing her inner pain.

The sight of her stole every notion he had to tend to Jack, the roughness of her physique and her joy to see him distracting him. Her russet skin was dirty; her hair was matted locks of black, although at certain angles, he found the deep shade of violet.

"Bartholomew?" Miriam addressed him again.

"I do not go by that name anymore," he said as his head turned away, the sound of his name reminding him of his charge. It was not his intention to sound so cold, but as glad as he was to see her, he could not bear the sight of her brokenness, and truthfully, he had not the time to rejoice.

"Bartholomew," she said, her tone dejected. "Do you not recognize your own sister?"

An abundance of guilt crushed Buck's infant conscience. Out of all the creatures in Euxinus, she had been the only one who had stood on his behalf, who tried to sway him from his madness. He, of course, had not seen it that way, nor had he fully understood what she had tried to do for him. But now, looking back on that moment when he had knelt in the palace atrium in front of the Council of Elders, the First and Second Grade orders of Breedlings, and even the Fates, he knew Miriam had tried to save him. She should never have been capable of displaying such affection, but somehow she had managed the feat, if only in that moment. He hung his head, realizing now what it had meant. She had done it out of love, the very same that Charlie had displayed for his cousin Jimmy—a loyalty unbreakable. Miriam had been capable of love before he even understood the meaning of it, and his thoughts tried to reconcile what that meant. Was she blessed? No—Annaliese had said there was no one else like him. So what, then? How was it possible for her to express emotion?

The questions would have to go unanswered for now. A smile tried to spread across his face, his admiration for his sister coming through tenfold, but he held it back, afraid it might be misconstrued.

"My pardon, Miriam," he replied with care, tilting his head toward her, his hands still holding Jack's injured hand. "It has been . . ."

"Are you here to take me home?" she asked quickly, hope brightening her face. "Have you made amends with our masters? Will the Fates grant me a reprieve?"

Buck swallowed hard. The thought had never crossed his mind that he would find his sister. Annaliese had mentioned she was in the Reformatory, but the chances of Jack ending up in the same cell as her—he could not even begin to tabulate the odds. Then again, maybe it was not that outlandish. It was possible the *Felis Caudaglobosa* assumed Jack was a Wicker based on the scent of his poisoned blood, and since Miriam's punishment decreed them as her charge, the balled-tail cat had placed them together. Buck nearly laughed at his dumb luck. With her here, he had a better chance of expediting Jack to the Apothecary's coffin. However, he suddenly felt a churn in his gut, an unease he did not like—could he trust her?

Buck studied her eyes again. They were still loyal to the Fates, a shroud of obedience consuming her pupils, and yet there was something else, a glimmer of emotion he was certain she consciously was unaware of, but one he knew well—the seed of disobedience. If he could convince her to come with him, surely he could do more than just liberate her from her cell. Maybe he could also help her break her bonds with the Fates.

"Have you come to take me home?" repeated Miriam, her voice impatient.

"Not intentionally," he replied, still trying to find the right words to say.

"I see . . ."

Buck heard the disappointment in her voice. "Miriam, it is not like that," he said placing Jack's hand on the Trickster's chest. If he was going to ask her for her help, he was going to have to tend to her fragile state first and give her his full attention.

"I see," said Miriam, again bitterly. "You care more for this Wicker than you do your own sister, so by all means do not let me stop you from tending to his wretched soul."

"Miriam . . ." Buck paused and rose to his feet, leaving the candle to watch over Jack. He tried to stretch out a comforting arm to her, but she refused him.

"No," screeched Miriam. She locked her arms around her chest. "You cannot be real."

"Miriam," Buck attempted again.

"No, no, no, you are only in my head, an apparition. Oh, by the powers, have I not suffered enough?" She paused. "Have I not been humiliated enough? Have I not done everything I have been asked?! This is all your fault!"

Buck stood shocked at her repulsion toward him. "Miriam . . ."

"Save your breath, Bartholomew. If the Fates see fit I remain here by not sending for me, then who am I to question their authority? We cannot all be as great as you, the Fates' most beloved," she added, with a surprising hint of venom.

"Miriam . . ." Buck tried again to interject, but she continued to strike him with her words, the Fates' treatment of her billowing out from pent-up anger.

"Have I not endured enough by being assigned the position to ferry the most detestable creatures to walk the four realms? Why are the Fates still displeased with me? How can they be if you are here? All I ever did was be your sister. I—" Miriam collapsed, hitting her knees hard on the stony floor, and threw her face in her hands.

Buck crouched in front of his sister, hesitant to embrace her, but he needed to prove he was real. He wrapped his arms around her and pulled her in close. Immediately, she buried her face in his chest. Her hands gripped his corduroy jacket, drawing him as close to her as possible. He felt her anger give way as she embraced their moment of reunion. Buck stroked her matted hair in an attempt to console her, his mind lost in thought about the Fates' cruelty. He whispered a hush as Miriam fortified her grip. *Like brother, like sister*, he mused as her body trembled. Having been through this pain himself, he understood her brokenness. It was not as raw as his had been when he had escaped, but it was nearing the breaking point. Buck felt an overwhelming responsibility to set her free, but he could not allow that to distract him, as heartless as it seemed.

"Miriam," he whispered. "Miriam, please, tell me what happened."

"No, Bartholomew, you tell me why—why did you do it?" She looked up, her swollen eyes pleading with him.

"Miriam, this is neither the time nor the place for that. The Reformatory walls are alive with prying ears. I can explain it all later when we are in safer quarters."

"No." She pushed him away. "That is what you always say. And I let it go because you are my kin, Bartholomew. I believed in you and followed your example. But then, then you left me." Her sobs resumed. "You left me, Bartholomew, alone in this miserable world."

"My dearest sister," said Buck. "What have they done to you?"

Miriam succumbed to the security of his embrace again, unable to sustain her temper, the fracturing of her personality neutralized by his presence. "After Serkan led you out of the palace, there was a wrath unlike any have seen in Euxinus since the days of the War of Wind and Flame. The Fates were beyond anger. They went after the Breedlings, questioning every last one, even the Lessers, but none of our responses were satisfactory. It did not matter what was said, how much we pleaded our loyalty—we were all punished in some way, most simply banished to the confines of their coffins. There was only a handful of us given charge during this time. Annaliese and her fellow Scar Healers had their continued standing charge. Me, I was sentenced with the task of retrieving Wickers from Eden, and a handful of First Grades were sent to retrieve amid souls with the highest energy profile, which is why so many have been abandoned to remain in Eden and denied trial." Her tears began to seep into his jacket.

Buck's mouth opened, prepared to ask more, his thoughts suddenly reeling. He took a breath instead, stowing the knowledge for later inquisition.

Releasing a painful sob, Miriam nestled her face deeper into his chest, as if she could stow herself away there and hide forever.

"Shhh," he consoled as she heaved.

"It was awful, my dearest," she continued. "I tried to appeal to the Fates that there was something wrong with you. I had noticed your aura was in flux, tainted. I thought you were infected—cursed, maybe—but in the moment I had not been able to identify the foreign markings. I pleaded with them to give me a chance to examine you better, but they refused. From there, I continued to defend you . . . not your action but your integrity, your loyalty. I knew there had to be a reason for your silence, a reason you could not yet say. I tried to see it in your mind's eye, but I could not reach you, feel you—something was broken within you." She curled her face back into his chest, losing control of her remaining strength, and sank farther to the ground.

Buck strengthened his hold on her.

"They sent me away on charge after charge, to track down the remaining Wickers seeking refuge in the darkened shadows of Eden. And, each time I returned, I stood tall in front of the Fates in all their glory. Every time, they asked me if I still believed you to be a loyal servant of their house, to which I replied you were the truest, and that when you had regained your tongue you would bear the witness and knowledge you possess. But now"—she paused and caught her breath—"now you have betrayed my words." She cried as if in some great physical pain, digging her fingers into his skin. "There is a change in you I cannot place, but I recognize it. It is stronger than before. You are no longer a member of my house." She pushed him away. "You have forsaken me and your kin, betrayed our masters. You have taken up servitude . . . in the house of a mortal?"

"Yes, Miriam, a mortal," said Buck, thinking briefly of Charlie. He lifted his hands to cradle her face. The tears from her eyes trickled down her cheeks, leaving their trail marks through the grime on her skin; the lavender was so faint, there was no cheer left. She was distant, ready. If she was willing, he could help her to leave this place, but first he needed her help—for as much as he wished to save her now, he would lose the only chance he had to save Jack, and he could not forsake him. Not even for her.

"Tell me why," she said.

Buck lowered his gaze. How could he make her understand without telling her his secret? It was not that he did not trust her to keep it, but she still answered to the Fates. With one command they would extract the truth from her, and she would not be able to resist.

"Please," she begged. "Why . . . why did you leave me?" She searched his face, trying to find the answer, hoping her suffering had not been for nothing.

"My intention was not to leave you," he said, his voice ever so gentle and sorrowful, filled with the promise of loyalty he had always shown her. "But I had no other choice."

"There is no choice but the will of the Fates," Miriam protested. She slowed her sobs. "You should not have been able to resist their questions. You should not have been able to keep the knowledge of your charge from them."

"As you say," said Buck. "But my dearest sister, you know how untrue your words are."

Miriam's face brightened with terror.

He smiled to reassure her. "There is choice. It may be far out of reach, but it is there, hiding under layers of obedience. You have already begun to feel its pull, though you may not realize what it means—but I do. I see it in your eyes, the loss of divinity, and I hope I can bring you to understand why it was necessary to do as I did. Why I chose to disobey. I never considered the far-reaching consequences my actions would have on you or the others. Now I can better comprehend the notion, but I do not regret it. I hope you will in time be loyal to me again as you have always been, in spite of the injustice that has befallen you because of me. That in time, you will come to realize I did all this to save us. That I did my charge as asked but could not in good conscience reveal what I learned. There would have been no neutrality in it."

"Then the whispers are true." Miriam held herself up as if finding new strength. Buck dropped his hands from her face. "You found them—those that were lost?"

"I found one," said Buck.

"Tell me," said Miriam, her demeanor changing. She sat back on her bare feet. "Was it as beautiful as the Apothecary describes them in his stories?"

"Miriam, I . . ." started Buck. The curiosity in her eyes burned with hunger.

Miriam's enthusiasm vanished. "You do not trust me?" Her voice was full of hurt.

"No." Buck took her by the hands. "It is not you who I do not trust . . ." He could not admit to her how dangerous she was to him.

It was hard to tell if Miriam understood, but regardless, she dropped the subject. "What will you have of me then, brother?" she asked.

"Help me," said Buck as he turned his head to Jack, whose skin had changed from pale white to red, the venom already working its cursed magic.

"Bartholomew, you want me"—she stopped in disbelief—"to help save your Wicker?"

"He is not a Wicker, Miriam. Jack is not what you think," he stammered.

"You cannot possibly expect me to believe he is . . ." she paused, her expression conflicted by the thought she was having. She shook her head. "It is not possible, Bartholomew, the Eden Wanderer is a myth. A creature described in poems to prophesize the return of the Lost Creators." She gasped, the realization forming on her face. "Even if you are speaking the truth, you do not realize what you are asking me."

"No, sister, I know well what I ask," said Buck, giving her a soft smile. "And I need your help. I cannot carry him myself, and in his condition I cannot have him stand as witness in the Hollow. I need to take him to the Apothecary. Please sister, I implore you." He fell back on his heels, kneeling in front of her.

"Bartholomew," she gasped. "What you ask, I am unsure I can give. No one has ever left the Reformatory without divine decree."

"But you were caught by a Coymorph," said Buck, pitting what he knew about Euxian Law against his sense of free will. "The Fates gave no decree you remain in captivity, did they?"

"Not that I am aware," said Miriam. "My Wicker and I were captured and brought here by a Coymorph, and Annaliese has since dispatched the foul creature. She tried to get me to leave with her, but my mind was so lost it pained me to think about liberation."

Buck's smile grew. "Then you are free to leave, sister," he said with encouragement. "You can come with me, the Apothecary can heal your ailments, and . . ."

"Can you take me away from here?" she asked, her voice cracking—she winced, the words going against her ingrained obedience. "Please," she whimpered. "Promise me you will take me away from here, set me free from this horrible place. Promise me you will tell me the secret of your escape, when walls do not have so many ears."

Buck gave himself no time for thought, his eagerness pushing the words from his mouth like some parlor trick. "I swear to you on my life," he said, realizing only after he had said it that there was a hint of emptiness in his oath.

"Then as you have promised, so shall I hold you to it." Miriam bowed her head, sealing their accord.

Buck kissed his sister's hand and rose to properly embrace her. He traced calming circles across her back, all the while hoping he would not betray his words.

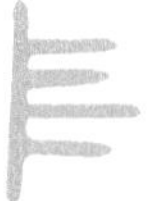

THE SPY REPORTS

"Ah, Master Chameleon," greeted the Apothecary as the reddish-brown tabby cat entered through the ebony doorway. "We were just conversing about your arrival." The eldest Euxian stopped stringing bundles of herbs on the piece of wire hanging from the kitchen wall. He brushed the cloak of his silver hair behind his shoulder in order to address the spy properly.

He watched the feline's pink eyes scan his other two guests: the Retrievers, Serkan and Jardina, keeping him company during this time of uncertain suspense. They had come under the guise of trial preparations in order to dodge the Fates, but they could only stall for so long. Both the Retrievers stared back at the cat with primal alertness, their black eyes posing a challenge, which was to be expected. Serkan was always trying to find a way to get into a fight with the Fates' spy. The Apothecary sighed, placing a hand over the triple star insignia of the Fates stitched into his traditional velvet robe. Gripping the soft fabric, he recited a curse in his head. He would have no squabbling, not now.

"Serkan, Jardina," the Chameleon finally addressed them.

"Master Chameleon," they responded in fluid unison, their voices carrying a hypnotic rasp, though its power had no effect on the Fates' spy. They nodded their heads slightly, their pointed chins piercing the air.

The cat entered the room further, making itself more visible. "My Eldest," greeted the Chameleon. It bowed low, touching its furry chin to the tiled floor and holding its position out of respect.

"Master Chameleon, my dear friend," said the Apothecary. His gray eyes were full of affection, as was the smile crossing the bronze skin of his frail face. "Please," he continued, rounding the counter, "you honor me too much."

Serkan snickered with a sharp fang cresting over his lower lip.

The cat responded with an angry hiss.

"Serkan!" scolded Jardina. She hit her mate on the back, disturbing his still wings—they twitched in response but did not open. "Many pardons, Master Chameleon," she continued, lowering her slender figure to the floor to meet the cat as an equal. "Serkan has grown restless in the wait for your return."

"As it appears," replied the Chameleon. It accepted the apology and brushed against Jardina's leg affectionately.

Jardina stroked the feline's fur with care so as not to cause the Chameleon any discomfort. The cat shuddered as its skin twitched against her chilled touch; she immediately removed her hand.

"Master Chameleon," she said, horrified.

"There is no need to worry. I am not harmed," said the cat as it circled back to the center of the room and sat on its hind legs.

"If it is all the same," said Jardina, rising from the floor. "I stand by my words. You know well how ill-equipped we are with waiting."

"Jardina, do not speak for me," growled Serkan. He threw her a brooding scowl but quickly returned his attention to the cat.

The cat's pink eyes danced with a hint of laughter.

"Do not stare at me thus, Master Chameleon," Serkan snapped, rolling his broad shoulders in an attempt to establish himself as the alpha.

"Do not threaten me, Serkan," countered the cat, pawing at the floor. Its whiskers twitched and its irises narrowed to deadly lines. "I am not your charge, nor a Breedling for you to command."

"You could have fooled me," said Serkan.

Catching the Retriever's gaze, the Apothecary gave him a disappointed expression. Serkan recoiled at the sight; his wings drooped, and after a moment he ruffled them before crossing his arms. The Apothecary bit back a chuckle, not looking to agitate Serkan's alpha personality. He needed the Retriever calm, and nothing tamed him better than harsh judgment.

"Why are you still dressed like that?" Serkan grumbled, addressing the Chameleon.

The cat observed its furry paws and then looked back at the winged Retriever. Smiling, the Chameleon batted its tail gingerly against the floor. "I've become rather fond of the feline appearance."

Serkan laughed. Even though none of the others joined in, the tension had at least lifted from the room.

"Master Serkan, Mistress Jardina, many thanks for standing watch with me," said the Apothecary, silencing Serkan's laughter, "but as per our earlier discussion, I must ask you now to leave."

"As you command, Eldest," said Jardina. She bowed, allowing wisps of her pixie hair to cover her face.

Serkan replied in kind, following his mate to the door and closing it behind them.

As the door latched, the tabby cat jumped onto the countertop and circled around the marble bowls of powdered herbs, placing its paws strategically in the open spaces. The Apothecary watched the feline closely, noticing the heaviness in its steps. A great burden weighed on the cat's conscience.

"Tell me what ails you," said the Apothecary.

The tabby cat finished the maze. "My Eldest." The Chameleon paused. "Are you certain I cannot be of more service?"

The Apothecary sighed. He had been over this with the spy before. It was in its nature to infiltrate and deceive—its loyalty knew only one allegiance, and that was to the Fates. He had risked enough already by asking the spy to track Bartholomew and to ensure the mortal Charles Reese was sought after by the Prince of Sea.

"Master Chameleon, how many times must I say you are not mine to command, nor are you in any way my servant."

"I say to you I am," said the cat. Determination gleamed in its pink eyes, its desire to know the First Euxian's secrets present.

"You flatter me, my friend, but I am not worthy of your loyalty. You are a member of the Seven and as such remain my equal."

Meowing mournfully, the cat pulled back its pointy ears. "As always, Master Apothecary, you know the right words to say. Pardon my curiosities."

"Serkan was right, you have been a feline for far too long." The Apothecary grinned, temporarily elevating the Chameleon's concern. "But that which the Fates order of you cannot be undone, for hard as you try, you cannot so easily fight against your chains of obedience. And soon you will not be able to keep our little conversations from our masters either."

In response, the cat turned its head away in shame. "I am aware of this, and I would rather perish than betray what little trust you have given me," it mumbled.

The Apothecary regarded the cat and knew the struggle within, which had grown increasingly hard ever since Bartholomew's betrayal. Even so, there were more immediate matters that needed their attention.

"Did Master Breedling make it safely to the Ferryman?" he inquired.

The cat acknowledged with a nod but kept its ears back. Its irises widened as it fought the urge to alert the Fates of the Breedling's arrival. Its fur bristled as it dug its claws into the countertop.

"And were you able to deliver my message?"

The Chameleon sat back on its hind legs and curled its tail in around its paws. "As per your wish, I tracked Bartholomew and his charge to the river. I was able to confront the Breedling and deliver your message regarding the mortal, and I told him the Prince of Sea has been given the charge."

"And do you believe Prince Moon will keep his word?"

"I believe he will," reported the feline. "Although, I do not know if he will be able to save Master Charles from himself."

"Your concern is noted," replied the Apothecary.

"But . . ."

The Apothecary held up his hand to halt the feline. "From what you have reported thus far, Master Chameleon, this Piece of Eight, as you and the Tales Teller have so insistently described him, poses no real threat to our mission. Until the trial of the Shepherdess has concluded, I will hear no more about the Breedling's Master." He regarded the tabby cat as it pulled back its ears before softening his stern expression. "And what of the Twins?"

"The Beloved Twins are in pursuit as ordered by your agreement with the Fallen Angel, Lady Vala."

"I see," said the Apothecary, stroking his round chin and retreating to his thoughts. In his endless planning, he had never once seen the Mistress of Heaven as a real threat, even though her ways were always more secretive in nature. After creating mortals, the not-so-heavenly Creator only sought to fight for their souls out of spite for Hades, continuing their unending sibling rivalry. Enlisting the Fallen Valkyrie, Lady Vala, had been a calculated risk—his first of the seven, for even now her loyalty still belonged to Everlyse. But it still remained a better option than orchestrating his fellow Euxian council members into small acts of defiance against the Fates.

"I trust Alyce and Lyes will keep to their sworn oath of service to Lady Vala, and that in turn she too will hold true to her word?" asked the Apothecary.

"And what if Creator Everlyse takes notice? What if she learns about . . ."

"My scheme?" The Apothecary shrugged, still unsure if the Mistress of Heaven had any inkling about the Eden Wanderer's prophecy. Even so, concern had recently plagued his thoughts, for now all his pieces were moving and a piece of eight was amongst his cast of seven, his well-crafted plan no longer his own. "It is possible," he admitted finally, echoing the Chameleon's concern. "If Everlyse does put herself on the board, it is possible the Beloved Twins and Lady Vala will be compromised. But Everlyse's hold on her Fallen is strained. And besides—"

The cat perked its ears.

"It was Everlyse who cursed the Fallen with the eternal protection of mortals and banned her from Heaven. The lofty deity would have to break her own word to fully regain control of her exiled Valkyrie, and after what she and Hades did to her— it is a sin not easily forgiven. Take heart, Master Chameleon, for I believe our course still shows promise. Now, where is Master Breedling?"

"Bartholomew and his charge advanced through the Mankato Scar some time ago, so I am surprised they are not here. You should have received them by now, but . . ."

"There was a disturbance," offered the Apothecary.

The cat's fur prickled along its spine.

"I am aware," he added. "The Coymorphs have been on the move for quite some time. The Herald reported a massive, well . . ." The Apothecary laughed. "A *jailbreak*, as mortals call it. Several Euxians abandoned their coffins along one street section in the valley, and one street is said to be flooded with a thin sheet of water."

The Chameleon gasped. "My Eldest, surely these are mere rumors. How can the likes of Sea return to Euxinus?"

Before the Apothecary could address the question, the front door of his coffin burst open. The Chameleon jumped and let out a hiss, startled by the noise as a girl in a mangy dress and dark purple hair entered. The Apothecary studied the intruder, her image almost a ghost to him, but he knew her—there was no way he could forget.

"Miriam," he addressed the disheveled Breedling.

"Please," she huffed, doubling over. "Bartholomew needs your help."

At the sound of her words the Apothecary stormed out of his coffin and into the quiet square. He saw Bartholomew knelt on the ground, a young man draped in his lap. Within a few strides, he towered over the two, and the Breedling looked up at him with a tired smile.

"I cannot take him any farther," said the Breedling with some difficulty. "He . . . poison . . . Wicker blood."

The Apothecary's eyes widened. "Is this?" he began.

The Breedling nodded.

The Apothecary bent down and lifted the young man in his arms, the heat of the body melting the cooler temperature of his own. He made his way back to his coffin, not bothering to check if Bartholomew was following him. Miriam came back into view as she walked out the front door, no doubt to assist her brother, although she could barely stand herself.

"My Eldest," spoke the Chameleon as he passed through the tea kitchen and into the healing room.

"Not now, Master Chameleon. You have your orders from the Fates. See to the invitations of Hades and Everlyse for Iona's trial. Our witness has arrived, and we cannot stall any longer."

"But how can he stand in this condition? Surely I can figure out something to delay my summons," said the Chameleon from the doorway, his voice shrouded with a need to be of assistance.

The Apothecary laid the Eden Wanderer on the bed and began to undress him.

"My Eldest?"

"Go," boomed the Apothecary, unable to conceal the worry in his tone. He froze at the sound of his own voice. He had never let such an emotion rule him, but there was too much at stake, and this—what had happened? He needed to speak with Bartholomew. But he also needed the Chameleon to go about his duty. They could not risk suspicion. "My pardons, Master Chameleon, I do not know what came over me."

"There is no need, my Eldest. I know the responsibility you have put upon yourself. I am not blind, and neither is the council. But as you have asked, I will conduct myself accordingly and fulfill the Fates' command."

The Apothecary heard the sour notes in the Chameleon's voice, but did not turn to watch the feline bow, his attention too focused on the bare flesh of the Eden Wanderer. He would smooth things over with the Fates' spy later. Bending lower, he grazed his finger along a thick black snake bulging from the covered wound on the Eden Wanderer's hand. He set his hands—one upon the man's chest, the other upon his forehead—and closed his eyes, reciting spells of healing under his breath.

"Can you help him?" came Bartholomew's voice from behind him.

In a rare moment, the Apothecary did not answer out of uncertainty. Instead, he curled his fingers into fists, abandoning his spells. Healing the Eden Wanderer in this state was going to take much effort and time, neither of which they had in ample amounts.

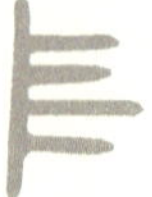

MADRID

EDEN, MIDWEST 1934

The night air was arid and lightning bugs dotted the sky. The coyote entered the grove of trees, crawling through the underbrush of Charles Reese's hideaway, and listened to him talk in his sleep. At times, his voice would register above a whisper, but when the fire of Hades—left by the mark on his shoulder—pulsed, the mortal would scream.

The coyote buried its muzzle and whimpered on each occasion.

With each wail, the coyote sensed his heartbreak—his pain was fresh, almost tangible. The agony of it all was not unfamiliar to the Son of Sea, having borne witness to such prolonged torture, but with Charles Reese it was different. The mortal's degree of resolve exceeded all others, for any other mortal would have wasted away by now—died simply from the loneliness or perished by his or her own hand. He was the last one, the sole survivor, and though the coyote cared not to admit the Chameleon had spoken the truth, it could relate.

The mortal's cries continued until they abruptly stopped.

Immediately lifting its head, the coyote sniffed the air— nothing, no smell or sight of an enemy. The coyote gained its legs to view the mortal better. Charles lay still, his eyes staring blankly skyward. Had its intuition misjudged the mortal? Was he dead? The coyote inched forward, leaving its hiding place. It looked briefly at the dim campfire. Before it could react, flames exploded and the mortal gasped. The coyote froze, ducking its head, unable to retreat without notice. It watched the mortal's frantic motions until Charles's eyes spotted it.

Charles reached for his rifle and sprang into a feasible shooting stance as the coyote retreated and repositioned for an encounter. Both were still, each waiting for the other to strike. When the next exchange came, the mortal held his guard, but the coyote managed to surprise him, forcing the rifle from his hands. It drove him into the ground, the pads of its large paws tingling with the heat emanating from the mortal's body, a minor irritation.

"Don't stare at me like that!" Charles cried. "Do what it is you came here to do. Take my life!"

The coyote's ears drooped, taken aback by the request. It would take little effort to end the mortal's suffering and free him of his plight, but it had to deny Charles his request. It was then the coyote felt a rare pang of sorrow, for it knew the road ahead for Charles Reese would be a litany of pain that no creature— whether Euxian, Hell-bound, Eden-made, or Heaven-sent— should endure. The cruelty of it sparked an obligational impulse in the coyote, its father's words reaching out from the past.

"Father, why did you create us?"

"Because, my son, without my sister I cannot protect this world on my own, nor the gifts my siblings so selflessly gave."

"The mortals?"

"Despite your misgivings about them, my son, Hades and Everlyse created mortals out of love, which I fear is why neither of them holds it any longer in their hearts. That is why I need

you. That is why the Animawalkers exist. But despite my reason, you are also my children. And while my voice commands you to protect them, my heart begs it of you. Will you help me protect the hearts of Wind and Flame?"

The coyote felt tears threaten the edges of its eyes, its heart conflicted. To allow Charles Reese to live was torture of the utmost cruelty, but to end his suffering was equal parts as cruel. For though the mortal's physical pain would cease, death would only be a brief respite. In death, it would be hard to argue against the claim Hades had on his soul. The coyote lowered its muzzle to touch Charles on the nose. It made no attempt to communicate, but somewhere a phantom voice seemed to pass through him. *The Breedling has made it back to Euxinus.*

The mortal fluttered his eyes, acknowledging he understood, and looked away, sadness and disappointment evident on his face. And perhaps, for a brief moment, a touch of relief.

It was in that relief the coyote saw the truth: Charles Reese was as fixed on dying as he was on living, but for the time being, he would not provoke death any further. The coyote raised its head and bellowed, its volume filling the vastness around them. It let out another cry, this time receiving an excusable response to solicit its leave. Without another look at the mortal, the coyote disappeared into the underbrush before doubling back on its belly to keep watch.

"I'm sorry," it heard Charles say.

The coyote continued to follow Charles Reese, keeping its distance as they traveled through the barren Iowan countryside. But as the days passed, it was clear the mortal was once again losing his conviction to live. He ate little, slept even less, and on occasion sought out trouble. He had managed already to get into three fistfights, each one marking his body with fresh bruises and superficial cuts but nothing life threatening.

By the tenth day, they reached the outskirts of the mining community near the Des Moines River. People displaced by the hardships of the Depression barricaded the town—men looking for work, women huddled in despondent packs, children running freely, their youthful dispositions not fully aware of the troubles of the world. The coyote managed to pass through them fairly unnoticed, camouflaging its movements.

Up ahead, a poorly built stage garnered the attention of a rather large, enthusiastic crowd. Behind it, towering banners waved in the rustling wind, depicting painted images of a bearded woman, a turtle boy, a flying trapeze, and snake charmers. The coyote paid little heed to the young man wearing a ringmaster's outfit who shouted at the crowd. The circus herald spoke of the amazing attractions coming soon to the town of Ames.

" . . . which is only twenty miles north," shouted the ringmaster. "Feast your eyes on recently discovered oddities, entice your sense of adventure with daring performances and exotic animals. Now, ladies and gentlemen, children of every age gathered, my next act is a pair who survived the Amazonian jungle. They fought against the odds where no man or woman can lay claim to have escaped. They battled giant poisonous plants, ungodly heat, predators of all shapes and sizes. Treacherous swamps, suffocating quicksand, disease. Together they tamed one of the mightiest beasts, the great jaguar. Please, put your hands together and welcome the Siblings of Flame!"

A terrible gasp shuddered through the crowd as a melanistic jaguar appeared on the stage, its stalking movement forcing every mortal into a mild retreat. The coyote shifted with them and then paused, its nose catching the feline's scent. It turned its gaze upon the stage as the jaguar perched itself on a round stool in the center and sat regally. Promptly, a male and female stepped out from behind the banners on either side the stage. They were dressed in the most peculiar garb, their faces concealed with stunning masks of flames, but their mortal appearances were unable to fool the coyote's powerful sense of smell—*weasel and hare.*

The coyote's fur bristled at the presence of Hades' demon generals. It had not seen hide nor hair of the three Octet members in centuries. It snarled as the jaguar, Tezcat, the high general and Hades' most trusted confidant, scanned the crowd, its yellow eyes searching the crowd.

"Greetings, one and all!" declared the female, holding her arms out wide. The gesture scrunched the doubled collar of the capelet around her neck; the corset of her costume dazzled from the rubies embellished on her hips, chest, and wings. Excess lace woven along the hips dangled over her bare thighs. "Please, come closer," she invited, magically producing a large hoop in her left hand.

The crowd inched toward the stage in response, cutting the coyote from its path to Charles. The coyote tried to squeeze through the extra spaces, but the zigzagged path led it closer to the stage as the entertainers introduced themselves.

"This is Chulda, and I am her brother, Stig," shouted the male with messy curled hair. He pounded his chest with a devil's walking stick, the scarlet tassels on the shoulders of his military jacket moving back and forth. The brass buttons on his jacket shimmered in the rays of the midmorning sun as though acting as spotlights.

The coyote watched the spectacle as Stig, with a grand exhale, breathed fire and torched the end of his stick. The audience oohed and gave a generous applause while Stig lit his sister's hoop. The scarlet flames danced around the sphere as Chulda held it in her hand, the sparks merely licking her skin. She twirled away like a ballerina and took her place right of center stage, holding the hoop. A hush fell over the crowd, their awe bordering on hypnosis.

Stig snapped his fingers, and on cue, the jaguar left its stool and leapt through the burning sphere. Chulda danced back to center stage, the curls of her auburn hair bounced playfully. With Stig's assistance she posed on the stool in a penché, holding out the fiery hoop. With another snap, the jaguar took a running leap, its muscular body flying through the fire and landing on all fours. The crowd roared with enthusiastic applause as the entertainers took their bows.

The praise continued with hoots and whistles, urging the act to produce another trick as two cigar girls came out from behind the banners and tossed bags of peanuts and popcorn balls. The mortals rushed the stage, sweeping the coyote in their wake. It rammed against the bulkhead, the force of the crowd crushing it against wood. Its bones ached under the strain, its body immobilized. Before it could gather enough strength to free itself from confinement, a warm grasp pulled it by the scruff of the neck and liberated it from its plight.

The coyote screamed as flames from Stig's cane pressed against its ribcage, fully aware its predicament was about to worsen.

The mortals in the crowd silenced their frenzy as Stig tossed the coyote across the stage.

Its body flopping into a heap, the coyote tumbled toward the edge.

"Wolf!" shouted one of the cigar girls, and both darted off the stage shrieking. The outburst rippled through the audience, prompting yet another retreat.

"Please, ladies and gentlemen," shouted Stig. "Don't be

alarmed! This mangy coyote is of no threat to you!"

"Madam, if I may," said Chulda, her voice dripping with sweetness, as she reached her hand out toward the child in front of her.

The woman, whose face was gaunt and dirty, her hair tucked under a yellowed bonnet, hesitated. Her dark eyes appeared fearful, but over them was a paralyzing glaze to follow the request like a command. Chulda insisted with an extension of her reach, and the woman, through no true fault of her own, sacrificed her child to the fiery sibling.

"Ladies and gentlemen, witness as this innocent child stands between two formidable foes," announced Stig.

The crowd responded with a collective gasp.

"Watch, as this Dog of the Plains attempts to rescue the child from the likes of an Amazonian King," continued Stig as his sister positioned the child center stage in her fiery hoop.

The coyote remained unmoved, its body in shock. It managed to tilt its chin, however, its yellow eyes fixing on the child caught in Chulda's trap. The audience was still again, their anticipation a mixture of awe and terror. Soft sobs came from the child as the flames sizzled, and in a timid voice it called out to its mother. As fear began to take hold of the coyote, time stalled, and yet what happened next was so sudden.

It was unclear where he came from, but Charles Reese appeared on the stage. He grabbed the child from its fiery prison and returned it to its mother. He then turned to confront the siblings, but was barely able to speak two words before they both stepped aside, allowing the jaguar a clear run at him. The mortal stood fearless, his stare spurring the exotic cat to take its best shot. He firmed his feet, his heels kissing the edge of the stage.

As the feline crouched, the coyote instinctually scrambled

to stand. The jaguar sprang off its paws into a charge as time snapped back into place—it collided with Charles, forcing them both into the crowd.

The mortals scattered as the boy slammed into the ground. His head bounced and a soft crack reached the coyote's ears. It leapt off the stage and took position at Charles's side, the jaguar mere inches away. A trickle of blood appeared from beneath the mortal's hair, his eyes closed, his expression vacant.

The coyote leaned in to lick the mortal's face as though a pet trying to rouse its master, but Charles Reese remained unconscious. It gave a worried whimper, not just for show, but in genuine concern. It was no match for three demon generals, not as a coyote. The only good his animal form provided was a shield of immortality.

In their making, the Black Tortoise had given the Animawalkers eternal life, but only to a point. As animals, the Children of Sea shielded their life force, which became their only defense against deadly attacks. Their creator, the Black Tortoise, had been too weak when the deity of Sea gave them life and had had only enough power to bless a select few with enhanced gifts—among them Coyote Moon. The use of those gifts, however, came at a price, for in order to use them, the bearer had to transform into a mortal, which left an Animawalker vulnerable to death.

The coyote debated whether or not to transform, unconcerned with the exposure or a care as to how many mortals would witness its metamorphosis. Before it could make a decision, however, it felt the battering ram of the jaguar forcing it away from Charles.

The two animals rolled in heated fury, the mortals creating a path for them. The coyote fell out of the tussle and quickly found its footing. It watched as a man and his elder son rushed forward and retrieved Charles Reese from the ground. They swiftly carted his unconscious body into the protection of the crowd, separating him from the Siblings of Flame, who at this point stood in bewilderment.

"Walker," hissed the jaguar.

"General Tezcat," growled the coyote, returning its attention to the exotic feline.

"I thought I smelt stale water."

Rather than acknowledge the insult, the coyote ran off into town, taking to the backyards of the nearby houses. It trampled through a pristine flower bed and a newly planted garden, knocked over the layout of a child's tea party, and barreled head first into a hedge. It was stuck for a moment, its fur knotting in the branches. It wriggled loose, but found itself caught once more by the strength of the jaguar, the demon general pinning it to the ground on its belly.

"I was not finished, Walker," snarled Tezcat. "Now, tell me your name, so that I may know which Child of Sea I have sent to join its fallen creator."

The threat released a distant disturbance in the air, stirring the wind and turning the sky a putrid shade of green. The jaguar roared as the coyote sank its teeth into its leg, drawing a bright shade of red blood. The sudden release of pressure offered the coyote the opportunity to weasel out of the demon's grasp and it took position to defend itself. Tezcat slashed and clawed at the coyote's face, but its blows missed. Countering, the coyote scratched the feline across the face. The jaguar sniffed, twitching its nose, then lunged at the coyote, this time embracing it and digging sharp claws into its back.

The coyote screamed and a close crash of thunder answered in kind, a streak of lightning illuminating the graying sky. The jaguar stepped away and watched the coyote fall.

"Is that all you are capable of, Lesser?" screeched Tezcat.

The coyote remained on the ground and whimpered, acting hurt. It lifted its eyes to the top of the hedge—a bold move, but it needed to study the closeness of the storm. It began to count as thunder rumbled again and watched the sky brighten. The coyote's count reached into the twenties, the lightning far off in the darkened clouds. It needed the rain of the storm, but unless it was willing to transform into a mortal in order to command the natural force, that rain would remain at a distance. Its fur bristled anxiously, ready to shed its animal visage, but hesitation stole its train of thought. To transform would reveal its true identity to the demon general, a secret it had kept from the hordes of Hell for several millennia. No one, save for the Apothecary and the Chameleon, knew a Prince of Sea still lived.

The jaguar took advantage of the coyote's distraction and attacked with claws and teeth, kicking and biting. It was a whirlwind of fur with no reprieve, pounding the coyote mercilessly. The coyote managed to get a few bats in, but for the most part remained defensive. Its continual cries called to the storm, but the clouds ignored its pleas.

Pinning the coyote once again, the jaguar sank its teeth into its throat. Dark blood mingled with sandy fur as the coyote relinquished its struggle. It pounded its paws on the jaguar's chest in a last effort to get some relief, but it only agitated the demon.

"Any final words?" grumbled Tezcat.

The coyote did not respond. It simply closed its eyes and waited for the blow that would immobilize, but not kill. The pain would be real, however, and the recovery would be extensive, the mere thought of which shot panic through the coyote.

The jaguar hissed angrily at its submission, but before it could tighten its jaw any further, a piercing crash tore through the air. The exotic feline immediately released the coyote, its eyes searching for the source of the sound.

At the other end of the yard, a teenage boy stared down the shaky barrel of a rifle. The jaguar roared furiously and took a few steps toward the mortal. The boy answered by cocking the gun and realigning his aim. Thinking better of its advance, the jaguar halted—it could surely take down the insufferable child but not nearly quick enough for him to miss his shot completely. It could take the hit, no matter how accurate, but the demon general could not afford the setback of an injury. Hades' orders were specific and did not include failure.

The jaguar snorted and batted its tail in protest, but all the same turned away in defeat and raced out of the yard without so much as a backward glance.

The teenager lowered his rifle an inch with a nervous sigh.

"What in tarnation is going on out here!" shrilled the boy's mother as the screen door slammed.

The boy looked over his shoulder and then back at the yard. He was ready to explain that he was trying to save a dog, but his eyes saw no sign of the coyote. The boy looked back at his mother at a loss for words. Without proof, she would never believe him.

"Answer me, boy," scolded the boy's mother.

He did not.

"Very well," she said before swearing up her own type of storm.

The coyote listened from its hiding place underneath a cluster of Miss Kim lilac bushes. The woman berated her son further before dragging him and the rifle back into the house.

After the coyote had waited long enough to be sure the boy and his mother would not return, it ventured out, limping toward the backside of a shed where a rain barrel sat. The coyote hoped there would be water in it, at least enough to heal its wounds. It lifted its paws with a grimacing moan and pulled with all its might. The barrel crashed onto the grass and liquid gushed out, dousing it with lukewarm water. It anticipated an immediate audience due to the ruckus, but neither the mother nor her son came to inspect the sound. In fact, the neighborhood had grown fairly quiet, the storm still lingering in the distance.

As the coyote snorted and rolled in the pooled liquid, the fiery venom of the jaguar sizzled against the clash of water, but it was more soothing than painful. The coyote shook out its sopping fur and walked across the yard towards the flapping clothes pinned between the corner of the house and a posted stake. Its pale eyes searched every window for any sign of eavesdroppers; when it could find none, the coyote reluctantly shifted its figure and stood tall on two legs.

With his hands, the man stole an undershirt, a vest, and a pair of pants. They were still damp, but that did not bother him. He buttoned the vest with fumbling fingers, not having used them in some time, realizing his attire was not quite suitable for the character of flesh he had chosen—*It will have to do for now.* When he finished, he contemplated grabbing socks, but it made little sense to wear them without shoes.

As he left the yard, he paused to double-check the windows, feeling as though someone was watching him. If there was, he saw no sign of the vigilant eyes. The man cursed under his breath and lifted his hand to the sky. He had no time to feel remorse or deal with the enlightenment of a mortal. He needed the protection of his creator's water, for with the coming of rain, the demons would retreat, hopefully long enough for him to find Charles Reese.

The man snapped his fingers, and in an instant, droplets began to fall from the sky. He proceeded to the front yard and began to walk back toward the edge of town. The crowd was no longer present, and the stage was vacant of its circus decorations. The man sniffed the air, the freshness of the rain blocking most scents, but not the smell of iron. He looked down at the softening ground, the water pooling craters into the mud. There was no trace of the red that had trickled from Charles Reese's head, but the smell of his blood was strong.

Closing his eyes, the man focused on direction, the image of two men dragging the mortal's unconscious body coming into view. He breathed in deeply and, with the second inhale, discovered the trail.

The man opened his eyes and darted off into the countryside.

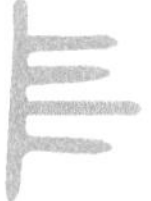

Herbs & Tea

Buck walked into the healing room and posted himself at Jack's bedside, leaving Miriam to linger in the doorway. He stared in horror as the Trickster's body began to convulse, the black snakes rattling across his naked body.

"What do we do?" he asked his mentor, feeling a great sense of helplessness.

"Place your hands on his chest," instructed the Apothecary.

Buck did as asked without question as the eldest Euxian placed a hand on the Trickster's forehead and took hold of his wounded hand.

"Miriam, dear, please come hold down his legs."

His sister squeaked, caught off guard by the request, then darted to the edge of the bed and pressed down on Jack's legs. Buck stole a quick glance at Miriam as her weakened arms absorbed the tremors.

"His skin is so hot," she said, showing her discomfort before turning away from the sight.

"That is the Wicker's Curse trying to take root," replied the Apothecary. "And no matter how bad it gets, Miriam, do not let go."

"Mm."

"Now, Master Breedling, do you recall the taming spell?" asked the Apothecary.

Biting his lower lip, Buck hesitated before nodding.

"Then close your eyes and with me speak the words."

Buck shut his eyes and softly recited the words.

"Again," said the Apothecary. "And with more certainty."

"Deep waters, calm sea, heal thy hurt with a cleansing wave. Purify the rage of Phoenix upon this body and restore the tranquil chill of ice within."

This time Buck felt a pinch in the center of his chest, and his breath hitched. His hands began to tingle as the temperature in his body dropped. A chill cycled through him, pulsing into his hands and into Jack. Miriam emitted a shocked gasp. Startled by her reaction, Buck opened his eyes and watched as the swelling of Jack's veins began to shrink, the blackness fading into dark blue.

"Again," said the Apothecary as the clash of fire and ice filled the room with a sizzling hiss.

Buck spoke the spell once more, this time with more conviction. A piercing chill settled in his core, causing his legs to tremble. He lifted his gaze to check if his mentor was having the same amount of difficulty, but to his surprise, the Apothecary's expression was serene. As the tremor climbed to his back, he feared he would not be able to hold on much longer. Closing his eyes, Buck concentrated on the flow of energy moving through him until it simply overwhelmed him. He collapsed to his knees, his elbows digging into the mattress. His hands slid to Jack's side as he breathed heavily.

"That will do for now," said the Apothecary, opening his eyes. "He will rest soundly for some time, but his healing is far from complete."

Lifting his chin from the bed, Buck saw the blackened skin

of Jack's palm and wrist in the Apothecary's careful caress. He creased his brow—they had not destroyed the curse, merely condensed the venom.

"You have every right to fear this, Master Breedling," said the Apothecary, placing Jack's arm against his side before grabbing the sheet, forcing Miriam to abandon her station. The Apothecary covered Jack's body as Buck pulled away.

"I am grateful, Master Apothecary," he said.

The Apothecary nodded, then turned his attention to Miriam. "You should be off, dear one," he said softly. "Go to the Tales Teller. She will draw you a bath and provide you with a change of clothes. She will conceal you for now, of this you have my word. Your escape from the Reformatory is not in violation of the Fates' law, but we will have to address the terms of your punishment at some point."

Miriam's face turned green with fright, and without a word she raced out of the room, her footsteps silenced by the slam of the door.

Buck had paid little attention to the interaction, his focus solely on Jack. He was reluctant to move, concerned the Trickster might spike another fever. Even with the swollen veils receded into his right arm, Jack's pale skin grew ashen, a symptom related to the rooting of a Wicker's Curse. Buck took hold of Jack's hand, the sheet acting as a barrier between their skin. Under his breath, he whispered—nothing coherent, no complete thoughts, just a string of words to let Jack know he was next to him.

"Come, Bartholomew," said the Apothecary after a while. "You need to replenish your strength before we try again."

Buck nodded and waited until the eldest Euxian was out of the healing room before following. He entered the tea kitchen and found his way to his usual seat at the counter, watching the Apothecary pour hot water into two silver beakers before grinding a few tisane herbs, all of which he knew by name. His gaze drifted to the wall, where tacked rows of wire housed drying herbs hung upside down, bundled together with twine. The first scent he picked out was rosemary followed by a hint of chamomile. It took him a little longer to identify the others, as there was not nearly as much to detect a proper scent—catnip, honeybush, stinging nettle, skullcap, and fennel. All the rest were scattered across the counter, creating an abstract picture on black canvas. In one pile, small purple berries from a cinnamon plant lay encased in a circle made of jasmine flowers and gardenias. In another cluster, rose hips, lemon balm, mint leaves, and orange peels decorated the counter. Buck tried to remember the specialty of each herb, but unfortunately his lessons with the Apothecary on remedies and healing teas had not survived his years in prison. On the edge of the island, a large bowl of water rested precariously; floating inside were a pair of orange hibiscus flowers. At the sight of them, Buck thought of Maddie and Father Van Lewen, his mortal breadcrumbs, and it sparked the litany of questions he had wanted to ask the Apothecary upon his return.

"Bartholomew," said the Apothecary.

"My name is Buck," he grumbled. He had been too distracted earlier to care about the usage of his Euxian name, but now that the commotion was over, he felt the sting of it. He looked at the Apothecary, his former mentor's face fully lit with an endearing expression.

The Apothecary crushed leaves in his palms, letting the dust sprinkle into the beakers. He stirred the concoction and placed one in front of him.

Buck did not reach for it right away.

"Many pardons, Bartholomew," said the Apothecary. "I mean

no disrespect, but the giving of a new name does not change who you are to Euxinus. You are still the same Breedling who begged the Tales Teller to let him read the histories of Eden, the same Breedling who rose to the challenge of any charge; the same Breedling who understood the true nature of loyalty. Until the court recognizes you are no longer a servant of the Fates, you will remain who you have always been: Bartholomew, Breedling of the First Grade."

Buck curled his fingers around the beaker. His hands instantly warmed at the touch, thawing the chill of his skin. He took a large gulp and let the hot water sear his throat, welcoming the discomfort in order to heat his core.

"What you have accomplished," resumed the Apothecary, churning a variety of herbs in the bowl, "is a feat of great importance to those of us who still hold esteem here in Euxinus. You are proof that free will can be obtained by the unwilled."

"But why me? How could the Black Tortoise possibly bless me?"

"To ask such a question is futile, Master Breedling. It is possible your chance encounter with the watery deity was merely happenstance. That you were in the wrong place at the wrong time—or, on the other hand, you were in the right place at the right time. Is it possible the Black Tortoise sought you out? Perhaps, but to presume so would be naïve. You know as well as I, Brother Sea had previously vanished from Eden, and between then and now, you are the only known creature to have made any contact with him. So your answer might be as simple as this: he was resting in the Nile River and he chose to rescue you."

Buck stole a glance at his hands, fingertips pulsing. He tried to view the aura around his skin, the flecks of coal dust, proof he bore the Black Tortoise's blessing. But he could not see it. "Then it is not a matter of knowing or choosing," he said, flexing his fingers. "My incident in Cairo is how you knew I would be the one; the one who had to fall, the one who would find Stingy Jack." Buck elevated his gaze. "You made certain the Fates chose me to seek out the Lost Creators."

The Apothecary's laughter was instant and unexpected, but Buck did not take the response as an insult. Instead, he felt a hint of foolishness.

"You give me far too much credit, Master Breedling. But I will admit you are partly right. When you returned from Egypt, you were unconscious. I tried every spell and concoction I knew to revive you, but you were not ailing from any curse or injury. It was only when I had requested the eyes of your sister that I discovered you had been marked."

"Miriam?"

"By that time, your sister had become keenly skilled at reading auras, having studied every creature within the four realms. She had surpassed even the Fates in such skill, built only upon her determination to serve them better. Before you left for Cairo, she had been diligently cataloging markings used by Hades and Everlyse and how they appeared in creatures, particularly Breedlings. This amount of meticulous work also became a resource for me in healing the ailments of your kin."

"And she saw it? The Black Tortoise's mark?"

"Not right away. First, she saw the residual, superficial marks left by Rachel's morningstar, and then she found the deep angelic wounds left by Mist. It was then Miriam detected a black stone nestled like a seed in your heart. Of course, she had no idea what it was, only that it was a foreign marker of some kind and feared it was the rooting of a Wicker's Curse. Very few Euxians, especially Breedlings, are familiar with the signature of the Black

Tortoise, for the Animawalkers are the only creatures left to carry such distinction and not many of them still exist. Even the Animilia have lost their spark of divinity. There are a few rare exceptions, of course, but not enough to be noticeable. When Miriam described it to me, it took me a moment to remember what it was, having hardly seen it myself in the years after the Black Tortoise's disappearance. Now, unlike before, your aura has shifted since you fell, and the stone has burst into dust, covering every inch of you, which I am certain is due in part to our Silver Wicker."

"You mean Maddie," said Buck, his hand unconsciously slipping into his pocket, fingers caressing the texture of the ribbon she had given him. His thoughts returned to the moment her lips had surprised him with a kiss.

"The same," said the Apothecary.

"Why did you bless her?" asked Buck.

"Even those among the cursed are still worth saving, are they not?"

Buck glanced over his shoulder absentmindedly, his eyes fixed on the door of the healing room where Jack lay resting. Not so long ago, he would have disagreed, but what he had seen that ill-fated stormy night had changed everything. If Iona Covington, a pure soul, could find it within herself to protect the cursed soul of Stingy Jack, then no soul, even that of Wind and Flame, was beyond saving.

"But, why?" he asked. "Why Maddie? Surely, the Fates' mandate to meddle in Eden affairs would have prevented such an incident." Buck waited for a reply, but the Apothecary said nothing. He returned his attention to the counter, not knowing what to expect—to his surprise, the Apothecary's head was hanging in a shameful gesture.

"My Eldest," Buck gasped. "Do the Fates know about her? Is she . . . ?"

The Apothecary held up a hand to silence his rattled nerves. "You should not speak so loudly, Master Breedling," he said in a soft voice. "And no, the Fates know not of my schemes. If they did . . ." He shook his head, not willing to share his thoughts of what the Fates might do to him. "The blessing of Madelina Petrovich was never so specific to her. I simply needed the right Wicker, and she was the one. My search began around the same time I discovered what had happened to you in Egypt. I knew you bore the blessing of the Black Tortoise, but any abilities bestowed upon you needed a catalyst to break forth from their stone casing. I had tried on numerous occasions to crack the stone, but my strength does not lean towards the element of fire. I had no idea my search would take so long, and after Miriam was charged with the retrieval of Eden's Wickers, I had to be even more discreet."

The Apothecary fell quiet for a moment, his thoughts reflective on his actions.

Buck knew the story already—the night the Apothecary had saved Maddie from the house fire that had destroyed her family. The eldest Euxian had taken pity on her, had seen in her a spark of humanity, despite her cursed blood. Her kindhearted nature had garnered his favor and bestowed upon her a blessed relic of the Black Tortoise, a totem to counteract her treacherous impulses and dull the fiery rage in her blood. He did not need to know how he found her; he was just grateful he had, that she had become one of his special breadcrumbs. Buck felt the corner of his mouth lift; at the thought of her doe eyes staring at him, he absentmindedly lifted his hand to press his fingertips against his lips as butterflies fluttered in his stomach.

"Judging by your expression, I see she left an impression."

The Apothecary's words broke him out of his reverie, and he pulled his hand quickly away from his face. He bit the inside of his mouth, embarrassed by his action. The Apothecary laughed, and—though it was at Buck's expense—the Breedling welcomed the lightheartedness.

"By the way," continued the Apothecary, "how did the Lady Mara fare? You did say the prayer, did you not?"

"Wait, how did you even know?" Buck shook his head. "Of course you knew, and of course I did. Just as you taught me, just as you said it to Father Van Lewen's dying mother. But I am afraid it did not work."

The Apothecary lifted an inquisitive eyebrow. "Bartholomew, your powers may still be untested, but from what you did mere moments ago with Jack, I have no doubt you saved her mother."

"Her mother?" Buck's jaw dropped. "Mara is Maddie's mother?"

"So you were unaware of the connection?"

"I . . ." At a loss for words, Buck trailed off, curling in his fingers. He had felt a fleeting connection between the two, seen it in the comparison of their faces, but had thought nothing of it.

"I am in your debt, Master Breedling," said the Apothecary. "You may not know this, but I had promised the young Madelina she would have her name back; because of you and in part because of Master Jack, reuniting her with her mother fulfills my word."

"It appears some things can be made right," said Buck under his breath. He lifted a hand to his face and brushed his fingers across his lips as they curled into a smile, hoping the reunion between mother and daughter had been a joyous one.

The Apothecary left him to his reflective thoughts once more as he began to prepare another beaker of tea.

Buck drank the remaining contents of his brew, his mind

building with more questions. "Tell me," he began, the words spilling out of his mouth. "How did you know Father Van Lewen would keep his word?"

"Bartholomew, you greatly underestimate the power of a promise," replied the Apothecary, pausing to test the tea he was creating. "Once a promise has been made to any supernatural creature, no mortal can break it—their free will is bound to it, like a Breedling to its charge. Choice is a mortal's strongest weapon against the forces of Hades and Everlyse, even Euxians."

"Does that mean you marked Father Van Lewen's soul?"

The Apothecary slammed the beaker on the counter, the bang forcing Buck to flinch. The pleasant expression faded from his face, his eyes burning with a hint of anger. "I do not adhere to the ways of Wind and Flame," the Apothecary snapped, then breathed to cool his bitterness. "For a time, yes, the mortal's soul was marked, but I did not try, in any way, to maliciously take Damek's soul from him or claim it as my own. We simply had an arrangement, a service for a service. I would not have entertained the idea if I had not seen the strength of his fighting spirit. Besides, once he fulfilled his promise, I released him from our bargain."

At this, Buck smiled. "I am glad you visited him. I am certain your words gave him peace of mind." He tried to remember the priest's long face with those thick cheekbones and sharp chin. He listened for his voice, its commanding tone binding him to his charge to find Stingy Jack. It was the end he held onto the most, the promise that one day he would reunite with Charlie. "What about the other breadcrumbs?" his voice spoke, his thoughts once again on his mortal master. "Is Prince Moon among them? Is that why you sent him to Charlie?"

"Master Breedling," thundered the Apothecary, "I thought I

taught you better, or has your loss of Euxian grace damaged your sense of secrecy?"

"What? No, I . . ."

"Then you will do better to remember that there are some things that cannot be so casually spoken of. With the trial of the Shepherdess approaching, Hades and his horde will be allowed into Euxinus."

"Yes, but he is confined strictly to the chambers," objected Buck, anxiety blotting his face. "There is no threat of him coming here. Please, just tell me he is all right."

"Your master is well."

This vague statement brought Buck no relief, but for the time being, he decided against pushing. The last thing he wanted was to put Charlie in any unnecessary danger, but there was one thing more he needed to know. "When I went to Chicago, you told me to stay with Charlie. Why? If Damek was your breadcrumb, why not just tell me to go to him? Charles Reese was not beholden to you. He was not a part of your secret plot."

A brief pause lingered in the tea kitchen, Buck waiting for his answer.

"Charles Reese was initially a means to an end," confessed the Apothecary. "I thought the young mortal would lead you to Damek straightaway, and when he did not, I sent the Tales Teller to charm him, not realizing the effect it would have on him or how he had already affected you. It was foolishness not to consider how you would change, and in my haste, I put in motion a confrontation what will forever plague Charles Reese. It was never my intent for him to cross paths with Creator Hades, let alone fall victim to his mark. But as I told both the Tales Teller and the Chameleon, my plot, as you say, is no longer mine; and in the end, Charles Reese still fulfilled the purpose I had envisioned for him."

"And you feel no remorse, no responsibility?" asked Buck, bitterness in the back of his throat. "You, me, the Tales Teller, the Chameleon, Hades; we are all to blame for his awakening"

"And yet, the same can be said of Charles. He could have left at any time."

Buck wanted to argue the point, but the Apothecary was right. Charlie could have denied him the opportunity to tag along. Let him fall into the clutches of Frankenstein or the Bogeyman. Left him in the care of Grocer Pawlak instead of Father Van Lewen. Or simply left him in the burning orphanage to perish.

"But that was not his way," Buck said, his voice somber. "Without him, my body would be ash and all your plotting would have died with me. He may have decided to save me, but he did not ask to be changed—to have the veil ripped from his eyes, to be marked, to be a master. If I had known saving me would have created such a future for him, I would have been more insistent he leave me to die."

"You must think very little of him, Bartholomew."

"I think no such thought!"

"Then speak no more of what could have been," said the Apothecary. "There is nothing overtly special about Charles Reese, in the sense that there has not been any supernatural influence in his life. What makes him unique is his humanity, for what he did can only come out of pure selflessness. A far greater force than that of Hades' anger, Everlyse's apathy, or the Fates' arrogance nurtured his kind heart and strong spirit. Such love has a way of ascending mortals to greatness or to great suffering. For Charles Reese, the double-edged sword is sharpest on both ends, and it will act as both his salvation and ruin. His heart would never have allowed you to suffer such a cruel end. He chose to save you, and for that I am eternally in his debt."

The Apothecary lifted his beaker in a toast.

Buck nodded and finished his tea. He understood what the Apothecary had said, but the truth of the words still left him unresolved. "Your wisdom knows no bounds, my Eldest," he said, offering a half-smile.

"You honor me, Master Breedling, but do not be so quick to call me wise, for if I were wiser I would have broken my bonds with the Fates long ago. I am not as strong as you."

"My Eldest, you cannot mean that," said Buck, overflowing with disbelief. He had never heard the Apothecary speak in such a manner.

"I do," said the Apothecary, a silent stir of offense in his voice. "I see where this may come as a surprise to you, Bartholomew, but remember—though I must serve the Fates, I do not consider them my masters."

"Then who do you call master?"

"The Tales Teller would say I am a slave to my ambition," the Apothecary replied, chuckling. "And she may be right. I have grown increasingly meddlesome since your incident on the Nile River."

"Is that who you call master? Do you serve the Lost Creators?"

The Apothecary merely turned his back and reached for the warmed kettle. He began to pour water into his beaker. "More tea?" he asked.

Auras

Buck wanted to push. The rationalization of the Apothecary conspiring on behalf of the Black Tortoise and the Golden Faun was incredibly plausible, but his mentor's demeanor told him it was a conversation for perhaps another time. Besides, he was too tired to ask, and he felt drowsy clouds forming in his mind. He thought of Maddie first, the image of her warm smile putting him in a blissful state of ease. She was saying something to him, but he could not make out the words, except for—*will you be my seventh?* It was then he heard Damek's voice ask the same thing, and he finally realized he had known all along how many breadcrumbs the Apothecary had created. Not only that, he felt a nagging memory buried deep within his subconscious—the voice behind the echoing words of the seventh. He could not remember what it meant or whose voice repeated it over and over like the tolling of a bell.

Buck swiftly removed himself from the stool, jolting himself from the drumming in his head, then crossed the tea kitchen and stood at the far window. Staring out at the Equadrian Square, he felt a sense of déjà vu, his mind trying to break the wall that barricaded the truth from him. As he braced against the window frame, a wave of fatigue crashed through him and he cursed under his breath. Whatever had been trying to surface had evaporated. He sighed, not overtly upset, for obvious reasons. The memory was hardly relevant to the task at hand.

His eyes caught sight of Miriam exiting the Tales Teller's coffin, her presence dramatically different from before—even her steps seemed lighter. Buck smiled at the sight of her, reveling in the prospect of her freedom from her bonds radiating this type of merriment once again. She walked slowly, pausing before the fountain as he pushed away from the window and returned to his seat at the counter. Closing his fingers around the refilled beaker, he took an immediate sip, mustering the courage to break the silence in the wake of his last question.

"I see you are both deep in thought as usual," said Miriam, a happy chime in her voice.

Feeling himself relax, Buck shifted on the stool, rotating his body in order to see his sister. She stood with hands cupped near the door, her ragged clothes no longer darkening her physique with misery. Her new dress was a rich burnt gold that was fitted at the top and flowy at the bottom. If she started twirling, he was certain she could make the skirt dance. Across her waist, a sash of black, stitched with hibiscus flowers, professed a statement of rebellion. Her velvet hair complemented the dress, its shade of deep violet falling over her shoulders, straight and untangled. Her russet skin was softer and refreshed, but despite the transformation, her lavender eyes could not hide her true feelings or the suffering she carried.

"How is the Trickster?" she asked, walking across the room.

"Still resting," said the Apothecary, preparing an additional beaker of tea. "Master Breedling will have to perform another patching spell now that warmth has been restored to his core."

"But that does not mean you have cured him."

"Not even close," continued the Apothecary. "No, Master Jack's injury will take more time, a luxury we do not have on our side, which means his demeanor will need careful watching at the trial."

"A fair assessment, my Eldest," agreed Miriam, bringing herself to the counter. "Brother, you will have to take heed of the Trickster's mood. I have witnessed the effects of the Wicker's Curse first hand on plenty of mortals, and I can tell you there may be a moment where he becomes destructively violent to himself and to anyone near him without reason."

Buck nodded, burying his face in his beaker. He did not want to think about the potential detriment Annaliese's blade might have on the outcome of the Shepherdess's trial.

Finished with stirring the beaker, the Apothecary placed it in front of Miriam. "Drink up," he said. "Chamomile. It will help you get a pleasant rest—the divine only knows the last time you had a restful slumber, dear. Now, if you will excuse me, I must step out for a moment and converse with the Tales Teller on the impending trial."

"She's in her study," offered Miriam, taking hold of the warm beaker. "At least that is what she told me to tell you."

Buck's face flushed. "Wait, what about Jack?"

"As I said, another patching spell should help keep him subdued for now. If you need to, I suggest using that trinket of his to boost your energy."

Without allowing him the chance to ask a question in reference to the silver cross in his pocket, the Apothecary removed himself from the tea kitchen and exited his coffin.

"How did he know?" asked Buck, eyes wide as he looked at the front door.

"Know what?" asked Miriam, taking a sip of her tea. Her throat hummed with satisfaction.

"How?" Buck paused, brow creasing as he turned back to his sister, judging whether he should say anything more.

"Bartholomew?"

Buck leapt off his stool and entered the healing room without explanation, Miriam calling his name again before her feet followed him. He took position once again at Jack's bedside and assessed his condition. The Trickster's skin was still ashen and void of any grotesque veins. The only blackness visible was the charred-looking flesh of his right arm. Buck gently rolled down the sheet to reveal Jack's chest, reached into his pocket, and pulled out the silver cross to the surprised gasp of Miriam.

"Bartholomew, how? Where? Is that . . ."

Buck chuckled inside at her inability to formulate a complete thought. "Yes, dearest sister, it is what you think."

"A relic of Sea." Miriam gasped again, before taking her post opposite him. "Bartholomew, do you know what this means?"

Buck pondered the question, but was too slow for Miriam's liking.

"It means you can set me free."

"What?"

"The cross, give it to me," she demanded, reaching out her hand.

Buck pulled the blessed object into his chest for safe keeping. He stared at his sister, dumbfounded by the wild twisting of her expression.

"Bartholomew, give it to me."

"No."

"Brother, you promised."

The pain in Miriam's words garnered his sympathy. He knew he had promised to help her, but this was not the way. He tried to tell her as much, but she would have none of it; he tried to talk her down, but nothing seemed to work. She was too eager and aware, neither of which would prepare her for her task to break her bonds. She needed to feel hollowed if she was to succeed; right now, she was too refreshed.

"You promised!"

"My dearest sister . . ."

"No," Miriam protested, sitting on the next bed to Jack. "The relic of the Black Tortoise can give me the will to choose. It can help me choose to turn my back on the Fates. Why will you not help me?"

"It is not that I will not help you, but it is not enough for you to have a choice, Miriam. Our obedience is rooted deep within us, and the only way to get rid of that is to rip it out. Touching this cross will not give you that. Besides, you already have the will to choose. You have it of your own volition."

"I have no such thing," shouted Miriam, her tone curt.

Buck threw his hands to his sides, nearly dislodging the cross from his grasp. A twinge of frustration swept his face and leaked into his voice. "Then how is it you were able to leave the ranks of our kin? To kneel before me and beg me to speak my truth? How could a Breedling of the Second Grade feel any amount of loyalty toward a traitor? You came to my defense, remember? You implored the Fates to read my aura. You shed tears for me without any regard to our created nature."

"And given the opportunity I would do it again!" countered Miriam, her volume matching his. "I will always defend you, always. But don't stand there and tell me I had a choice. It was an impulse, an overwhelming feeling to protect you. There was nothing I could do to combat it, nor was there any way for me to express it."

"Then you understand," said Buck. "I too felt as you did. That feeling is what prevented me from speaking the truth. I could not turn such knowledge over to the Fates."

"Regardless of whether I understand or not, you had no right . . ." Her voice trailed off, the statement unfinished. Her arms pressed in an embrace around herself, her face uncomfortable.

Sighing, Buck felt his fit of anger deflate. He could not tell what had come over him, only that it might have something to do with the transfer of energy coming off Jack.

"Just do what you came in here to do so you can quiet him," said Miriam, her gaze turned away.

Buck looked at his sister. Her expression was full of frustration—or maybe it was anger. She was conflicted, on the cusp of breaking but not ready to shatter. He had denied her temporary relief from her suffering, and he felt a sense of remorse over it. As he should.

Dropping his chin, he stared at Jack. The Trickster seemed so peaceful, but the pulse from his injured hand gave off an aura of toxicity. The negative energy was affecting Buck's mood, probably Miriam's as well, and he did not particularly like the feeling.

Buck set the cross on Jack's chest, his eyes checking Miriam to see if she would try for the relic again, but she was content enough not looking at him. He placed one hand on the cross and the other over the blackened skin, wincing at the sudden heat sting but gritting his teeth, fighting back the discomfort. He hesitated, his eyes once again trying to see the flecks of coal dancing about the ivory skin, but to no avail.

"It is there," said Miriam, still not looking at him. "The dust, I mean."

Buck lifted his gaze just enough to see she was holding back an amused smirk.

"You never were any good at seeing auras," she teased, the lightheartedness in her voice dispelling the tension in the room.

"How did you do that?" he asked. He was not fully at ease, but he did feel less agitated.

"Practice," Miriam replied, shrugging. "I have had to learn how to adapt in order to survive the growing weight of being around Wickers for the last two Eden centuries." Her gaze was soft, yet somber.

Buck looked down immediately, his guilt over what had happened to her gripping him.

"But you know that is not all I see," she continued.

His nerves teetering on the verge of fear, Buck remained still. He had not spoken about his encounter with the Golden Faun because he did not trust the influence the Fates still held on her. But by his own words, he had said she had the ability to choose, created by her own will. So, really, what did he have to fear from her? As long as she was nowhere near the Fates, his secret was safe, and there was no place safer for her to be than in the confines of the Apothecary's coffin. Besides, the secret only needed to last until after the trial.

"What does it look like?" he asked.

"Sparks of gold, like comets in Eden's night sky," said Miriam, unfolding her arms and placing her hands on the bed. "Her mark is by far the most dazzling, and I imagine the magnetism of the Golden Faun is quite the sight to behold."

"It is," said Buck under his breath. He did not bother to raise his head, but lifted his eyes high enough to see Miriam checking her wrists, no doubt able to see the weblike binding of the Fates' hold on her. He remembered how heavy that binding had become in the end and knew by the exhausted expression on her face she wished to be free, like him. She did not press him further about the Golden Faun; it seemed enough for her to confirm the earthly deity was the one he had found.

After a moment, she rose from the bed and stood opposite him once more. Her eyes studied the Trickster, no doubt trying to crack the coded aura of Jack's soul.

"It is strange," she finally said. "Despite all the fiery markings on his soul, Stingy Jack does have a dark spot in the center of his chest. Oh, the fire sits there, perched on top of his flesh, but it cannot penetrate any further, as though another force is protecting the very core of his being."

"And you cannot see past it?"

Miriam smiled, lifting her gaze to meet his. "No. It is a marking I have never seen before, but I am certain it is the product of the divine. Now, why not do what the Apothecary has asked so we can go back to enjoying our tea?"

Smiling in agreement, Buck returned his focus to Jack and began to recite the Apothecary's spell. He felt the familiar pinch in his chest before the chill settled in his core. He produced the words five times before his legs began to tremble. The infected skin sizzled and steamed from the clash of temperatures, but he held back his discomfort. Closing his eyes, he thought of Maddie and the spell she had inadvertently planted in his skin, the strange mixture of heat and power. He tried to recreate the sensation, building it with the words of the only healing prayer he knew. He scrunched his eyes tight, digging deep for the recognition, intense pressure building inside him.

"Bartholomew."

He heard Miriam's voice call him but could not break his spell-making in order to respond.

"Bartholomew, that is enough," came Miriam's voice, concern shrouding every syllable.

Eventually, his voice gave out, and the tightness in his chest began to steal his breath. He felt so cold.

It was hard to know when her arms embraced him or when he was no longer on his feet, but at some point Miriam held him in her lap. He managed to open his eyes, his teeth chattering uncontrollably, a coursing pain mingling with the numbness. As tears began to form in his eyes, he felt her hand take hold of his; he responded, gripping it tightly.

With her free hand, Miriam rubbed her fingers across the back of his head and neck, drawing figure eights. "Shhh," she whispered, running her hand through his wispy brown hair, keeping her strokes long and light.

Fatigue washed over Buck as his eyes grew puffy and red from the tears.

Miriam hummed a charming reflective melody to soothe him, but it had little effect on the distress of his body. He blinked the stinging water from his eyes, the chill and pain increasing tenfold. She pulled him in closer, smothering him with her warmth, but it did little to break his icy fever. Buck attempted to speak, but the words stuck in his throat.

He watched her eyes closely, until something stole her attention. Unable to turn his head, Buck relied on his peripheral vision, he saw the blurred image of the Apothecary standing in the doorway, his ageless face unreadable. He crossed the floor anxiously, a sense of fear mounting on his face, then knelt gracefully next to the Breedling, examining his face with his hands.

"Is he all right?" Miriam asked.

"Not at the moment," said the Apothecary, putting his arms underneath Buck and lifting him from the floor. "He went too far."

"What does that mean?"

"The cooling force he summoned from his link with the Black Tortoise has turned his insides into ice," the Apothecary replied, placing Buck on the vacant bed and beginning to strip him of his clothes. "Miriam, dear, please go in the kitchen and douse one of the cloths with water from the kettle; it should still be warm, so take care. Wring it out and bring it to me. Also, grab his beaker of tea."

Miriam went and did as asked, or at least Buck assumed as much, because he could no longer see her in the healing room. He watched the Apothecary diligently, trying to fend off the clouding fatigue pulling him under. The eldest Euxian clapped his hands together and rubbed them fast before placing them on either side of Buck's cheeks. It was an instant shock of warmth, prompting alertness. The Apothecary proceeded to repeat the action, placing his hands on the Breedling's neck, shoulders, breast, lower ribs, hips, thighs, and feet.

"This is only a temporary fix, Master Breedling," said the Apothecary as Miriam handed him the beaker of tea. "Just long enough for you to drink this," he added, lifting Buck's shoulders to help him drink the tea.

The temperature was no longer scorching, but it did penetrate the chill.

"There," the Apothecary continued, placing Buck's head on the pillow. "Rest now. The Chameleon has not returned with Everlyse and Hades yet, so there is some time for you to recover your strength."

Buck felt the warmth of the moist cloth as the Apothecary fanned it across his chest. Miriam leaned over and kissed him on the forehand, her touch loving and fragile. He offered her a small smile before falling asleep.

Healing Room

Waking from a dreamless slumber, Buck batted his eyes. The light in the healing room was faint, several expired candles giving the room a sense of night, but he did not mind the dimness—he was simply grateful it was not dark. Buck allowed the familiar black ceiling to come into view, though unlike his former prison cell, the tourmaline crystal above glistened with imaginary stars. He took a moment to snuggle in the security of the bed, curling the cotton sheet under his chin and digging the back of his head into the downy pillow. He invited the serenity, unable to recall the last true moment of peace he had felt, and left his mind still so as not to allow a thought into his consciousness. He used the respite to temper his breath and secure his feelings. He needed to be ready, unwavering, and focused.

Finally, Buck drew back the sheet and rolled his head, resting his right ear on the pillow. In the bed next to him, Jack lay tucked under white silk covers, his skin now a pale shade of green. Buck smiled, glad to see the Trickster's symptoms had changed. The Wicker's Curse was subsiding. Out of the corner of his eye, he caught the shadow of the Apothecary standing in the arched doorway and tilted his head back; he watched the eldest Euxian cross the room, his black velvet robe sweeping the floor.

The Apothecary carried a small silver tray with two beakers of steaming herbal tea, the scent of honey and rose hips filling the room. Buck pushed himself up against the wall.

The Apothecary set the tray on the small nightstand between the two oval beds and moved back to the doorway to gather the bamboo chair—a gift Jardina had given him upon returning from a charge in the Eden Orient. He placed it equally between the beds before taking a seat. After fixing his robe, he gave Buck his attention, pulling back the silvery strands of his long hair from his eyes and revealing a warm smile.

"It has been a while since I have had so much excitement," said the Apothecary.

Buck smiled at his mentor's attempt to lighten the mood. He wanted to reply with something witty, but his voice was not prepared. Instead, he used his hands to gesture his thanks. Looking about the room a little more, he noticed the third bed to his right was empty. He turned back to the Apothecary with a flash of panic.

"Not to worry, Bartholomew. After you fell asleep, I examined her before sending her to bed. The energy in the room was compromising her, so I sent her to rest in the upstairs quarters. Like you, she must regain her strength if she is going to have a chance at succeeding with her escape. Did you tell her what needs to be done?"

Buck gripped the sheet. "Not entirely," he said, twisting his expression as guilt settled back into his thoughts. "I refused to tell her how I escaped. Not because of what it entails, but because I broke her heart once already and could not bring myself to break it again. Besides, she is not ready to hear what I have to say."

"It is not a little thing you will ask of her, nor will it come so easily to her. She is not like you, Bartholomew," the Apothecary continued. "She is not looking to escape because of some higher calling or charge. Plus, you had the blessing of two Creators on your side. She does it for reasons that are more selfish than yours, although survival in any form has merit." He paused to consider his next words. "Her loyalty to you, which in truth is the clearest notion of love I have encountered in any Euxian apart from the council, will be enough to help her endure the fall."

Shying away, Buck returned his attention to Jack. He knew the Apothecary was right, but he was also wrong. It had never been his mission that drove him to escape, not if he were being honest with himself. The moments of isolation had broken him, his pain too much for him to endure. He had escaped out of necessity to survive. The Apothecary's letter had given him the tool needed after his fall to remind him of the other reason—the promise he had made the night Iona Covington died—for without it, he would have all but abandoned his mission to stay alongside Charlie. He held onto that thought, blissfully wondering what adventure he and his new master would have encountered, but nothing came to mind.

It was then that he wondered if it would be the same for Miriam—if somewhere in Eden a mortal waited for her. Would she too turn away from the one mortal who could give her existence meaning, as he had done with Charlie?

Buck shamefully dropped his eyes to his lap, unable to hide his expression.

"Fear not, Bartholomew. All will come to resolution in the end. Granted, maybe not fully in the way we might expect. For instance, the Trickster is not quite how I had envisioned him, but it makes sense that the Eden Wanderer would turn out to be Hades' mortal rival. The amount of scarring is also more than I anticipated, both on his flesh and in his soul. Out of all the pieces in my design,

Stingy Jack was the most foreign to me. My 'wild card,' as the mortals say. Pain shrouds his essence like armor, burying truths he has long forgotten, so that even the Tales Teller cannot reach them. As for you, Master Breedling, your transformation is more impressive than I could have imagined."

Buck lifted his head as the Apothecary reached for a beaker on the silver tray and handed it to him.

"Drink this," he said. "It should be cooled enough now—lukewarm, as you prefer."

Cupping his hands around the beaker, Buck blew the steam away from the top and breathed in the aroma of honey and rose hips. He sipped the warm liquid as it ran down his parched throat, leaving an aftertaste of rosemary. Clarity evaporated the fog around his thoughts, returning a flood of images he had held locked away: Iona's sorrowful face in the flash of lightning, her tears indistinguishable from the raindrops. He stared at her and lost himself in her eyes. Slowly her pain became his, and her plea became a standing command. He felt his eyes swell, her agony as fresh now as it had been that stormy evening. Buck released an unsteady exhalation before taking a deep breath and drinking the rest of his tea. He slammed the beaker on the tray, the contact creating a forced chime, then held his position, focusing strictly on combating the flood of emotion. His grip became tighter.

"Do you mind?" groaned Jack's voice.

Buck immediately lifted his chin, his line of sight finding two blue orbs. "Jack."

The Trickster blinked in response, but his tired expression gave way to a spark of pain, the skin on his brow wrinkling as he squinted. He took a shallow breath and reopened his eyes.

Buck smiled, hoping to mask the mess of sadness on his face. He did not need Jack asking questions he was not ready to answer.

"Buck, what happened?" Jack forced the words through tight lips. "I remember—being really hot, and then everything was numb. There was so much pain."

"You were cursed, Jack. The poison on Annaliese's blade was Wicker blood."

"Cursed?" Jack's gaze fell away.

He watched the struggle unfold in the Trickster's expression as he tried to remember what had transpired. Buck had not asked Miriam to explain their interaction in full, but he had an inkling it had started defensively cordial, mellowed, and then deteriorated into dangerous hostility.

"The butterfly," said Jack into his pillow, piecing together his thoughts. "The Coymorph." A small pool of drool escaped the corner of his mouth. He did not even get to his encounter with Miriam. "The cross?" Jack tossed his head from side to side as he struggled to move, unable to sit up. "Buck, why can't I move?"

"Jack, calm down," warned Buck, peeling back his sheet and forgetting his nakedness. He forced himself off the bed, unprepared for his legs to give way. He collapsed instantly, but the Apothecary caught him before hitting the floor.

"I think it best you stay in bed a little longer, Bartholomew," said the eldest Euxian. "You have not fully recovered your strength."

Buck let the Apothecary put him back in bed, laying him down rather than sitting him upright. The security of the sheet returned upon his skin and he felt relaxed.

"Now, as for you, Master Jack," said the eldest Euxian as he took the Trickster by the shoulders and pulled him up. "Your trinket is here on the stand."

"Give it to me," Jack demanded.

The Apothecary appeared uncomfortable for a moment

but seemed to regain his composure quickly. "I will not," he said sternly. "Your trinket will remain here until you have the wherewithal to collect it yourself. Now, drink this."

"Do as he says, Jack," said Buck, his gaze once again on the sparkling ceiling, although, from the corner of his eye, he saw the Apothecary tilt Jack's head and press the beaker to his lips. Jack made a horrified face and spit out the tea the instant it hit his taste buds. The Apothecary gave him no chance to recover and forced the cooled medicine down his throat. Jack gasped when the last of the liquid left the beaker and choked on it, coughing violently as his skin color softened to its ghostly shade. When the fit abated, the Apothecary tucked him back into bed.

"I will prepare another brew," said the eldest Euxian, then dismissed himself from the room.

Despite his need to move, Buck remained still. He opened his mouth, but no words came out. He swallowed, his throat suddenly dry. He could not quite explain the onset of nerves, only admit that he had them.

"What happened to the girl?"

"Annaliese?"

"No, Miriam," said Jack.

"She is upstairs resting," replied Buck, before clearing his throat. "About Miriam—she is my sister. And before you say anything, I do not know exactly what happened between you, but . . ."

"It's all right, mate. Nothing happened—well, except for me collapsing into a heap ridden in pain. All things considered, it was about time I got some just desserts."

"But you did not deserve it." Buck turned his head and found Jack already considering him with an uncharacteristic expression.

"And that is where we differ, Master Breedling," said Jack, his tone flush with defeat. "Fer all that I have done, what is one more curse to a creature as detestable as me? Some might say knowing one's true nature is the first step to becoming a better man, but such a thing is not within my grasp."

"If I may," interjected the Apothecary as he reentered the room. He placed the silver tray once again on the nightstand, three beakers present, then took Jack by the shoulders and hoisted him up, leaning him against the wall. The sheet fell away to reveal the scars on the Trickster's chest.

Buck closed his eyes, unable to look at them, a sense of shame filling him for having observed something so private.

The Apothecary draped a white robe over Jack's shoulders and helped him dress. "It is all right, Master Breedling," he said. "You can open your eyes now."

Buck did as instructed and watched as Jack inspected the cloth bandage wrapped around his right forearm.

"Best leave it on," instructed the Apothecary. "At least until after the trial. We do not need to give Hades any more fuel to use against you. Now, drink this. It will restore your strength." The Apothecary placed the hot beaker in Jack's hands. "You too, Bartholomew," he added, moving Buck into a sitting position before handing him a beaker. He reached for the third beaker and returned to his chair.

As Jack took a sip, his cheeks instantly turned a pale shade of pink. He pulled the beaker from his lips, his thoughts readable on his face.

Buck kept his gaze on his lap, breathing in the scent of rose hips and honey.

"Seeing how Bartholomew is still not himself, you may ask of me any question, Master Jack, and I will entertain a reply," offered the Apothecary.

"Why did ye call him Bartholomew?" asked Jack, his voice hoarse.

"Because that is his name—at least that is the name he is called here in Euxinus. And although he was given an Eden name by his new master, I do not recognize such a name until it has been written into record."

"You mean Charlie Reese," said Jack as he stole a glance at Buck.

"Indeed," replied the Apothecary. "But surely, this cannot be the only question you wish to ask."

Jack curled his fingers around the beaker. "Tell me," he spoke, lifting his eyes to the Apothecary. "Tell me about this place, Euxinus. Tell me about the Lost Creators Buck seeks. About Hades and his sister Everlyse. Tell me why I am the way I am. Tell me about Iona's trial, what I need to do, and how we can win. Tell me everything."

The Apothecary raised an eyebrow and shifted his gray eyes to the Breedling.

"There has not been enough time to explain everything," said Buck, sensing his mentor's gaze, his voice gruff and hollow.

"Then it is best to start at the beginning, I suppose, and if that is the case, such a lesson warrants a certain level of storytelling I cannot offer you."

"Wait, so you are not going to answer my questions?"

"I never said I would answer them," said the Apothecary. "I said I would entertain a reply. Besides, the Tales Teller is better equipped to tell you the legacies of this world, and once you understand those, I will tell you what it all means for you and Iona in our present." The Apothecary rose from his seat. "Finish your tea. Once you are done, Master Breedling will escort you across the square."

"Wait, you're not even coming with us?"

"It is not that he does not want to, Jack," spoke Buck, being careful to choose his next words wisely. "Where we are going, the Apothecary is not allowed."

"He can't go into another coffin?"

"Not exactly," said Buck, staring at the eldest Euxian's pained face. "He cannot enter the Tales Teller's library."

Jack opened his mouth, but the Apothecary offered an answer before he could question.

"The mystery of that is not a topic you need to explore, Master Jack. So, if you want your initial answers, you will go with Bartholomew and call on the Tales Teller." The Apothecary looked at Buck. "When next we meet, Master Breedling, our interaction may not be as familiar. I have left the ornaments of your station on the empty bed. Master Jack, the white robe I have provided will suffice as your attire at the trial. Till then." The Apothecary presented a cordial bow.

Buck returned the gesture with a nod and watched the Apothecary take his leave. His eyes lingered on the doorway for a moment until he no longer felt the eldest Euxian's presence. He wasted no time and chugged his tea, then threw aside the covers and found the strength to get out of bed, although his legs wobbled underneath him as he stood. Staring at the decorations spread on the snowy sheet, he traced his fingers along the crescent moon patch stitched on the gray robe. A twist in his gut brought about a sense of longing he wished were not real. With the Fates there had been security, no fear or want for anything. He would never have had to question the way of things nor feel that he needed to ask questions. To have it end as it did—he shook his head, pushing the regretful thoughts from his mind, for there was nothing to regret. He had made the right choice, because it had been his choice to make.

"Buck, what's wrong?"

Buck tilted his head to the side. "Nothing," he answered, then turned away again. "Just thinking about old ghosts."

"Ghosts?"

"It is only a figure of speech, Jack." Buck picked up the robe and threw it around his shoulders, staring at the remaining decorations lying on the bed—the insignias of his Euxian station. He balled his hands, angry with himself for fearing what lay ahead, the truth he would have to tell.

Buck felt the Trickster place a hand on his shoulder, giving him a hesitant pat. The gesture was sincere, but it made the moment awkward. Jack retreated abruptly as Buck turned to acknowledge him. He was stunned to find concern on Jack's face, the Trickster's usual defenses more transparent due to the Wicker's Curse. The emotion was underdeveloped, partly because he was trying to hide it, but it was the same expression he had displayed for Danny O'Toole, the red-headed spitfire they had rescued on the streets of Minneapolis.

Jack stuffed his hands in his pockets, his stature uncomfortable, his skin shifting once more to a pale green.

"I almost forgot." Buck approached the nightstand, gathered his trinkets from his clothes—Maddie's orange ribbon and Charlie's harmonica—and stuffed them inside the hem of his robe. He refused to appear in front of the court without Charlie's presence. He reached for the silver cross and handed it to Jack. "Best to keep this with you," he said with a smile. "If something goes awry, it will be your best source of protection from Hades or his demons. I am uncertain if it will have the same effect on angels, but they are not currently a threat to you."

Jack took hold of the heirloom, and instantly his skin shifted back to its ghostly shade. "And what about ye?" he asked, placing the cross in his pocket. "I mean, will any of those give ye protection?"

"These are merely symbols to be worn at the trial. This robe pays tribute to the Squabbles of the Hollow, imitating the gray color of their scales. The four tassels that will go around my neck represent the Elements or the Creators—scarlet for Hades, azure for Everlyse, gold for Earth, and black for Sea. The three-star insignia over the left breast signifies the masters I once served. The crescent moon patch signifies my station among my kin, Breedling First Grade, the highest honor. A willow patch symbolizes the Scar Healers, those charged by the Fates to heal Eden Scars. It is not a role I have played often."

Buck paused and observed the silvery green willow. He had not thought about the connection before, but he suddenly felt a burst of ironic laughter build inside him. He looked at Jack, whose eyes lingered on the weeping tree, pain breaking across the Trickster's face.

"Jack . . ."

"It was Iona. It was the symbol she used to brand her sheep with in order to identify her herd." Jack wrapped his hand around the brand above his wrist. "It was the only thing of hers left I could carry with me after she died." He paused, his eyes fighting back tears. "When this is all over—the trial, I mean—ye will tell me how it happened."

"Jack, I . . ."

"I know ye know, Buck, so yer avoidance is futile. I can see it plain on yer face. Ye were with her—maybe not at the end, but ye were there. Ye saw something." Jack cleared his face of all emotion, his stare hardening. "Promise me that once we have saved her, ye will tell me what happened to Iona that night?"

Buck kept his gaze on Jack's eyes until he could not stand

the sight of their intensity. He felt cornered, unwilling to fulfill the Trickster's request, despite his previous promise to explain everything. His breaths became labored as he remembered this sensation. It was the same terror he had experienced when Charlie challenged him to reveal Hades' true identity. And just as before, like a coward, he fled the healing room, passed through the tea kitchen, and opened the front door. He took a deep breath and gazed out into the well-lit square, his eyes scanning the four coffins on the opposite side. Off to the left, what was once the seventh member's coffin appeared more decrepit than when he had looked out the window moments ago, its stone bricks cracked, the foundation wasting into dust, the dark-tinted glass cracked, the peak roof caved in. What he had seen earlier had been nothing more than the mere echo from his memory—*the seventh*. The word haunted him for a moment but faded as he stepped out into the glowing square.

All around the circle, the tall lanterns housed bursts of scarlet flame. He drew away from the Apothecary's coffin and approached the fountain. It towered above him like a grand mountain peak rising from the very heart of the Land of Dark Sky. Its slopes were smooth, carved out by the cascade of water that once occupied its center like lava rushing into the sea. Around the base of the volcano, four island pillars posted a direction. On each pillar was a majestic statue, personifying one of the elemental spirits— phoenix, heron, tortoise, and faun. Buck's eyes remained on the faun, its statue posed on four hooves, its head slightly turned, its ears perked as if ready to listen.

Buck knelt on the cobblestones and peered over the edge, expecting to see his reflection in the base, but the pool had long ago lost all water. He reached his hand into the empty pool and ran his fingers along the bottom, feeling the cool grit of earth as he scooped some into his hand. A soft breeze floated down from the peak and whirled around the mountain. It swept across his hand and forearm, but it never reached beyond his elbow, for the base of the fountain was its boundary, caged to remain eternally around a fake volcano, a dry sea, and dead earth.

Buck locked the earth in his palms and folded his hands together. The corner of his eye caught the beam of blue, the radiance of the Euxian moon trying its best to penetrate the warm glow of the square. He tilted his head to gaze fully on the glow of the Fates' palace, but for some reason, its radiance was not nearly as grand as it used to be. Turning back to the fountain and squatting on his heels, keeping his hands on the ledge, he tried to think of something to say, something that would be appropriate, but nothing came to mind. He lifted his gaze to the faun once more, her ears still ready to listen.

"Forgive me," he breathed and hung his head in shame, unable to stomach the sight of the lost deity. He tightened his fists around the earth until it began to escape through the cracks of his fingers, then dropped his hands into his lap and closed his eyes to stem the tears. In the sleeve of his robe, the harmonica came loose from the hem and brushed against his skin—*Charlie*. Buck began to hum the sober notes of Jimmy's Lullaby, freeing his mind to speak in silent prayer.

By Tortoise and Faun, Earth and Sea, may that which was lost, be saved. So that no longer lost it shall remain.

"Buck," came Jack's voice.

Buck released the tension in his grip and unfolded his hands, the remaining earth sprinkling over the stone. He rose to his feet and faced Jack. "Yes, Jack, when this is all over. When we have saved Iona, I will tell you what happened. I swear it on the life of my master."

"I shall hold ye to yer word."

Buck sighed. "I expect nothing less."

They stood for a moment in silence; then his ears detected the distinct sound of water, and he stole a glance at the peak of the volcanic mountain. Glistening along the slope, a single stream trickled into the empty pool, the smell of fresh rain lingering in the sulfuric air.

The Library of the Tales Teller

Jack stood outside the threshold of the Tales Teller's coffin, a ghostly presence whispering to him beyond the open door. It did not hiss or feel malicious in any way, but there was something about it that seemed all too familiar to him. The serene whisper of someone he knew? Jack, oddly insecure, felt a chill ghost along his back. His injured arm began to tremble, and he pulled it in close to his chest, the sleeve of his robe falling into the bend of his elbow. He stared at the cloth covering his skin. What did it look like underneath? Was it black as if burned by fire? He began to unconsciously pick at the bandage.

"Jack, stop." Buck grabbed his curious hand, the Breedling's cool touch pulsing a wave of calm through him.

"How bad is it?" he asked.

"It is of no consequence now."

"To me it is."

"The Apothecary and I were able to concentrate the poison in your forearm to keep it from taking root, but, Jack, there is no quick way to extract a Wicker's Curse. The bandage acts only as a formality to hide the condition," said Buck, the Breedling's face a shade paler in the dim light. He let go of his arm and went inside.

Jack followed, but again he found his feet hesitant and remained at the threshold.

From the brief explanation Buck had given him, Euxinus had become a desolate and dark place, a dead world. And while the aesthetics around him mirrored such words, he could feel a sense of life underneath waiting to burst forth from the ashes. He could not identify where the feeling came from, only that it seemed to be a thought conjured by something else.

Jack took a deep breath and entered, the door closing on its own behind him.

A mere foot inside, he found the quaint layout was similar to the Apothecary's dwelling. However, instead of a tea kitchen, the open room to his left was a tidy study, littered with candles. In place of a stove was an ornately carved desk made of Euxian lava rock, the etched characters difficult to make out from a distance. Instead of dried herbs hanging from wires, there were stocked shelves of stone tablets, scrolls of parchment, folded pieces of hide, and leather-bound books filling the space of the interior wall. Under the front window, a small wooden credenza stood with both doors open to the full extent their hinges would allow. Inside were hundreds of small ink bottles.

Inching closer to the staircase directly in front of him, Jack caught sight of a ghostly figure gliding down the steps and redirected his gaze. The lady in white descended the stairs with flawless elegance. At first, he was uncertain she was real, but he blinked a few times and each time the image remained the same. She was dressed in a long, free-flowing dress with full-length georgette sleeves. Its corset, made from crushed velvet, displayed the three-star insignia stitched into the fabric like a brooch, silver crystals dazzling the trim. Her skin was fully transparent, making her face invisible to him. The cloth framed the rest of her body.

"Welcome, Master Jack," spoke the lady as she stood directly in front of him. Her skin shifted to a pleasant cream, allowing feline features to appear. On either side of her flat nose, silvery whiskers sprouted from her cheeks. The glow in her slit eyes was a muted harvest yellow, and her mortal-like lips were a pale pink. Adorning her head, a pair of pointed cat ears were alert to detect the softest of sounds.

"Madam Teller," said Buck, presenting his Euxian elder with a courteous bow.

"Bartholomew," she said, her voice pleasant and warm. "I see your suffering has rewarded you with many blessings."

Buck nodded in reply, his solemn expression breaking into a knowing smile.

"Shall we begin?" asked the Tales Teller, moving toward a pair of closed doors, its archway similar to the entrance of the Apothecary's healing room.

"In there?" said Jack. He stared at the Tales Teller, then looked at Buck. "Ye can't be serious? The library of an ancient world fits in a small room?"

"Who said it was a small room?" challenged the Tales Teller, her whiskers twitching as her lips formed a smile. She opened the doors and invited him to enter.

Jack walked through the door into a circular room large enough to fit a grand cathedral, although he could see no hint of flame to brighten the empty space. Instead, the lighting was nothing like he had ever seen before. Along the circumference of the wall, streaks of luminescent purple reminded him of the splatter markings of paint on canvas; looking down at his hands, he saw their pale shade glowing purplish blue. He walked a little further across the floor, craning his neck back to the dome ceiling that rose higher than the roof of the Tales Teller's coffin, and traced the patterns on the ceiling as though they were constellations. One formation in particular made him think of butterfly wings.

"What is this place?" he asked, his voice filling the quiet.

"We call this room the Tortoise Shell," replied the Tales Teller.

"Because of the dome."

"To the naked eye, perhaps," offered the Tales Teller. "But moreover, it gets its name based on speculation that this is where the Black Tortoise hid himself during the collapse of the Elements and before the creation of Eden."

"Fascinating," said Jack. "And the paint?"

"It is not paint," said Buck, stepping out from behind the feline woman, the scarlet glow of candles behind him.

"It is blood."

Jack lowered his head, his whimsical expression deflating. "Blood?" He waited a moment for the two supernatural creatures to explain further, but when neither did, he purposefully walked over to the wall for a closer inspection. He lifted his hand on impulse to touch the glowing residue.

"Best leave it be," warned the Tales Teller.

Jack steadied his arm. "Why? It's just blood."

"Fatal last words," said the Tales Teller. "Well, maybe not fatal," she added with an airy laugh. "Exposure to the deity's blood has been known to drive any creature mad or, in some instances, make it fall into a dark despair. The Apothecary believes that, while in isolation, the Black Tortoise experienced both and may have inadvertently harmed himself in order to stem the feelings. It is a chapter of Euxinus missing from the formal history, and no one, not even the Fates, knows for certain. But we do know the blood to be that of the Black Tortoise, because his children, the Animawalkers, bleed this very same shade."

Butterfly wings, thought Jack. It was then he realized Annaliese's companion was an Animawalker. He heard the ghostly voice return in his ear, the whisper spurring him to reach out. A pulse in his bandaged arm warned against the action. He sensed fear in the fire that lingered in his veins and pumped his fingers into a fist.

"Jack, leave it," insisted Buck.

This time he did not listen and placed his injured palm on the wall. A rush of loneliness spiraled through him, forcing him to drop to his knees. Jack felt himself spinning, though his body remained still, and closed his eyes to nullify the motion and reestablish his equilibrium. Instead, his mind opened up to a memory that was not his own. He felt the maddening sensation of anguish force its way into his chest, and from it a scream rose.

He braced his hands against the floor, but it was not enough. Jack began to smack his hands repeatedly against the stone as though the force would break it down. He felt the ache build in his arms and the numbness in his hands. He went faster, the steady beat reverberating in his head. Everything began to hurt, and when his body could no longer withstand the invasive memory, it departed.

Jack came to a halt on his hands and knees, panting. The garbled vocals near him made it feel like he was underwater. The Breedling's worry struck him like an expected wave, the sincerity in it grounding him. He tried to engage the muscles in his neck, but he was too weak to put forth the effort, and his head hung like dead weight.

"I understand," he huffed.

"What, Jack? What do you understand?" asked Buck, his voice directly in front of him.

"Ye"—he swallowed hard—"ye were right about the Black Tortoise. He was here, in this place, alone. For so long. He—" Jack paused, collecting his thoughts. "He lost everything. His home, his siblings, his love. What did they do?"

"Who?"

"The Fates? How, how could they overpower such a mighty deity? I don't understand. Buck, how is this possible? How . . ." Jack's body began to tremble. He closed his eyes. The soft voice still whispered to him, but he could not make out its words.

"That is what we are here for," said Buck, offering two reassuring hands. "To teach you about Euxinus, like you asked. Knowing the beginning will help you understand your importance in this story. For without the Eden Wanderer, there is no return of the Lost Creators."

"Thanks for the vote of confidence," huffed Jack, the Breedling's touch pulsing ripples of calm through him.

"It is not confidence you need, Trickster," scolded the Tales Teller, hooking her arm under his right arm and hoisting him off the ground without warning.

"Madam Teller!" exclaimed Buck as Jack bellowed.

"On your feet, Stingy Jack," said the Tales Teller, her tone unexpectedly cutting through him.

Jack wobbled on shaky legs but managed to remain upright, if only to prove he had the strength.

"You are weak, Stingy Jack," scolded the Tales Teller, her skin casting a shade of red. In the luminescent light, however, it appeared a dark purple, almost black. "Your soul is broken, your heart missing, and your emotions unpredictable. You wear your suffering shamefully on your skin and your deeds haunt your rest. You are a creature of great importance, the foretold Eden Wanderer, and yet you know nothing of your role."

"Then tell me," Jack snarled, the Trickster stirring in his voice, but he took a deep breath to steady himself. "I'm ready to listen."

The Tales Teller smiled. "What you ask with confidence I shall grant," she said. "All I ask in return, Master Jack, is that you embrace everything you are about to see and hear. Only understanding will prepare you for what is to come and the witness you must provide."

The Tales Teller snapped her fingers, and the room echoed with the scraping of rock against rock. In the center of the room, the floor opened up and a beam of reddish orange rose to the peak of the dome. The Tales Teller drifted across the space before disappearing into the glow.

His confidence waning, Jack took another deep breath. His body felt raw, and an angry burn in his forearm rekindled its fire.

"I am here, Jack," came Buck's voice as the Breedling took hold of his hand.

"I don't know if I can do this," Jack admitted. He instantly hated himself for verbalizing his weakness.

"You can and you will," said Buck, tightening his grip. "Just keep thinking about Iona. Her face, her voice, the love you feel for her. Put that in the center of your mind and weather the rest. I would give you another moment, but once the Chameleon returns it will be time."

Jack nodded and let Buck lead him, not trusting himself to make it on his own. He leaned over the opening, his eyes readjusting to the new wave of light. Below, a spiral staircase descended several feet underground. He could not see the Tales Teller, only the grated iron and the light breaking through its cracks. He let Buck venture down first and followed, bending lower to ensure he maintained his balance. Bracing his hands against the surprisingly rough walls, he paced himself; he felt rising claustrophobia nag at him, but he kept his eyes fixed on the opening beneath him.

"This way," said the Tales Teller as Jack stepped foot onto a balcony.

He felt the warmth on his face first before noticing the blazing scarlet fire burning from the ceiling, its flames reaching downward. Absentmindedly moving forward, he felt his hands take hold of a rail that blocked him from plummeting. He ventured a gander into the supernatural library below—each level angled to the right, giving it the dizzying pattern of a seashell. He felt queasy but held his gaze long enough to see the white twinkle at the deep heart of the spiral.

Jack pushed away from the rail and caught up to Buck at the end of the balcony. They descended another flight of stairs and stood on the first platform of the library. From the floor rose hundreds of individual shelves that held leather-bound books. Jack approached one to inspect the cover and read the embossed title, *The Fisherman's Son*. He was tempted to remove it but thought better of it and let the book keep its secrets.

"What are all these?" he asked as they began their descent.

"The library of Euxinus houses all the stories of every creature in its borders as well as volumes on Hades' Octet and Everlyse's Valkyrie. There is also a selection on various Lesser Demons and Cherubs, the lowest-ranking creatures in Hell and Heaven, who have either perished or demonstrated a level of uniqueness beyond the limits of their station. The books you see here are the tales of mortals who in death became amid souls. As you may notice, some of the covers appear burned while others have a weathered look. This is to indicate which deity was granted the soul upon the conclusion of its trial."

"And the pristine ones?" asked Jack, thinking of *The Fisherman's Son*, his curiosity temping him to retrace his steps and open the book. He held his feet firm, however, and reengaged his attention toward the Tales Teller.

"Those are a rarity in this library," she said, the warm orange shade of her skin both patient and thoughtful.

"Yes, but what does it mean?"

"It distinguishes a reprieve," said Buck.

"Souls that are given rebirth," Jack guessed.

"The same," said the Tales Teller with a smile, leading them further through the library.

"What about Spirits?" asked Jack. "What was it you said, Buck? Mortal souls who retain their free will in death?"

"They are here as well," offered the Tales Teller. "Eden's catalog does extend to editions on Spirits, Wickers, and every known Seer."

"Seers? What are those?"

"Like Wickers, Seers are a special bloodline of mortals who possess variant abilities to see visions," offered Buck.

"They can see the future?"

"Not exactly," continued the Tales Teller. "The sight of a Seer is fairly limited to their immediate surroundings and the individuals closest to them. Their visions only extend so far into Eden's future, the furthest being a year. In some rare instances, a Seer may have glimpses into the life of a single mortal, but such an occurrence has not happened since Eden's Great Flood."

Jack opened his mouth, prepared with a barrage of questions, but he took too long to speak.

"Put them out of your mind for now, Jack," added Buck. "Seers have no role to play in what is at hand."

"All right." Jack stuffed his hands in the pockets of his robe, dissatisfied. He made a mental note to revisit the conversation later.

The spiral wound tighter as the pages of books gave way to the scrolls of ancient times in Eden. They did not sit on outward shelves but rather inside holes in the wall, and their sheer number was overwhelming. The small cubby holes eventually gave way to pillars of stacked stone tablets, and the warm glow from near the first platform of the library shifted to a white hue. Jack's eyes readjusted to the brightness; he felt as though he were steadily approaching the silvery glow of the moon.

"The Council of Seven," said Jack to no one in particular as he observed the seven stone tables decorating the circular basement wall. He read each aloud: "Apothecary, Tales Teller, Chameleon, Jardina, Serkan, Herald, Keeper." Jack recognized the first three but was uncertain about the rest. He was about to ask, but Buck ushered him to the middle of the small space.

"One more floor to go," said the Breedling.

Jack climbed down the ladder and bent low as he made his way through a narrow passageway. The silvery light ahead grew in intensity so that when he exited, it was hard to know the size of the space. He tried lifting a hand to shield his eyes, but no matter where he looked, the white glow reflected off the glossy lava rock.

"Be mindful of your footing, Master Jack," warned the Tales Teller, her voice an odd distance away.

Heeding the warning, Jack managed to inch his way around a few sharp stalagmites, holding his focus until he tripped over his own feet and landed on the jagged floor. His hands fortunately braced his fall, protecting his legs from injury; he felt a helpful pair of hands grip his arm and allowed them to assist him. He kept his eyes partly closed and briefly made out the blurry image of Buck's figure.

"Here, Jack," said the Breedling. "Close your eyes. I'll lead you the rest of the way."

Jack made no objection, carefully moving where Buck guided him.

"All right, Jack, you can open your eyes," said Buck, releasing his hold on him.

"Are ye sure?" asked Jack, the white light trying to penetrate his eyelids.

"Open them, Master Jack," said the Tales Teller.

Jack opened his eyes to blinding nothingness.

"Do not close them," said Buck, his voice quick. "Let the light see your eyes."

"See me eyes?"

"Just trust me," said Buck.

Jack inhaled to combat his natural instinct and kept his eyes open. He waved his right hand, searching for Buck, but the limb simply moved through air. He called the Breedling's name, then called again, his voice creaking, but there was no immediate response. He released a panicked breath, and in response, he felt the Breedling's calming touch slide into his hand.

"Don't let go," he said, his voice surprisingly frazzled.

"Do not close your eyes," said Buck, and he squeezed his hand.

Jack felt the reassurance and waited for what seemed like hours. If it were not for Buck anchoring him in this bright void, he was certain he would have gone mad.

"Euxinus," came the Tales Teller's voice. "In the unwritten history of the universe, there is no known beginning. The realm of Euxinus simply was. The Fates lived on the slope of a mountain covered with earth, although nothing grew on it, and from their vantage point they looked out upon a vast sea. A joyous wind danced throughout the eternal night sky, and the only source of light was the vibrant flame at the volcano's peak. In the earliest chapter of Euxinus, the Fates lived in harmony with the Elements, until the trinity grew tired of endless eternity and sought to create a greater world to suit their vanity."

At the corner of his eyes, Jack saw the beginnings of pencil etchings, drawing for him the image that the Tales Teller conjured with her words. He could see everything clearly now, as though he were staring at a canvas. Euxinus came to life with splashes of color appearing—scarlet, brownish gold, black, and wisps of blue. The Fates took shape on the mountainside, though he could not describe their form, only that they shared similar features with mortals. The Tales Teller gave no further description of them, so the image was more or less his mind giving them a familiar shape. Jack's breath hitched in his throat, the images beginning to smear and change as the Tales Teller continued the narrative.

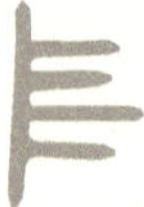

Collapsing Elements

The new image in front of Jack was what he knew Euxinus to be—a dark world. The seabed was dry, and volcanic flame replaced the blue glow of the Fates' palace. The mountain was bare, the atmosphere of the scene dead. Jack felt an odd sense of—was it sympathy? Sadness? Anger? Loss? He could not quite make out whether the feelings were his own or whether the Tales Teller's words had stirred them within him. The Fates had destroyed the Elements in their truest forms, harnessing their powers, and forced the immortal siblings to shed their appearance.

Jack watched as a fiery Phoenix, an elegant Heron, a delicate Faun, and a great Tortoise appeared on the canvas. Each one was the spiritual embodiment of their physical forms: Flame, Wind, Earth, and Sea.

"This marked the start of a new age," said the Tales Teller, "ushered in by the Fates' greed and unforgivable sin."

"And what happened after the Elements took their new forms?" asked Jack as a raging fire ignited in the image of Cemetery Valley, melting the jagged rocks until they were smooth. He felt intense heat emanating in the space around him.

"Without consulting his siblings, the Scarlet Phoenix took it upon himself to retaliate. As you can see, it is here Flame's anger took root, and it was solidified when his sister, the Azure Heron, sent a gust to extinguish the inferno running wild in the valley. Furious with his sister, the Scarlet Phoenix went straight on to attacking the palace. But at this turn, his brother, the Black Tortoise, stopped him."

Splashes of black and red collided on the canvas as the heat against the Trickster's skin diminished. Rage fueled the actions of the Scarlet Phoenix as it attempted to combat its weaker brother. In the midst of their fight, the Fates fled to the shelter of their palace and blue wisps of wind supported the Black Tortoise. The combat was a miraculous sight. The swirls of colors collided but never melded, each one maintaining its own identity.

"With two siblings combined in force," continued the Tales Teller, "the Scarlet Phoenix sought out the aid of their sister, the Golden Faun, knowing the spirit of Earth could sway their siblings into abandoning their protection of their betrayers, but the empathetic deity was nowhere to be found."

A cry rang out from the canvas and caught Jack off guard—he jumped with a timid yelp. The Scarlet Phoenix threw back its head and bellowed another cry, a tragic plea resonating in Jack's ears. It was a haunting sound. For the first time, Jack felt a sense of pity for the fiery deity. Under the circumstances, he would have done no differently, fighting back against those bent on harming him or those he loved. The Scarlet Phoenix's anger did not come from a place of vengeance; it came from a want to protect. He felt the deity's heart break, betrayal gripping him—the birthplace of the Devil.

Jack wondered if Hades remembered this moment—the true reason he lost his will to feel love. Did he even care? Or was there a part of him that longed to return to himself, to release himself of his burdensome anger? Jack shook the thoughts from his head, cursing his moment of weakness under his breath. The Devil did not deserve his sympathy.

"It's no more than he deserves," lashed Jack's tongue, the Trickster vocalizing his inner disgust.

"You speak of Hades and how he is now," said the Tales Teller. "But Flame did not deserve what happened to him or his siblings. He did not deserve to be slain, betrayed, or forsaken by his family."

"Although, in the Golden Faun's defense," interjected Buck, "she had disappeared and could not, whatever the reason, come to her fiery brother's defense."

"He made a choice," argued Jack, heat pulsing underneath the bandage on his arm.

"If I recall from your legendary escapades, you too made a choice, Master Jack," said the Tales Teller.

"I did no such thing," said Jack defensively.

"So you have always been a Trickster?"

Jack heard the challenge in her voice as the white canvas began to paint four different worlds for him to view—Euxinus, Hell, Heaven, and Eden. He did not want to answer the Euxian historian, because he was uncertain. He could not remember being anything but the way he was, and yet when flashes of his mother crossed his mind, a sense of longing filled him. It had nothing to do with his mother, which he found odd. Rather, it was the absence of something he could not name.

"It is understandable for you to relate to the Scarlet Phoenix, Master Jack," said the Tales Teller.

"I share . . ."

"That is enough, Trickster!" shouted the Tales Teller. "You will bite your tongue."

Jack opened his mouth, but a sudden stab of ice prevented him.

He looked down at Buck, the Breedling's lips moving quickly. The chill spread, once again subduing the Trickster, and he felt calm again.

"Thanks," he sheepishly mumbled.

"You were not yourself," offered Buck with a reassuring smile. "Remember, focus your feelings on Iona. Do not let the pain of others become yours."

Jack wanted to ask what he meant by these words, because he was finding it exceedingly difficult to pinpoint his mood.

"Shall I continue?" asked the Tales Teller after giving Jack an adequate amount of time to readjust.

"Please," said Buck, answering for him.

"As you can see, Master Jack, it was at this time the universe became larger," said the Tales Teller. "In retaliation for his act of villainy, the Fates tore a hole in the universe and banished the Scarlet Phoenix to live in the fiery desert sands of Hell. This did not, however, diminish their paranoia, and they feared the others might turn on them. And so, in the same vein, they exiled the Azure Heron to the snowy lofts of Heaven."

"And what of Eden?" Jack asked, finding his voice.

"It was not long after their banishment of Flame and Wind that the Fates realized their mistake, for upon their new world they gazed and saw how empty it was without the Elements. But, too prideful to admit their guilt, the Fates sought their only source of recompense. Beyond Hollow Mountain, the Fates tore a third hole in the universe; into it they released what was left of the four Elements and fashioned a world of night and day, boundless water, fresh air, and vast tracts of earth. They called it Eden."

Tears swelled in Jack's eyes as the glorious world he knew unfolded in its infancy. It was hard to believe the Fates could have created such a place after having failed with their own. But unlike

Euxinus, which had turned sour by their greed, Eden had been a gift, a means for the Lost Creators to seek refuge from their vanity, a place they could rule as their own. But as precious as the gesture was, their gift soured, for it only provided a battleground for the sibling rivalry between the Scarlet Phoenix and the Azure Heron.

"And what of the Black Tortoise?" Jack asked.

"What of him?" asked the Tales Teller in turn.

"During the banishment of his siblings, is that when he sought refuge in the room above? Why did he not just go to Eden when it was created?"

"Jack," whispered Buck.

Feeling the shakiness in his legs, Jack pressed his hand against his chest. He began to feel dizzy as a shiver ran up his spine. Pressure built in his head, and he tried desperately to keep his eyes open. He heard the Tales Teller sigh, and without warning she appeared in front of him. She placed her hands on his temples, her feline eyes staring intently at him. He did not understand how she was doing it, but after a moment the throbbing subsided.

"There, that should hold you until the end," she said, standing next to him as the muted canvas came back to life. "To answer your question briefly, it is unknown why the Black Tortoise did not just seek refuge in Eden. He eventually left the confines of his self-inflicted prison, but it was not until after the War of Wind and Flame."

"And the Golden Faun?" asked Jack.

"The spirit of Earth has not been seen since the collapse of the Elements. By word of the Fates, the story dictates her soul drowned in the sea."

"But shouldn't they have found her in the seabed?"

"It is a logical question, Master Jack, but the Golden Faun

was never found. Her and the Black Tortoise's collective absence in Eden left the virgin world open for occupancy, which led to the rise of three armies. Still feeling exposed and vulnerable, the Azure Heron began to create creatures that would obey and protect her from any further, unforeseen wickedness from her brother or the Fates. The Scarlet Phoenix did the same, but his creations came out of his hurt and anger and became a weapon to exact his revenge."

"So Eden became their battlefield," interjected Jack as the landscape of Eden expanded before him. The canvas displayed an invisible battle dotted by slashes of scarlet and azure. Off to the left, in the shadows of the Euxian landscape, he watched the figures of the Fates grow restless in their palace, fear emanating from the illustration.

"Not long after the fight began, the Fates began the construction of Cemetery Valley and the building of the seven coffins before creating their grand army. The Apothecary and I were the first to inhabit the square, each given a specific charge—his to heal; mine to account the battle to come. Sequentially, the Fates began to create the ancient creatures, as well as the Herald and the Chameleon, who became the messenger and the spy of the army."

"Remember, Jack, you saw some of them in the street," said Buck.

"Giants, great wolves, behemoths, monocorns," said Jack as the images appeared on the canvas, the creatures not nearly as impressive as they had been in the flesh.

"Collectively, the Fates had created us to intercede on their behalf and maintain the balance between the warring siblings. We were a preventative measure to keep them subdued in their current states and deny them the chance to gain strength. Upon our arrival in Eden, however, the armies of Heaven and Hell dug into our ranks, the Scarlet Phoenix persuading the dragons to join him and the Azure Heron coaxing the great wolves to side with her."

With the snap of the Tales Teller's her fingers, two tall winged creatures appeared, their flesh pale as a full moon and their wings as black as the Euxian stone.

"To prevent any further defections, the Fates created the Retrievers, Serkan and Jardina, to keep their army faithful. They became the two most feared creatures in Euxinus, the bounty hunters, charged with the retrieval of the disloyal. With their keen instincts, the Fates were able to purge the army of its defected creatures."

"And what happened to them?" asked Buck.

Jack glanced to his side and found the Breedling's expression rather puzzling. Did he not know this already? Jack studied his face—it seemed he was trying to answer his own question, but whatever it was, the attempt of self-discovery failed him as several creases appeared across his brow.

"That is not like you, Bartholomew," said the Tales Teller. "Do you not remember your studies?"

"I do, but—" Buck visibly bit his lower lip. "I mean, I know their carcasses filled Cemetery Valley, but I do not remember what happened to them after that. It is as though something stole my memory, or perhaps I have forgotten it?"

The Tales Teller hesitated to answer, which caught both Jack and Buck's attention. The feline historian appeared flustered, her skin shading pink and her slit eyes calculating how to proceed.

"Is it bad I do not remember?" asked Buck.

The Tales Teller laughed at this, neither Jack nor Buck finding the humor in the question. "Not at all."

Jack watched the pinch in the corner of her lips.

"To deal with their deceased creations," she resumed, "the Fates created their final creature of the Coffins of Seven, the Keeper. It was her sole charge to give last rites and care for the slain. Her life, however, was very brief, as the Scarlet Phoenix captured, tortured, then executed her. In retaliation toward Flame's heinous act, the Fates sent legions against him, but the fury of Flame was not to be conquered, not in this way, so they pulled back their army, never to have it set foot in Eden again. Both the deities took their retreat as added insult to injury, but there was not much they could do about the matter—neither of them truly had the strength. Instead of fighting to the death, they both chose to survive, conceding for the time being. Thus the War of Wind and Flame ended. The estranged siblings returned to their respective realms to refortify their spent energies while the Fates continued to purge the ranks of their warriors, until only the most loyal creatures remained."

Mortal Will

The cries filled Jack's ears instantly—animalistic and indiscernible, all melding together. The agony present in them was heartwrenching, and with his free hand he clutched his chest. The other crushed Buck's hand, squeezing tightly to the point Jack was certain he would break it. The noise deafened all other sound around him. He tried to stand his ground, fight back against the onslaught, but the pain became his own; he collapsed to his knees and his eyes filled with tears. Unable to hold them back, he felt droplets of rain. In front of him, the colors began to run on the canvas. It was as though he had broken a magic spell, the white light flickering like a flame at the end of a wick and blowing out. The white glow retreated, its intensity reduced to a single orb in his peripheral vision, a moonstone.

Jack let out a cursed scream to expel his invisible attacker, the soundwave blasting out into the cavern surrounding him.

The sound stretched on and on—Jack gasped, having held the piercing note for too long. Puffing a few breaths, he closed his eyes, allowing the water to sting the dryness away and welcoming the moment of respite the darkness gave his eyes. He continued to hold Buck's hand but relinquished some of his grip and was again able to feel the pulsing calm emanating from the Breedling's touch.

Jack took a deep breath, released it, and opened his eyes. The glow from the moonstone lit the cavern, its pure light reflecting off the glossy lava stone walls. He took a moment to get his bearings. When he was ready, he stood.

"Jack," came Buck's voice.

"I'm fine," he replied, his voice strained. He coughed, clearing his throat before continuing. "Did ye hear the screams?"

"I did once, but it appears they no longer affect me the same as they did in the past. The only cry I heard was yours."

"There were so many of them," said Jack, a level of sympathy once again rising within him. "Who are they?"

"The dead," offered the Tales Teller.

"Ye mean the ones the Fates executed?"

The Tales Teller's face flushed a somber blue, her ears and whiskers drooping. "The same," she said, her stance uncomfortable and her gaze off to the left.

Following her eyes, Jack took in the grandness of the cavern. It was not nearly as high as the dome of the Tortoise Shell, but it expanded farther. It was hard to discern the true distance with all the heaps of bone staked to the ceiling. Jack swung his leg to readjust his stance and face the mass grave head on. The bones were unlike anything he had seen, massive in scale, some long as Romanesque columns and just as thick.

"There are so many," Jack managed.

"What you see, Master Jack, is only the start, for the bones of the first Euxian creatures end here. This cavern is a massive tunnel that circles the entire Equadrian Square."

"What on earth for?" he asked, returning his gaze to the Tales Teller.

"An interesting expression, but here it would be, 'What in Euxinus for?'" said the Tales Teller with a weak smile. A ray of sunlight beamed across her left cheek, but the rain clouds brewing across her skin quickly engulfed it. "To answer your question," she continued, "it became a warning. A constant reminder to the Euxian Council that our lives are at the mercy of our Masters and that our gifted autonomy, though eternally ours, can still be crushed."

Jack thought about her words, his mind finally understanding the level of supernatural wonder around him. He could now see beyond his rivalry with Hades—that his existence was important because of what the Fates did to the Elements, although he still did not know exactly why or how. He just felt connected to it all.

Looking back at the scattered bones, he felt his silent heart beat a single pound of grief for the slain. He loosened his hold on Buck's hand and nonchalantly released himself from the embrace. He took a step forward, then another. He reached out but became nervous of having another fit. The thought forced him to stop, his fingertips almost touching the decolorized bone.

"What will I see?" he asked, keeping his arm steady.

"Only suffering, Master Jack," said the Tales Teller. "The War of Wind and Flame was merciless and brutal, neither side willing to compromise. What you will see will be unlike anything your mortal mind can comprehend."

Jack pondered the proposition, his fingers drawing subconsciously toward the Euxian remains. He felt the impulse to follow through but curled back his fingers and retreated a step.

"I'm all right, Buck," he said aloud, sensing the Breedling's concerned gaze on the back of his neck. He turned away from the mass grave, the glow of the moonstone a welcoming sight. "I don't need to see such things," he concluded. "I need to know how I came to be, how Iona and I are connected to all this. Tell me, Madam Teller, what happened next?"

The Tales Teller placed her hand on the moonstone. The light pulsed, projecting a circular image of Eden. It was similar to the canvas, except this time it was more reminiscent of the Gettysburg Cyclorama Jack had seen at the 1933 Chicago World's Fair. He walked through the shadowy image, entering the inside circle, and spun slowly, taking in the illustrated scene. Everywhere he looked, animals began to appear on land, in air, and under the water. At first they were limited, but as they began to multiply, their numbers seemed endless.

"It was at this time the Black Tortoise appeared in Eden and began to populate it with the presence of his own creations. He named his children Animawalkers and their offspring the Animalia—animals, in your mortal tongue."

"Wait," objected Jack. "How did he get there?"

"It is a mystery," replied the Tales Teller. "And despite the appearance of the Animawalkers, the Black Tortoise remained hidden due to his weakness." With a snap of her fingers, all the imagery vanished. With an additional snap, a black swan appeared, beautiful and majestic. Its presence was strong, commanding, and regal. It stood alone near an expanse of sea, gazing out into the open air.

"Who is that?" asked Jack, feeling an odd sense of recognition.

"That is General Vala, or Lady Vala, as she is more commonly known. She is one of Everlyse's Valkyrie, one of five generals, the highest ranking angels of her army. Each one takes the form of a swan in Eden."

"Swans?"

"What did you think angels looked like?" challenged the Tales Teller.

Jack opened his mouth but did not bother to answer. He had always assumed angels were more akin in appearance of mortals with wings. And yet, he thought as a blue heron appeared next to the swan, birds *were* a more logical choice.

"In the aftermath of the War of Wind and Flame, the Azure Heron fell into a deep depression," continued the Tales Teller. "Her Valkyrie tried to lift her sorrow with lavish gifts, but nothing eased the loss she felt. The war had proven how selfish she and her brother had become, squandering their energies when they could have been searching for their lost siblings. She lay in bed for months in her lofty citadel, her passion to live waning. The angels feared she would fade away, but not her beloved Vala."

"*Then honor them.*" Jack heard the resonating command of the black swan. "Show them you still care, show them you are still worthy of their love."

Jack watched the spirit of Wind smile at her child, then together they went to Eden, much to the jealous dismay of her four Valkyrie sisters—Tove, Bree, Idun, and Mist. The Azure Heron collected earth and water, molding together two forms of clay, and breathed life into them. She named them Adamov and Ava, the first two mortals of Eden. And to commemorate her gift, she shed the image of her spirit and became Everlyse.

Jack marveled at the sight of a tall Norse woman with long, blue hair falling around her broad frame. She was naked, her skin the shade of fresh snow. She kissed the pair of mortals on the forehead and left them to acclimate with their surroundings. Rotating his eyes around the circle, Jack watched the story of their early beginnings unfold, until it stopped on a scene of Adamov and Ava entertaining Everlyse with a lavish meal. In the distance, at the base of the sloping hill, an orchard covered the lowland, and amongst the pomegranate trees a fiery phoenix stood spying.

He gasped. "Wait, why is Hades still the Scarlet Phoenix?"

"Because, in order to ascend, the Master of Hell needed to

bestow an essence of himself upon mortals—a gift."

"Gift? What gift could a cruel-hearted creature like that possibly give?" asked Jack, practically shouting the question. He felt a twist of hatred festering in his stomach and clenched his fingers, his face burning before it turned a pale shade of ash.

"Jack," said Buck, keeping his voice even and calm. "Take a deep breath—all is well. You need to breathe. Think of Iona."

Jack closed his eyes and calmed his breathing. He remembered Iona, sitting underneath the shade of a tree, her hand stroking the pelt of one of her lambs. He listened for her soft hum, the melody of her voice, extinguishing the fiery surge of anger. The color in his face changed back to a warm red, his demeanor softening. He uncurled his hands but kept his eyes shut, his mind's eye focusing on his love as he posed his next question.

"What did Hades give?" he asked in a soft voice.

"Their souls," replied Buck.

Jack felt a laugh build in his chest, his lips cracking into a smirk. He let the chuckle out, finding ironic humor in the Breedling's reply. For how else could the fire deity have made such sport out of manipulating mortals? It was near-impossible to resist Hades' charm or his penchant for self-destruction.

"And what of Adamov and Ava?" he asked, redirecting the conversation.

"At first, the two mortals were happy, and for a time they acted as a reminder to Hades and Everlyse of their truce," said the Tales Teller. "Adamov and Ava were inseparable and adored the deities, but they only saw Everlyse as their true creator. This, as you can imagine, drove Hades mad with jealousy. Bitter about his sister's new pets, he plotted a scheme to destroy her bond with them."

Jack opened his eyes, his sight falling upon the shifted illustration of the cyclorama. Everything the Tales Teller had told him was in sequential order. He rotated his feet again, taking in every frame, until he came upon the last, a scene the Euxian historian had not described. It depicted a joyous reunion, Everlyse embracing her fallen brother the Black Tortoise. A great celebration charged the image, thousands of animals in attendance, Hades and the mortals included. Then, the images shifted, revealing Adamov and Ava kneeling before the great turtle. The Black Tortoise pressed its head against each of them, akin to a knighting ceremony, but Jack understood the meaning.

"And what gift did the Black Tortoise bestow upon mortals?"

"He bestowed upon them the only power he had left, the gift of free will, which would be both a blessing and a curse. For it was the catalyst Hades needed in order to drive a wedge between Everlyse and the mortals."

The cyclorama reset again and began to design the next segments of the story. As the invisible artist drew, Jack turned to the Tales Teller, her soft yellow skin beaming like a haze-covered sun.

"And what of the Black Tortoise?" he asked. "What happened to him?"

"In the wake of his gift, the Black Tortoise retreated to the depths of the ocean to regain his strength."

"Wait, why didn't he ascend?"

"Such knowledge is unknown, Master Jack, but it is believed the spirit of Sea was simply too weak to make the transformation, which left Hades the most opportune moment to execute his devious plot."

The Tales Teller clapped her hands, bringing to life the new illustrations.

"In the night, Hades visited Ava and whispered in her ear falsehoods of an attack on Everlyse. Come morning, Ava awoke in a cold sweat and tried to tell her husband of the nightmare, but he ignored her words. She held firm to her instinct and, unwilling to see any harm befall her creator, sought counsel with Vala, urging the Valkyrie angel that Hades meant ill against their beloved creator. Seeing the love the mortal had for her Mistress, Vala agreed to speak with Everlyse. But unsettled by the waiting, Ava formulated her own plan to strike first.

"All that morning, beside her favorite pomegranate tree, Ava dug a deep hole in the earth, filled it with water, and covered it up with a sheet of thick leaves. That afternoon she coaxed Hades into playing a game of hide-and-seek, which the conniving deity accepted. Hades counted as Ava ran through the orchard and hid behind her tree. As Hades drew closer, Ava jumped out into the open and challenged the deity to chase, darting off like a rabbit. Hades pursued, but managed only a few feet before falling into the hidden pool. He screamed in pain as he tried to evaporate the water beneath his feet, steam rising from the crater. Ava watched in triumph, unafraid of Hades or his threats. She stood tall and told him she would let him go free if he promised never to return to Eden. At this, Hades ceased his struggle and laughed. The mortal was craftier than he had given her credit for, underestimating the power of free will. It mattered not, however, for he was more delighted that she had done all his work for him.

"When Everlyse discovered Ava's treachery, she immediately freed her wretched brother. She could not bear the thought of losing another sibling, no matter how detestable Flame had become. Furious with Ava, Everlyse relinquished her protection and devotion to the mortals. Ava fell to her knees and pleaded with the Mistress of Heaven to undo her punishment, trying to explain she had only wished to protect her from Hades, but Everlyse would not hear of it. Adamov held Ava in his arms and watched as the heavenly deity vanished, never to return to Eden."

"And what of Vala?" asked Jack, coming upon the last frame.

"In the end, Everlyse blamed Vala for the creation of such treacherous creatures. As punishment for her counsel, Everlyse cursed her beloved Vala to act as sole protector of the mortals and cast her out of Heaven. To Vala's credit, with the help of the Cherubs she did keep Adamov and Ava safe from Hades for a time, but their offspring were not nearly as cautious as their parents. Vala learned of Hades' villainous plot to have Abel killed days before it happened. She confronted Hades and received no mercy as the Master of Hell set her black feathers aflame."

"Did she die?"

"Nearly," replied the Tales Teller. "But the Black Tortoise saved her and nursed her back to health, although she would never again be able to take the form of the majestic black swan."

Jack was not surprised that Hades ended up getting what he wanted as Buck explained the fullness of the fiery deity's victory. Hades had discovered the true power of his gift, unlocked by the free will the Black Tortoise had bestowed. Mortal souls possessed immense power that could replenish his depleted strength.

"As mortals multiplied," resumed the Tales Teller as the cyclorama reset the illustrations for a final time, "Hades' curse on Cain's bloodline encouraged acts of violence that began to choke the sanctity of the earth. It was one of many dark periods in Eden's history, but there was a sliver of light, for on the shores of the great sea, a kindhearted mortal by the name of Nova fell in favor with the Black Tortoise. Taking pity on the mortal and his family, the Black Tortoise charged Nova to build a massive fortress on a high peak and gather as many creatures as he could to shelter. After three years of building and gathering, Nova and his family, along with a plethora of creatures, sought shelter as the great storms began. The Black Tortoise blanketed the earth with purifying waters in the hope that it would prevent Hades from setting foot in Eden to collect any more mortal souls. He held the water high for as long as he could, his Animawalkers protecting every mountain peak not subdued by water, but after two Eden years, the waters began to recede and the Black Tortoise lost his powers, leaving his children and the remaining mortals without a protector. Rumors spread afterward that the Black Tortoise had drowned in his own waters or had lost all power and became one of the Animalia. Upon his entrance into Heaven, Nova told Everlyse that before the flood, the Black Tortoise had seemed melancholy, his grace leaving him, the image of his soul fading. He tried to reassure the Mistress of Heaven that the rumors were not true, hopeful the now-lost deity had washed up on a shore and become a man.

"Everlyse wept for her brother and swept a cold wind across Eden, fostering the first Ice Age. When her mourning passed, her winds subsided and Eden thawed, bringing with the warmth an age of balance. It was within this second coming of mortals, seven generations after Cain and Abel, that the Fates created Breedlings, a race of creatures who mirrored the image of mortal children, charged with the task to obey without question, without a sense of self or feeling. And thus with their soulcatchers, order amongst the four realms reigned, the Fates' neutrality keeping the power struggle between Everlyse and Hades even and stagnant."

"At least until now," said Buck.

Jack interrupted the exchange between the feline woman and the Breedling. "You mean because of what you have discovered—about the Lost Creators, I mean?"

"Hades and Everlyse have only been allowed to gain more power based on what the Fates will allow. This is partially due to mortals having long forgotten the days when the angels, demons, and deities were among them. This delusion of their sight has made souls weak. But now everything has changed." Buck looked at the Tales Teller as though trying to get permission.

"What?" asked Jack.

"I would be lying to you if I said nothing, but as we discussed, Iona's part in this story must wait until after the trial," said Buck.

Frustration rose up in Jack. "Ye've tossed me around long enough, mate!"

"Master Jack," offered the Tales Teller, as she placed her hand on the moonstone. The light flickered once more, and the circular screen vanished. She stood upright and faced Jack, her posture confident and authoritative. "It is understandable for you to have questions, but given your poor state, one heartache at a time is enough. If you still wish to save your fair lass, you must forget the secret Master Breedling has had to bear all this time. He will explain when Lady Iona's soul is safe. In the meantime, we must prepare you for the trial. Come, we will retire to my study."

Jack twisted the fabric of his robe as the Tales Teller began to make her way up the ladder. His body threatened to produce a tremor, his skin falling ashen once more. Inhaling deeply, he concentrated on Iona's face. He heard Buck call him as he began to climb, but he did not bother acknowledging him. Instead, he fixated on the threat before him. His beloved was in danger, and only his witness could prevent her from the clutches of the warring deities.

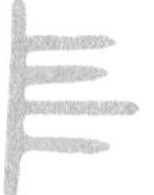

Last Tea

The Apothecary stood in the study with his hands crossed behind his back, his eyes wandering around the room. He was tempted to review the materials stacked neatly on the Tales Teller's desk, but he refrained. He trusted her enough to know she had gathered everything necessary for the trial. If all went well, however, she would not have to use any of it. Then again, the Trickster was unpredictable, and everything was contingent upon his behavior.

"Master Apothecary," came the Tales Teller's voice.

The Apothecary turned to look at her as she entered alone, not followed by the Breedling and the Trickster. "There is no need for that," he said, addressing the bend of her ears and the nervous shade of her skin. "All is well, but the Herald has made his summons."

The Tales Teller nodded and went to collect her things. Her hands trembled as she did, her nerves increasing rather than easing. The Apothecary attempted to comfort her, but she pulled away.

"Please," she said. "Your touch will only cause me more discomfort at this point."

"As you wish." The Apothecary returned to his previous stance and watched her. "How was the lesson?"

The Tales Teller picked up the stack of materials and pressed them against her chest, staring at him with a questioning expression.

"There is no ulterior motive to my inquiry, Madam Teller. I simply wish to know if the Trickster . . ."

"Stingy Jack," she said. "The mortal listened to the stories, the monster fed on the energy."

"I see. And do you think it will be enough?"

"Enough? What more do you want from him?" She slammed the books, tablets, and scrolls back onto the desk. "I have told you time and time again my concern on this issue. The layers of the Eden Wanderer are always in flux, and you cannot count on any of them, whether it be to do as you ask or keep a promise. And now, Annaliese's blade has inflicted him with a Wicker's Curse and he . . ." She cried in frustration. "There is something wrong with him."

"The place you cannot reach," interjected the Apothecary, his interest in her rant piquing. He knew well about the blind spot in Stingy Jack's history—there was a point in his youth, before his mother was murdered, that was blocked from the Tales Teller's sight. He had his speculations as to what it was but had never shared them with her, for obvious reasons. There was a piece of Stingy Jack missing, an important piece, and it had nothing to do with Iona Covington.

The Tales Teller shifted her gaze, trying her best to present stable composure.

"Is everything all right?" asked Buck, the Breedling's voice unsure.

The Apothecary chuckled in an awkward attempt to cover the tension in the room as he shifted his weight. "Pardons, Master Breedling, Master Jack, but we must take our posts in the Hollow," he said.

"Then the moment has arrived," said Buck. His eyes dropped, his expression in a state of panic.

"Not to worry, Bartholomew," said the Apothecary, seeing right through him. "Master Chameleon has yet to return from Heaven, so there is still time to educate Master Jack on the trial proceedings."

At this, Buck lifted his gaze with a smile.

The Tales Teller once again collected her materials, but she did so without conversation. She simply bowed to the three of them and took her leave.

"Well, then," began the Apothecary, extending an invitation for Jack and Buck to claim the empty bench against the wall. "Did you learn all you needed, Master Jack?" he asked.

"Enough," replied the Trickster in a low voice as they sat down. "It's easier in my understanding of what this place is and how everything began. Why—for the most part—Hades is the way he is." He grumbled the last part through clenched teeth.

"And do you have sympathies . . ."

"No," screeched Jack. "I have no sympathies for the Devil!"

The Apothecary nodded in acknowledgment. "And what of your feelings towards your place in all this?"

"I," Jack huffed, fully aware of the Apothecary's sly way of changing the subject. "I know no more about my role in all this than I did when I came here. But"—the Trickster paused, the tightness in his voice releasing—"I do feel connected to it somehow. My immortality was created with purpose rather than without, and yet I feel as though there is something missing."

"Iona?" asked Buck.

"No this is something different, something that doesn't involve her. Do ye know what it is?" Jack focused his full attention on the Apothecary.

The Apothecary felt a sudden unease under the Trickster's gaze. It was Jack asking, but also Stingy Jack, the villain within him waiting for the answer as well. It was though the Trickster wanted the Apothecary to give him an excuse for mistrust, but what he truly needed was for Stingy Jack to trust him. He cleared his throat, handing the Breedling and Jack a beaker of tea to delay his answer.

"I know not what is missing from your being, Master Jack," he began. "And such discovery will have to wait. What is important now is your connection with Iona. So, let us take in our Last Tea with knowing purpose and prepare you for what is ahead."

"Last Tea?" said Jack, the Trickster's suspicion accepting his words for the truth that they were.

"No need to worry, I do not mean it to be *your last*," said the Apothecary with a chuckle. "The Last Tea is merely a ritual conducted in honor of every witness set to stand for an amid soul. It is a rarity, for you are one of a few dozen offered this distinction, but the only witness actually capable of drinking his tea."

"As always, dear friend," said Buck, cupping his hands around his beaker, "your mastery is greatly appreciated." He took a sip of his tea and hummed, satisfied by the flavors of ginseng and orange peel.

The Apothecary nodded, acknowledging both sides of the Breedling's compliment—one for wisdom and the other for the brew.

Jack folded his fingers around the beaker and sipped. He shook his head as the taste locked itself in the back of his mouth, then stuck out his tongue and made a disgusted sound.

Buck elbowed him in the ribs and scowled.

Jack scowled back, ready to fight, but the Breedling withdrew his attention.

The Apothecary smiled at the exchange, the scene a welcome respite from all the dismal things he had seen lately. He admired the underlining friendship between the Trickster and Breedling, he felt a sudden hint of sadness that neither of them saw it, but was hopeful they would come to discover it. Maybe after Bartholomew finally spoke his truth about Iona and what he had discovered the night she died.

"Master Jack," he interjected. "Do you have a question?"

"I . . ." Jack lifted his gaze. "Is it true that we can save her?"

The Apothecary regarded the Eden Wanderer for a moment, the melancholy on his face settling in place, fear building behind his eyes. "I can only say you might, Master Jack. I know it is not the answer you wish to hear, but the truth of the matter is despite your presence, your character is in question. You may be able to present yourself as worthy, having passed the three trials, but your past discretions will paint you as undeserving."

"Then what am I supposed to do? Buck has made it clear that she's in danger because she knows about the—" He bit his lip, suddenly keenly aware that whatever the Breedling had already told him should not be repeated aloud. "Please," he said with a heartbroken tone. "How can we stop Hades and his sister?"

The Apothecary took a sip of his tea and thought about his plan one final time. What he needed from the Eden Wanderer, Stingy Jack could not give. He needed the Trickster. "There is no *we* in this matter, Master Jack. All this falls on Bartholomew's shoulders to see through."

"Then what am I supposed to do?" repeated Jack.

The Apothecary braced for the Eden Wanderer's reaction.

"Nothing," said Buck in a low voice. "You are to do nothing."

Jack sprang off the bench, spilling some of the warm tea on his hands. "Then what the bloody hell did ye bring me here fer?

What good am I if I'm to do nothing?"

"Jack . . ."

"No, Buck, I won't play by yer rules anymore. Now start making sense of this. If ye are the one who can do something, then why do I have to be here?"

"Master Jack, that is quite enough," boomed the Apothecary. He only needed the seed planted—not a bloom, not yet. Jack tried to continue his rant, but the authoritative tone in the elder's voice rendered him mute.

"Now, as I was trying to explain," the Apothecary continued. "Before the trial even begins, the Hollow is called to assemble. Following, the Tales Teller will begin with introductions, which is then proceeded by the Breedling's Formality. Simply put, it is the oath all Breedlings say, stating their name, rank, masters, and the extent of their charge. This moment is the only time a Breedling has true freedom to speak. Granted, none have ever taken the opportunity, for none have ever possessed such will, but Bartholomew does, and with it he has the chance to prevent the trial from even happening."

"But my Eldest," objected Buck, rising from the bench. "I would have to admit I am no longer in the service of the Fates."

"And you are not," said the Apothecary.

The Breedling straightened in a panic. "But to admit I follow the orders of a mortal under the crests of the Black Tortoise and Golden Faun? Surely the Retrievers will be compelled to cart me away the moment I speak such words of betrayal. How can you be certain the Squabbles will not find me a liar?"

"Master Breedling, calm yourself. In the Hollow you will have nothing to fear from the Coffins of Seven, but I cannot say the same for the Squabbles. They are the most impartial of any Euxian, which is why the Fates have entrusted them with the post of jury. That being said, you still lose nothing by speaking your truth. If the Squabbles believe you, the trial will commence as planned; if they suspect you and none can bear witness to your claim, the trial will be rejected."

"Why?" asked Jack. "How does Buck admitting he's no longer a servant of the Fates get Iona a reprieve?"

"Because the testimony of the witness is a protected right by the laws of neutrality. If Bartholomew speaks his truth, but there is doubt as to what he says, then the Hollow has taken away your voice. If a Breedling is not allowed to present the witness, the Council of Seven grants the accused an obligatory reprieve."

"Ye mean . . ."

"Yes, Iona would be released without question," said the Apothecary. "But this stratagem is not foolproof, for there is the matter of Hades."

Jack choked as he tried to swallow and talk at the same time. Tea shot out of his mouth, raining all over the floor. "Dammit," he swore, coughing until he dislodged a pocket of air in his throat. "That foul serpent is always getting in the way. If yer concerned, then why even get me hopes up?"

"Hope is all he can give us," said Buck. He looked sideways at Jack. "Hades is a threat to this plan because he can bear witness to my connection with Charles Reese. What may save us in this regard is Hades' vanity. To corroborate my story, he would have to admit his dealings with Charlie and how the mortal bested him. It is not something the Master of Hell will admit lightly, especially in the presence of his sister. It will come down to his hatred for you or his pride."

The Apothecary watched the Breedling shy away, his thoughts no doubt on his young master.

"Yer betting on Hades' pride being stronger than his hatred for me," said Jack, clearly perplexed by the plan. "Are ye delusional? Hades has swallowed his pride plenty for the sack of trying to best me."

"Indeed," said the Apothecary. "But burying his pride in the face of a rival, even his most hated one, is nothing compared to outing himself in front of an audience he deems less than him. Hades is smart and knows that no matter what he does, the truth about his interaction with Iona will be spoken before the Hollow. Hades is not the threat. Everlyse is the one we have to worry about if the plan falls through."

"How do we sway the Mistress of Heaven?" asked Jack.

"There is no trap that can be set for the apathetic deity," said Buck. "Everlyse is clear of any transgression when it comes to the life or death of Iona Covington. This puts her in favored standing. The only thing that may be able to combat it is the love between the Trickster and his Shepherdess, but even that may not be enough."

"And there is nothing else?"

"Short of Everlyse and Hades attacking each other, no, there is nothing more," said Buck, being cautious with his gaze.

The Apothecary watched the Eden Wanderer's reaction closely. Jack crossed his arms and pulled back some of the sleeve on his robe. It exposed the bandage on his arm, a sliver of blackened flesh peeking out from underneath. The appearance of the Trickster flickered across the Apothecary's vision, the evolution unfolding sinister thoughts on Jack's face.

"Jack . . ."

Jack turned his head, his lips curled. "There is only one way I can be useful if Hades intervenes. I'll pit those siblings against each other. I will make them fight. I will force them to destroy your Hollow if it means neither of them can claim Iona."

The Apothecary held back his smile, satisfied with the Trickster's proclamation. It was not merely a threat but a promise. If, or more like *when*, needed, Jack would unleash his inner demon and let him wreak havoc.

"If that be the case, Master Jack, then the Trickster within you will earn his merit," he said, giving Jack a bow. "Now, if there is nothing more, I must take my leave." He set his beaker on the desk, then added, "Oh, I need not remind you, Bartholomew— the Equadria is a safe place of passage, but nonetheless due to the nature of the trial, do be careful. As I told you before spies can be anywhere. Keep a sharp eye."

The Apothecary offered a final smile of encouragement and took his leave, closing the door behind him. He walked a few steps across the square but stopped in front of the darkened seventh coffin—the Keeper's former residence. Kneeling before the door and bowing low to the ground, he pressed his forehead in prayer.

"May that which you promised with dying breath come to pass," he whispered.

He cried for a moment, the loss of the Keeper still fresh in his memory despite the distance in time. All his plotting, the secrets, the dealings had come to this moment. Everything rested on the Eden Wanderer, and if he failed, if Iona fell into the hands of Wind, all was lost. Not just the mortal's pure soul, but the lost deities, and ultimately any hope for Euxian freedom.

Summoning Wind

The courtyard was white as always. Ice sculptures decorated the frozen garden where no plants would ever grow. Everlyse stood in the center of the walk, her body-length hair collecting flakes of falling snow. Her gaze lay fixed upon the image of what appeared to be a wounded faun, cowering in fear, its head tucked into its legs, its body curled in on itself. To the untrained eye, the faun looked as though it were sleeping. But Everlyse knew the truth, her immortal wind having carved the monument. The faun was actually crying, its body in pain. It was the moment the Golden Faun had appeared, the spirit of her sister Earth. She had watched the whole heart-wrenching scene unfold as the Fates ripped her from the mountain's slope. She had hovered over the space where earth met sea and borne witness to the birth of her death as her scattered form sank deep into the sea. She had been unable to save her sister.

She had not then made the promise to herself, to never feel so helpless again, nor was it later when the Fates destroyed her ethereal form and banished her from her home to the frozen world of Heaven. Instead, she embraced her place in the universe by making the most of it, creating a new home. She started with her citadel and its high-spired tower, shaping the landscape around it, smoothing the courtyard into a garden, and shoving the mountains into the distance. She spent time carving ice sculptures to post throughout the garden, totems of her life now gone, and in the center, she placed the image of her sister as a reminder to keep her in her heart.

When her surroundings were as she liked, she had created the Valkyrie, her most trusted companions. She had given them magnificent wings to fly with her, and soon she raised an army, the Cherubs being last. Throughout this time she was at peace, happy on occasion, but whenever she laid eyes on the faun, her demeanor would instantly change and she would mourn her sister all over again. And still she had not made the promise to never be helpless again. What triggered her transformation was Ava, one of the first mortals to whom she had given her breath of life.

Everlyse stared coldly at the statue, remembering the moment she was no longer able to feel and her heart had become indifferent toward her sister's memorial. It had been the instant Ava had tricked Hades into her trap of pooled water. Everlyse had heard his scream rise within herself, their sibling connection still strong enough to sense danger. Seeing Hades suffer brought back the painful memory of Earth; she could not stand the sight of her brother being tortured, as much as she had grown to hate him. She had rescued him and punished Ava, her mate Adamov, and Vala for their wickedness. And from then on, she sealed her heart and lost all feeling.

"Mistress," greeted a singsong voice.

"You are late, my Beloved Twins," said Everlyse, contemplating if she should shatter the ice sculpture into thousands of pieces.

"Our apologies, Mistress," chirped the red-breasted blackbirds as two appeared within her line of sight, posting themselves on a bird stand.

"And what news does Lady Vala send with you?"

"As instructed by our Lady, we followed the Breedling Bartholomew. With his guidance, the Trickster Stingy Jack, the Eden Wanderer, has completed the three tasks of a witness," said Lyes.

"And they have both entered Euxinus," reported Alyce.

"And on the other matter?" asked Everlyse, her gaze shifting to the two passerines.

"The rumors are true, Mistress," chirped Alyce.

"It appears Master Breedling does know the whereabouts of the Lost Creators—or, at the very least, one of them," confirmed Lyes.

Everlyse felt a pounding in her chest, a pang she had long ago thought she had silenced forever. A flicker of hope—if in fact hope was what it was. She could not recall the feeling but knew it once existed in her. She turned away from the two Cherubs, hiding her reaction as she lifted a hand to her breast. Pain began to restrict all conscious thought, threatening to overwhelm her with dead emotions. For a brief moment she felt her breath leave her and her mortal eyes watered, each dropping a single tear. She lifted her hand to wipe them away before dismissing the red-winged blackbirds.

Alone once again, she raised a strong wind and whipped it through the courtyard, its tail slicing the faun in half. She did not watch it fall, only heard the two pieces as they shattered on the ground. Pain rose in her throat; ill-equipped to deal with such grief, she wailed, her voice shaking the snow loose from the clouds.

"It is nice to see you still feel, Creator Everlyse," came a feline voice.

Everlyse tightened her hold on the whip and launched it at the Euxian spy, twirling her body in a magnificent swirl of blues.

The reddish-brown tabby cat easily dodged the attack and swiftly repositioned itself on top of the pedestal upon which the faun once stood.

"How dare you stand in her place!" shouted Everlyse and readied to cast her whip.

"Mistress," objected the voice of her faithful general. The trumpeter swan landed in the snow in front of her, its breast raised, ready to defend.

Relaxing her prepared fighting stance, Everlyse stripped herself of the unwanted emotions. Straightening, she and regained her regal posture, taking a few steps forward and aligning herself with the swan. She then placed her hand caringly on the creature's head, praising Mist for her interference—for, given the chance, she would have started a war by dispatching the Fates' spy.

"You have come unannounced, Master Chameleon," snapped Mist, her feathers flustered.

"It appears I have," said the tabby cat, swishing its tail unthreatened.

"Inconsiderate . . ."

"General Mist," reprimanded Everlyse, her voice fully recovered. "That is no way to address an emissary of the Fates."

"But Mistress!" Mist protested, craning her neck.

"You are dismissed, General," commanded Everlyse, her expression indifferent, but only to save face in front of the present parties.

The elegant swan bowed low, touching her bill against the snow, and left, taking flight.

Everlyse did not watch her faithful servant leave, her gaze fixed on the intruder. "Speak your piece, Spy."

"And what piece might I speak?" asked the Chameleon.

"Do not mix words, Master Chameleon, nor misinterpret my

earlier display. I may not allow my high general to speak to you in such a manner, but that is not to say I will refrain. What you have come to say could have easily been relayed by your Herald, so speak now or I shall strike."

"Many pardons . . ."

"I seek not your empty apologies, Euxian."

"As you wish," said the tabby cat, sitting tall on its hind legs. "I have come to summon you to the Hollow."

Everlyse released a chuckle, the burst more annoyed than playful. This summons was a run for the least of the Euxian council, the Herald, not the Fates' prized spy. There was something more to the Chameleon's visit, and she knew she had to be cautious.

"And the soul in question?" she asked.

"The trial is set for the Lady Iona Covington."

"The Trickster's lover?"

"The same."

Everlyse delayed her response. She knew very little about the ill-fated shepherdess, other than her affiliation with the unscrupulous mortal Stingy Jack and her brother Hades. The cherubs had only provided her with rumors, as the circumstances of her death remained unknown. It was only more recently that her Beloved Twins had reported the news that the infamous Euxian traitor Bartholomew, Breedling of the First Grade, was with the mortal at the time of passing and that between them was a shared secret—a secret her brother was willing to vie for against his Eden rival. She regarded the feline, ascertaining the Euxian's motives, then uncurled her whip and knowingly attacked, wrapping its lash around the feline's neck. Everlyse drew closer and picked the creature up by its scruff.

"What secret does the Shepherdess share with the Breedling? Is she acquainted with my lost siblings?"

"To the latter, I cannot speak," croaked the Chameleon. "I can only speak to the former."

"Then speak true," said Everlyse.

"The rumors, as they have been delivered, state Master Breedling knows the whereabouts of a lost sibling, but which, he has not said. You threaten me to learn for certain, when the only certainty lies in the Breedling's head. Your quarrel is not with me, Mistress."

Everlyse threw the tabby cat across the courtyard, her whip letting it loose. The feline landed on all fours in the snow, its fur spiked along its spine. "No," Everlyse said, her true feelings surfacing into words she had only dared speak once to her beloved Vala. "My quarrel is with your masters, the very ones who killed my sister, my brothers, and me. The trinity we called friends who destroyed my family and banished us from our home. You may not know the truth, but I shall root it out, even if I have to side with Hades and render the Hollow to rubble."

"Then I shall notify the council you will be present," said the Chameleon, dipping its head low, its chin touching the snow. It lingered no longer than needed before running off toward the distant mountains, disappearing from sight before it reached the edge of the courtyard.

Everlyse stood statuesque for a long while before conjuring the wind to resurrect the pieces of the broken faun sculpture. She worked meticulously to fix her mistake, but it was far too damaged. With a mighty gust she blasted the pieces from her sight, projecting them in every direction. She wanted to scream again, but this time she held it in, her apathy swallowing her exposed feelings.

"Mist," she said, having sensed the returned presence of her general, the magnificent swan perched atop the sculpture behind her. "Gather my conclave."

"And our orders?" asked Mist.

"You will escort me to the Hollow for trial and you will listen attentively. For if I decide to put my lot against my brother and this Trickster, I must know every part of this story I currently do not."

"As you wish, Mistress," said Mist and flew off toward the citadel.

Everlyse placed her hand on the empty pedestal, searching for the pang of hope, but to her dismay, it was gone. She tried to stir her feelings again, but those too had fallen dormant once more. She wanted to make a promise, say something out of respect, but she could not find it within herself to do either. All she could do was prepare for the unknown: a soul that could not be claimed by Wind or Flame, a fallen soulcatcher with a strength of will no Euxian possessed, and an amid soul rumored to share a universe-altering secret. A Trickster, a Breedling, and a Shepherdess.

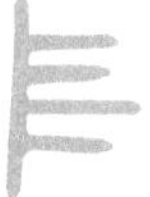

Squabbles Hollow

Jack collapsed at the top of Hollow Mountain, the hike more strenuous than he had anticipated. He felt like he had reached the peak of a high Tibetan temple. He rolled onto his back, out of breath. The air was much thinner at the top, void of the intense sulfur smell in the valley. Jack stared up at the eternal night sky; while it was empty of stars, the blue hue from the Fates' palace glowed brightly. He lifted his head high enough to see the Euxian moon, its beam acting like the spot of a lighthouse, parting the darkness. He slowly sat up, his calves screaming at him from the climb. Glancing down, he felt a sense of vertigo and closed his eyes; after he dared to pry them open again, he surveyed Euxinus. None of the streets were lit save for the scarlet-flamed torches along the Equadria directly below. He wondered if that meant the escaped Euxians were back in their respective coffins.

"Buck, do you think the Coymorphs have caught all the escaped creatures?" he asked between labored breaths, his ears pounding the heavy drum of the rhythm his heart once kept.

"From the darkness below, it would stand to reason all have been accounted for," said Buck, standing next to him.

"Will they be punished?"

"I cannot say with any certainty, but I will venture a guess that the Fates will be more concerned with figuring out how they all managed to get out in the first place. Plus, I'm sure the appearance of water in the valley will have them paranoid. It will not take them long to piece together the incident with our arrival."

Jack felt a sting of panic in the chest. "Will they come after us?" He looked up at the Breedling.

"Of that I am certain," said Buck, his gaze fixed on the Fates' palace.

Jack noted the curling of the Breedling's fingers, his hand balling into a fist. It was a show not of nerves but of strength, a willingness to fight.

"I do not know when they will try to come, but they will, sure enough, after the trial is over," Buck added.

"Then where will we go?" asked Jack.

The Breedling's shoulders drooped. His hands unclenched and he lowered his chin. Uncertainty filled his emerald eyes, though he did his best to hide it.

"We will worry about that after," said the Breedling with a weak smile. "Now." He reached out his hand. "Shall we see to the saving of your Shepherdess?"

Jack smiled at that, making Buck's eyes grow wider; he took the Breedling's hand and gained his feet. His legs were still a little sore, but at least the throbbing had stopped. Turning with Buck toward the Hollow's entrance, he paused a moment to take in its splendor. It reminded him a great deal of the grand Pantheon temple in Rome, but with a few deviations, particularly the illusion of water running down the walls. Pillars stretched from the summit to the benevolent dome circling the outside of the chamber, and torches lined the pathway through the portico to the arched doorway.

As he passed under, Jack eyed the peak of the arch and saw

the three-star insignia established in superiority in the center. On either side, two symbols added to the crowned decoration of the portico. To the left was a great tortoise standing in the center of a tidal wave, and beneath it were wisps of wind swirling about a regal heron. On the right of the Fates' insignia, a graceful fawn lay underneath the protection of a tree while an open-winged phoenix, engulfed in flames, lorded over it.

At the sight of Hades' crest, the charred skin on Jack's arm tightened. Venom pulsed up to his shoulder, the Wicker's Curse twisting his emotions. He felt his skin with a building rage and gripped the sides of his robe for some control.

Buck paused at the entrance and looked back at him, concern clearly filling his face. "Easy, Jack, stay calm," he whispered, retracing his steps. "You cannot allow yourself to be triggered by the mere sight of a symbol. Now relax. If you cannot hold your composure now, then seeing Hades in the Hollow will undo you."

"I'm trying," growled Jack.

"Try harder."

"Do ye have any idea how hard this is?"

"No, now concentrate."

"Argh," Jack blurted in frustration. He could not push back the spread of the poison. He was not directly looking at Buck, but he could not figure out why the Breedling was just watching him struggle. Or maybe he really did want him to try to overcome the fever. Sweat began to pearl his brow, and he felt the heat in his neck. At that moment, Buck took action, sneaking his hands inside Jack's robe. The direct contact made Jack groan, but he did not pull away. Cooling ice tamed the fire, and he hoped it would hold for the remainder of the trial. His voice cracked as his body shuddered with a refreshing chill. He gave Buck a weak smile as the Breedling released him.

"Thanks," he said, his voice hoarse and unsteady, his steady temperament restored.

"Do not go soft on me now," said Buck with a nervous laugh.

Jack shoved the Breedling playfully and managed a chuckle.

Buck smiled. "Are you ready?"

"Do I have a choice?" asked Jack sarcastically.

"Of course you do," said Buck. "With free will there is always a choice. You just have to be prepared to suffer the consequences."

"I didn't mean it like that," Jack replied, rolling his eyes. Clearly, the Breedling had no concept of humor. Right hand reaching for Iona's brand buried under the bandage, he sighed. "Yes, Buck, I'm ready."

"All right, just follow close behind me—and remember, once you pass through the arch, keep your voice silent and speak only when addressed."

Jack nodded and gestured for the Breedling to lead the way.

Through the arch, night gave way to an artificial day. All along the inner shell of the Hollow, circular bowls of fire radiated with intensity. The light collected in the dome above, which hung over the inner amphitheater of Hollow Mountain. They descended the stairs to the witness stand below, where two black marble chairs sat boxed in by a guardrail. On either side of the railed balcony, two circular basins were aglow with restless flame. A cool breeze wafted about, bringing with it a scent of snow, which combated the reek of sulfur.

Jack took his seat next to Buck. He fidgeted for a moment to get comfortable before stealing a glance at the Breedling, taken aback by his straight posture and his confidence. Seeing Buck like this reassured him. Settling on a suitable position, Jack looked beneath him at the vacant, ornate pulpit in the center of the floor. His eyes drew to his left, where black-robed creatures filled in stone bleachers behind an ornate throne donned with snowflakes, plumes, and feathers.

He let out an unexpected gasp as his vision fell upon the voluptuous goddess occupying the seat. She was tall and upright, her hair was a long, flowing gown of thick, baby-blue curls. The roundness of her cheekbones, which bore a glow of freshly churned butter, made her chin seem small. Her pursed thin lips were a chilled purple, her nose slightly button-like, and her deep blue eyes held a burdened history of anguish. A celestial, azure robe covered her thick neck and broad shoulders, as well as the defined bulk of her arms and the wealth of her bust. The stitching pattern on the robe, done in variations of blue, depicted the grace and beauty of a heron playing with the wind. Jack's jaw nearly dropped open in disbelief.

Everlyse—her name alone did not do her elegance justice.

A sudden tap stole Jack from his reverie, and he turned to find Buck's expression warning him not to stare. Sitting up against the back of his chair, he turned his head forward just in time for the procession to commence, all in attendance rising to their feet.

As Jack rose, he caught a flash of scarlet out of the corner of his right eye and hastily prevented his line of sight from drifting any further. He thrust his hand in his pocket and grasped his mother's cross, its calming energy immediately having a subduing effect on him. He lifted his attention to the high balcony of the chamber as, one by one, large, alligator-like heads appeared over the ledge resting above the glow of fire surrounding the Hollow. Their metallic gray scales shimmered in the torchlight, their catlike ears perked to listen. One of them ran its snakelike tongue along the ridge of its nose.

Below the Squabbles unfolded a stage topped with five thrones, each one engraved with a distinct symbol. From left to right, the first one depicted an eagle, the second the side profile of a lizard, the third a flower. The fourth and fifth each held one bat wing, which if put together would create a full wingspan. From the shadows, Jack recognized the Apothecary immediately as he took his seat in the center, a tall silver staff gripped in one hand. To his right, a male and female with mortal qualities sat—the male covering the left wing, the female the right. They were both dressed in the same gray robes as the Apothecary, the three-star insignia stitched over the left breast, and around their necks was a white, braided rope with tassels. Their albino skin and alert black eyes made Jack's skin crawl. Their shoulders did not touch the backs of the thrones, their furled wings preventing them.

Jack shifted his attention to the opposite side of the stage as a tall bird of prey perched on the eagle-crested throne, its lethal talons curled against the edge. The bird opened its magnificent wingspan, then settled, nestling its wings into its sides. Its eyes gleamed as they moved across the chamber, eventually, like those of the male and female, landing on Buck.

The last to take the stage was a creature the likes of which Jack had never seen before. It was much smaller than the bird of prey, but its presence was nothing short of intriguing. The reptilian features of the creature were so distinct and unusual, Jack could only liken it to a lizard. The creature's arrow-like head was proportionally larger than its long body, its thin prehensile tail like that of a monkey swinging upside down. The creature's horn-like projections, the large crest on the top of its head, and its parrot-like feet equipped with sharp claws defined it as a distinct predator. Its Kelly-green scales enhanced the pink color of its eyes, which scanned the entirety of the Hollow in a circular fashion.

After the five members took their places, the Apothecary rose. The first Euxian's face was indifferent, his expression cold. He did not speak but pounded his staff like a gavel seven times. Jack followed the Apothecary's gaze down below, as the Tales Teller emerged from beneath the witness stand. She was still in her white dress, a gray cape draped over her shoulders, the three-star insignia stitched visibly on the left side. She took residence at the podium and stowed the stack of materials she was carrying underneath. The Apothecary banged his staff once more, gathering the attention of the Hollow.

"As the speaker for the Masters of this land, to whom we, the Coffins of Seven, pledge our unending devotion, we act as mere representatives of their glory. To the Hollow, I present the Herald; the Chameleon; the Retrievers, Jardina and Serkan; our sister the Tales Teller, whose lips will bear the truth; and I, the Apothecary, sole presider to these proceedings."

Jack watched as the six creatures took a ceremonious bow.

"As always, we welcome Flame and Wind to this neutral chamber where we bear witness to the truth and pay tribute to the wisdom and verdict of the Squabbles. Creator Everlyse, your beauty and wind are as always a pleasurable presence." The Apothecary bowed to Everlyse, and she responded in kind. "And to you, Creator Hades . . ."

Jack inched his eyes to the right to find Hades sitting on a throne of engraved flames. His pallid skin beamed in contrast against his black hair and scarlet celestial robe. The robe was several hues of red, with a patch shaped like a phoenix stitched over his right breast. Jack pulled his eyes away as a churning in his stomach tried to rouse his anger. Gripping the cross in his hand again, he focused on the Apothecary.

" . . . your gift of flame is as always a comforting sight," resolved the Apothecary. He presented Hades with a bow, which the Master of Hell returned without reluctance. The Apothecary then banged his staff three more times. "We are called to order here in this sacred place to hear in testimony the truth of the victim whose promise of life was stripped away. Here, Iona Covington will be given voice to speak, though not with her own, for we, the servants of the Fates' neutrality, will determine her afterlife." The Apothecary made another thunderous pound and returned to his seat, resting his forearms on the sides of the throne.

The entire Hollow sat in a single motion—Jack followed suit a second too late as the Tales Teller lifted her head to look up at the witness stand. Her slit eyes widened into large circles, revealing two different colors, one yellow, one orange. Her lips parted, allowing the sound of a deep alto voice to fill the Hollow.

"Master Breedling," addressed the Tales Teller. "It would please the Hollow to hear your voice. Please, make your presentation."

Jack watched Buck rise out of the corner of his eye, the Breedling's posture transformed by confidence. He knew the trick he was about to execute was a fragile one and that the Breedling needed to mask every inch of doubt and nerves from his demeanor. Jack was not sure how long the façade would last, but he was keen to the fact that Buck was not a seasoned con artist. Hades knew it too, he was sure of it. He would see right through Buck quicker than the average mundane mortal.

Jack closed his eyes as Buck stepped forward. He needed to let him try his way first and trust in the plan. But in the back of his mind, the Trickster laughed at his gullibility. There would be only one way to ensure Iona's safety, and he was willing to unleash the Trickster when the time was right.

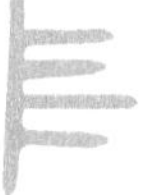

Formalities

Buck stood at the rail, his posture straight and his face poised with a knowledgeable expression. He had done this so many times before that the Formalities of the trial were second nature to him, but standing in the Hollow for the first time since his fall from grace, he felt different. The familiar rhetoric would not serve him well because he could not recite any of it. His insides twisted, and he did his best to keep the discomfort from bleeding onto his face. He could not show any sign of weakness.

Buck tried to sneak a deep breath, but every eye was watching him. He felt Jack's gaze on him and sensed a change in the Trickster's demeanor. It felt wrong—calm, almost. Buck wanted to turn his head to gauge his expression, but the time to do so had passed. He placed his hands on the rail and finally breathed.

"Everlyse," he began, presenting a respectful bow. She returned the gesture in kind. "Hades." He did not change his tone when addressing the Master of Hell and performed the same gesture, making sure to not make direct eye contact. Hades bowed willingly in reply. "Highest Council and Elders of Euxinus," he added, presenting another bow forward. The Squabbles and the Council returned his gesture. "I stand before you, Bartholomew, Breedling of the First Grade—"

Buck stopped, a flash of panic filling him. He knew what words should be next . . . *in servitude to the Fates, Rulers of Euxinus, for it is to them I bring this charge before the Hollow.* But they were all wrong. He started to rub his thumb against his finger, unsure how to proceed.

"Master Breedling," said the Tales Teller. Her voice was clear and indifferent.

"Buck," whispered Jack.

Buck lifted his eyes and confidence returned to his face. "Many pardons, Madam Teller; it seems my years in a Reformatory cell have made me second guess myself," he said, hoping by the grace of Eden that he would be able to get through this part. "If it pleases the Hollow, I shall begin again."

"A pleasure it would be, but mind your hesitation, Master Breedling, for you know well the consequences of deception," said the Tales Teller in warning, her whiskers twitching.

Buck bowed and began again. "I stand before you, Buck, Breedling of the First Grade. I come to you in the service of the mortal Charles Reese, Master of Eden." He pulled the scarlet and azure tassels from around his neck and let them fall over the balcony as a roll of gasps filled the Hollow before giving rise to whispers. "And it is by his command I bring this charge before the Hollow as witness to the amid soul, Iona Covington."

Buck gripped the three-star insignia and tore it forcefully from his robe, throwing it down at his feet as the Squabbles perked their catlike ears in disbelief. The members of the council sat still, neither acknowledging the other. It was only the hooded angels and demons that gossiped incessantly.

BANG, BANG, BANG!

The Hollow became still as the attention shifted from the witness stand to the balcony.

"Master Breedling," boomed the Apothecary's voice. "You will do well to speak the truth."

"Whether or not you accept it, my Eldest, it is the truth. I would never dishonor the neutrality of these proceedings, because to do so would find me in contempt, forcing my charge to defend his position without counsel. I *have* broken my bond with the masters of this realm, yes, and in doing so, I have found a new allegiance. But that is not to say I have changed, for I am still a Breedling, a soulcatcher, and in order to fulfill my created purpose I must have a master. Charles Reese is that master—by the power of the oldest of Eden Laws, we are bound by sacrifice."

"Master Breedling, you would do well to keep your tongue," warned the Apothecary.

"But my Eldest," said Buck, continuing to play off the Apothecary's lead. "It is for Eden such proceedings are carried out, and such laws cannot be overlooked because they are not deemed appropriate for this land. I ask pardon for my blatant honesty, but what I have said is true. I cannot prove it to you. I have no credible witness to bring forth, for you know as well as I that no mortal can survive in Euxinus." Buck acknowledged the Retrievers. "Even if you were to send Serkan and Jardina to find him and question him, there is no guarantee for a successful charge. You have only my word, and if that is not satisfactory, then I call to strike. If you do not take into account my charge, my witness, Stingy Jack, the trial is then forfeit and a reprieve consequential."

"Upon the strength of hellfire!" said Hades in objection, gaining his feet.

Buck glanced over at the fiery deity and pressed his palms into the rail, ready for the Scarlet Phoenix to overturn their ill-conceived plan. He was hanging onto an ounce of hope that Hades would not admit defeat against Charlie, relying on the villain's vanity. But such hope was folly. Buck peered at Jack and caught sight of the raw rage festering on his face, his fingers gripping the armrests of his chair. He moved to place a hand on his shoulder, to keep him in his seat but also to soothe his temperament. He looked at Hades, and the mere glance made his heart sink.

Hades tilted his chin just enough to exhibit a glimmer of satisfaction on his face before turning to address the Hollow. "Master Apothecary, pardon my outburst," he bowed, "but if it pleases the Hollow, I can vouch for Master Breedling's account to be what he says."

Buck's hand dug into Jack's shoulder, surprised Hades had not even hesitated. The Devil would rather give himself away than give Jack easy victory.

"Creator Hades," the Apothecary's authoritative tone warned, but Buck noticed his eyes falter. Jack had been right—their plan was about to fail.

"I know there is doubt," said Hades. "However"—he lifted a long finger in objection—"while gathering souls in the city streets of Chicago, I happened along Bartholomew and his young master, Charles Reese." Hades shifted his line of sight and stared at Buck for verification of his story.

All Buck could do was nod as the Squabbles began to hiss overhead.

Hades smirked, then continued to address the Apothecary. "Master Charles, a fine mortal—gifted, really—bested me in a deal upon our meeting." Whispers spread in the Hollow amongst Everlyse's angels, but Hades did not let it give him pause. "Yes, it is true. I have been known from time to time to be bested by mortals. Take Master Breedling's charge, Stingy Jack," he offered, exposing Jack's presence further to the Hollow. "As the Hollow will soon discover, he and I are most at odds with each other."

"Creator Hades, it is not the custom of these proceedings to rely on outside testimony. Your words have no meaning here unless you have some reliable proof."

"Ask the Breedling," said Hades with a cross hiss.

"Creator Hades!" the Apothecary's voice thundered. "Give me viable cause to question and I shall oblige."

"The mortal received a token out of our deal," said Hades, producing the cherrywood harmonica. "Naturally, I could not part with my prized instrument, too sentimental and all, but I did leave Master Charles with a replacement. My spies have told me that the young master passed it on to his squire."

The Apothecary softened his tone and looked at Buck, his face stern to mask the rising discomfort. "Master Breedling, are you in possession of such a token?"

Buck quickly thrust his arm tightly against his body, the harmonica pressing into his side. He should never have brought the blasted trinket with him. How could he be so stupid? Panic flooded his face, his creamy shade turning slightly green. He hesitated for a moment but then pulled out the instrument from the hem of his sleeve and held it out in the palm of his hand for all to see. "Yes, my Eldest, this is the token won by my master against Creator Hades." Buck tried not to let his voice sound defeated, but his eyes showed the sickening truth.

"Very well." The Apothecary returned to his seat, his gray eyes showing Buck no sympathy. "Let it be stated in the record as verified by the witness Creator Hades, the Breedling once known in Euxinus as Bartholomew now stands before us changed and free. In the House of Eden, his new master, Charles Reese, a mortal, has graciously bestowed upon him a new name, and he will henceforth be known to all as Buck." The Apothecary paused. "It would please the Hollow, Master Breedling, if you would properly introduce your charge."

"Certainly." Buck placed the harmonica back into his robe and removed his hand from Jack's shoulder. The Trickster had settled once more, but he still had an uneasy feeling about him. "May I present to the Hollow Stingy Jack, once a mortal of Eden and lover of the accused Iona Covington."

"And by what manner do we receive this witness?" asked the Tales Teller.

Buck bit the inside of his mouth, the nerves tumbling through him again. He looked at the Retrievers, worried now for Jack's safety. They were in uncharted territory, and he had no way of knowing if the Apothecary had been truthful with him about the Fates' intentions. Within a single blink, the Retrievers could leap from the balcony and have Jack and himself in custody.

"Master Breedling, I shall not warn you again about your hesitation," cautioned the Tales Teller.

"By manner of Eden, Madam Teller," replied Buck.

"By manner of Eden? You mean Spirit?" asked the Tales Teller.

"No, Madam Teller, Stingy Jack is more than a Spirit. He is a soul of flesh, the Eden Wanderer."

An outburst erupted as both angels and demons rose in protest. Buck knew what this meant to them—that Jack was indeed proof the Black Tortoise or the Golden Faun had blessed him, which meant that at least one of them was not as lost as once believed. Hades had known this for quite some time, but judging by the outrage from the demons in attendance behind him, he had not shared such knowledge with his underlings. As for Everlyse, if she had not known it already, she knew it now. Buck looked up at the stage. The Retrievers were on their feet, unfurling their thin translucent black wings, their stances at the ready to advance.

The Apothecary rose from his chair to call the Hollow back to order, but the volume only increased. He banged his staff on the stage and shouted, his deep voice breaking through the chatter.

"SILENCE!" he roared.

It took the Hollow a little longer to settle, but once the echo faded, the Apothecary resumed.

"Serkan, Jardina, return to your seats," ordered the eldest Euxian, his focus solely on the Retrievers. They both folded their wings back behind their shoulders and reluctantly sat, their black eyes ever more vigilant of Jack.

"Master Breedling," said the Apothecary. "Do you have any proof to your words?"

"If I may have the use of one of the Herald's talons, then I can prove to you what I say is truth," said Buck, knowing the sight of Jack's blood would be proof enough, for spirits did not bleed.

"To what purpose have you asked for such an unthinkable gesture?" challenged the Apothecary.

"To prove Stingy Jack bleeds the red blood of a mortal."

The Apothecary pounded his staff. "Master Breedling, you try the neutrality of this Hollow."

"Master Apothecary," offered Jack.

Buck turned in horror as Jack stood, speaking out of turn.

"Master Breedling!" shouted the Apothecary. "Do not test the resolve of this Council or we will hold you in contempt! Now see to the silencing of your charge's tongue."

"Jack," whispered Buck as the little color he had in his skin morphed into stark white.

"Let me do this," said Jack, keeping his voice at a whisper, and, without blessing, addressed the Apothecary. "Master Apothecary, I have the proof ye need, if it would please the Hollow." Again Jack did not wait and unfastened his robe. He let the soft comfort of the white fabric fall down his arms and held it at his elbows, exposing his naked skin for all in the Hollow to see. A roll of gasps followed, even from those on the stage above.

Buck kept his gaze forward, unwilling to look at the dismal patchwork on Jack's flesh. He had seen it once already and the sight of it would only upset him again.

The Apothecary pounded his staff as Jack refastened his robe before returning to his seat.

"Master Breedling," he said with less command, his poise stolen from him by the sight of Jack. "One more indiscretion from you and I will hold you and your charge in contempt of this Hollow—is that understood?"

"Clearly, my Eldest," said Buck.

"Then let the evidence stand that by his own admission, the witness Stingy Jack has given verification to his status as an Eden Wanderer and must therefore be questioned on thought and feeling throughout the course of these proceedings, for such that it is he maintains free will." The Apothecary banged his staff twice. "And thus conclude our Formalities—Master Breedling, you may return to your seat as the Tales Teller commences with the telling of the evidence."

Dipping his chin in acknowledgment, Buck returned to the chair, giving Jack a reassuring wink even though everything about their situation was disastrous. Seated, he inched his hand over to Jack and grabbed his hand tightly, for what was next would be hard to bear. All the skeletons were about to fall, but if they managed to endure it together, maybe the pain would be worth the price.

The Tales Teller's voice opened, transcending the Hollow to a different time and place. It was the same technique the Ferryman had used, blacking out all the immediate surroundings. With her voice she brought to life ghostlike figures, animating them as she told the story of how Jack came to be the Trickster known far and wide as Stingy Jack. She did not read all of his indiscretions, but the list was enough to be damning, and this only covered his mortal life. The Tales Teller's voice carried on into Jack's first meeting with Hades and how he had tricked the trickster.

"It was the moment that bonded the two, their rivalry more violent and self-absorbed than that of Wind and Flame," read the Tales Teller.

Buck waited for whispers to rise again, but in the break of the Tales Teller's story, no one made a sound, her voice too captivating to raise a quarrel. She continued with Jack's second meeting with Hades and what had transpired in the orchard. The scenery around them blazed with angry flames, consuming every tree. Buck's heart sank. It was no secret to him who Stingy Jack was—he had heard all the rumors and accounts of his deeds—but to see them unfold around him . . . he shook his head. He could not let the Trickster's past deeds sway his emotional attachment to Jack.

"And thus, the mortal Stingy Jack tricked the Devil for a second time," concluded the Tales Teller as the glow of the chamber returned. "In the year that followed, the Trickster spent most of his time avoiding capture, until at last he met his end. He was thrown into the stockades in the middle of a village square and was starved. And on the night he died, he awoke as the Eden Wanderer, the mortal of flesh that cannot be claimed."

This time whispers broke in the Hollow, the Squabbles overhead the most vocal. Buck kept his attention on the podium below, the Tales Teller's translucent skin shifting a pale shade of green. Whatever she had to say next was about to lift the tension in the chamber—a barrage was about to begin. The feeling was familiar, a rising discomfort, a seeded worry he had experienced only once before. He tried not to think about it, but the more he tried, the stronger the memory formed in his mind.

A Red Herring

"Master Breedling," spoke the Tales Teller.

"Yes, Madam Teller," replied Buck, her address pulling him out of his head and back to the task at hand. He sat up straighter to bolster his confidence.

"On the day of Stingy Jack's death, it is noted in the account a child took pity on him and gave him a drink of water. In the Trickster's history, there are only a few instances in which secrets surround him. While in service to the Fates, during your initial charge on this matter, in all your travels and research about the Eden Wanderer, did you omit such knowledge?"

"What?"

"When you were placed before the Fates to give your account of the Eden Wanderer and the Lost Creators, was one of the secrets you held the truth of his transformation?"

"Madam Teller, I do not know what you are talking about," said Buck, taken aback. "I was not there the night Stringy Jack lost his mortal life, nor do I know anything about a child."

"We shall see," said the Tales Teller, turning to address the side of Heaven. "The court calls General Mist for questioning."

"Madam Teller," objected Everlyse. "What manner of questioning do you have for my Valkyrie? We have no connection to this foul immortal soul."

"Save for but a moment," said the Tales Teller. "For is it not true, Mist, you were present in the square upon the night in question?"

The trumpeter swan rose to address the Euxian historian, its delicate feathers ruffling with a hint of discontent. "I was present on the night," she replied. "As was Creator Hades."

"A fact that goes without saying," grumbled Jack under his breath.

A collective amused hiss responded from Hades' demons.

"Be still," boomed the Apothecary's voice, silencing the hyenas. "Madam Teller, please continue."

"General Mist, on the night in question, why did you come to retrieve the soul of Stingy Jack?"

"I—" began Mist, pausing for a brief moment as though she did not recall the actual reason. "I was summoned."

"Summoned?" questioned the Tales Teller. "By whom?"

"I cannot say."

"Cannot or will not?"

"I do not know, on the honor of my Mistress," swore Mist. "All I can recall is that I sensed a great force that needed further investigation. I arrived in the square to find Creator Hades standing over a deceased mortal body. It was a puzzling sight, for it was not what I had expected to find, nor was I prepared to discover the soul was still within the mortal's body. I examined the soul of Stingy Jack and found it undesirable for the claiming of Heaven."

"But only at first," taunted Hades.

"Yes, it is true," spoke Mist, not playing into the Scarlet Phoenix's tease. "Creator Hades did make me rethink my initial assessment once he was rejected from claiming his soul. For while

I was unable to see past the twisted scars left by Flame on the cursed mortal, there was a hidden energy buried underneath. My sin was curiosity, and I paid the price for it. In my attempt to retrieve the soul of Stingy Jack, an energy blast rejected me. I was propelled through the air for my trouble. After that, I saw no further need to entertain Hades, so I left. Of what transpired beyond that time, I am unaware."

"And the blast," pressed the Tales Teller. "What was it like?"

"A typhoon, it . . ." Mist cut herself short, bringing the tip of her wing to her beak in realization. "You knew." Her gaze carried across the chamber to Hades.

"Whatever do you mean?" baited Hades with a mischievous grin.

"Mistress, please, I did not realize," said the swan, bowing its head at Everlyse's feet. "Please pardon my transgression."

"General Mist," spoke the Tales Teller. "Such a display is improper in the Hollow. What is the meaning of this?"

"I can tell you," said Hades, rising from his seat. "What your high general failed to realize was that the energy that had struck her the night Stingy Jack died came from our dearly lost brother."

"Lies!" shouted Everlyse, her fingers bracing the armrest.

"Such a thing is not possible for me to do in this chamber, dear sister," said Hades. "My tongue only speaks truth here, you know that."

"Creator Hades," said the Tales Teller.

"I can prove it to you if you like," said Hades, moving his gaze to the witness stand. He manifested a spark of flame in his hand and lifted it.

Buck sprang to his feet and positioned himself in front of Jack in a protective stance. He stared down at Hades, the deity's fiery eyes revealing a sliver of maddening sadness. There was context behind it, but Buck could not tell if it was in relation to his lost brother. Hades increased the flames in his hand, the emotion growing brighter on his face. No, this was something different, a fresh wound. Something else had happened. Buck pounded his hands on the rail in protest, hoping the Apothecary would take his lead.

"Creator Hades," spoke the eldest Euxian. "Your demonstration is not necessary."

"Oh, but I don't mind," said Hades.

"Be that as it may," said the Apothecary.

"Let him," spoke Everlyse. "I wish to see the truth of this Eden Wanderer."

Hades broke out in a chuckle, his flame ready to fire.

"My Eldest, Jack is not on trial here, he is the witness," shouted Buck. "You cannot let him do this. You . . ."

"Master Breedling," said the Apothecary, an unease creeping into his voice. "The motion has been seconded, so unless you have something more to say that will settle the issue, I have no choice but to let Hades have his way."

"But . . ." Buck turned to Jack, the Trickster's expression unreadable. "Jack, give me your cross," he whispered.

Jack did so without hesitation, handing over the sacred relic of Sea.

Buck thrust his hand out, his fingers gripping the silver cross, hoping he could use it as proof enough to sway the council to forgo Hades' challenge. "Here's your proof. Jack is in possession of one of the last remaining relics of Sea, an heirloom given to him by his mother at a young age before she was killed and left him an orphan."

"That is all quite fascinating, Master Breedling," said Everlyse. "But no relic has the power to mark a soul."

"You take no interest in Eden, so how would you know such a thing?" challenged Buck, placing the relic at his side. He needed to get them past this inquisition. This was not about the Black Tortoise marking Jack. This was about uncovering the true reason for his being, the truth about Stingy Jack's transformation into the Eden Wanderer. *Was it possible then*? he wondered. Did the Tales Teller already know? Had she spoken her words the way she did to warn him to derail the conversation? Did she know the truth about the child she had mentioned? Or was it even a child?

"My Eldest," he said, lifting his gaze once more. "Stingy Jack cannot be marked directly by the Black Tortoise, for he has been missing since the Great Flood. In all my searching there is simply no trace of him anywhere, save for this relic and two others; the heart of sea, which is in the care of the Seers, and the vial necklace, which was entrusted to a healer. It is possible, having possessed the object for so long, the energy connected with Jack's soul? Would it not seem plausible? For how else could a mere mortal trick the Master of Hell?"

The jaguar next to Hades roared in protest despite the insult discrediting Jack's miraculous feat, when in fact Buck's agreement did pose a great deal of sense.

"So then you admit it," said Hades. "You do know where our sister hides."

"Although it is true I was asked to discover the whereabouts of the Lost Creators, that is not to say I know where your sister hides, only that she is not lost."

"So you admit to denying this knowledge to the Fates," said the Tales Teller.

"I did not deny them anything, for it was not mine to give," said Buck.

"Then what of the girl," shouted Mist. "This Shepherdess is

the one who knows."

A great chorus arose in the Hollow as the sides of Heaven, Hell, and Euxinus all began to speak at once. The noise was deafening, but Buck endured it, remaining at his post in front of Jack. He was glad for the distraction, all focus shifting away from him knowing anything about the child that visited Jack the day he died. He took a breath and pondered the Tales Teller's breadcrumb. She had brought it up for a reason, if only just for him. To realize something important.

It was then the epiphany struck him. Iona—the child in question was Iona. This had nothing to do with the blessing of Sea, this was about the blessing of Earth. And the Tales Teller was trying to prevent it from reaching Hades and Everlyse. But then again, maybe it should?

Buck tried to think quickly about his next move. He knew that short of Everlyse and Hades fighting, the verdict would fall in favor of the Mistress of Heaven. He needed more time. Time enough to get his thoughts in order, because he needed more than just his words. He needed a distraction.

As though on command, he felt a cool wave pulse against his palm, in response to his plea. He lowered his eyes, the gleam of the cross winking at him—*water*. Buck turned to Jack and thrust the relic into the Trickster's hands.

"Listen carefully," he whispered, bringing his lips close to Jack's ear. The instructions were short; when he was done, he pulled back and waited for a sign of understanding.

Jack nodded and rose from his seat.

Buck stepped out of the way.

"Master Apothecary," spoke Jack, his voice even.

The Apothecary pounded his staff and, after several minutes, was able to quiet the Hollow just enough for Jack to speak over the tamed chatter.

"There is no need for Hades to force a demonstration of my connection with the Black Tortoise," said Jack. "I can perform it on my own."

The Apothecary leaned forward. "To do so will not change anything in these proceedings."

"Be that as it may, if this is not put to rest this trial cannot continue." Jack placed the cross on the rail and pressed his hand down on it.

Buck held his breath, hoping he was right. He thought back to the moment he had picked up the cross after Jack had dropped it in the street.

"We are waiting," taunted Hades.

Jack did not respond.

Buck bit his lower lip, second-guessing himself, but then a waterfall trickled over the railing.

At first it was merely a shower of droplets; then it grew into a steady stream. It crashed onto the floor below, the whole surface becoming a thin pool of water. It was not enough to be threatening, but it still made the demons cower slightly. The full Euxian council rose from their chairs and looked down onto the floor, the Tales Teller pulling up the hem of her dress.

Jack grinned wickedly at them, but when he spoke, his voice was even and calm. "Is there anything else?"

"No, Master Jack," said the Apothecary, the ancient Euxian's expression genuine. Buck knew none of them had seen the likes of spontaneous water in Euxinus since the War of Wind and Flame.

Buck shifted his gaze and watched Jack lift his hand, tiny flecks of coal dust dancing about his skin. Once the cross no longer had contact with the black stone, the water ceased. Jack returned the relic to his pocket and wiped his wet hand against his robe, then straightened his posture. There was something oddly regal in the way he stood—another façade of his personality, perhaps? But to Buck it all seemed too natural. It made Buck wonder at the possibility of Jack being the Black Tortoise, but the Apothecary's voice stole him from his thoughts.

"This demonstration, though miraculous, will be stricken from the proceedings, as it has no bearing on the trial of the amid soul." The Apothecary and the six other members of the council retook their seats.

"Master Apothecary," cited Everlyse, the heavenly deity on her feet. "With your permission, I would like to approach the stand."

"Creator Everlyse, the issue on this matter has concluded," said the Apothecary.

"But . . ."

"You will not get your way, dear sister," came Hades' voice, the fiery deity sitting once again on his throne. His posture was slack and annoyed. "The Euxians care not of our dearly departed siblings, not in the way that you and I care."

"Lies," spat Everlyse. "I am not the one who wishes to control them."

Hades shrugged. "If that is what you tell yourself. Regardless, there is no need for you to dig into Jack's soul. Our brother's mark is present in him, and if you care not to believe my words, then you have the words of your Valkyrie."

Buck kept his eyes on the heavenly deity, gauging her reaction to Hades' words, and for the first time, there seemed to be a crack in her apathetic armor. He could not be certain, but there seemed to be a trace of hope in her eyes. The inquiry she had started came with a sense of longing, and he felt she was looking for something else—a different mark.

Everlyse relinquished her stance and sat on her throne, her demeanor once again stony. A breeze filtered in the Hollow as a show of her dissatisfaction, but it went unacknowledged.

There seemed no good place to pick up the pieces of the proceedings, everything having gone so array already, but somehow, the Apothecary managed to interject his voice through the tension of the room and urged the Tales Teller to continue.

Amid Soul

The Tales Teller placed her hands on the podium and lifted her gaze to the witness stand, surveying the Breedling and the Trickster, both still on their feet. She had tried to engage Buck in an open confession, but it appeared he truly did not know about the child. She looked down at the pages of Stingy Jack's storybook, silently reading the dialogue between the little girl and the confined Trickster as they exchanged words. At one point, Stingy Jack had asked for her name, which she had freely given—*Iona*.

The Tales Teller was not surprised that Jack did not remember this meeting or the gifts she had given him—a few crusts of bread and some water. The food had sustained him for another day, but it had never really been about the trappings of mortal nourishment—it had been about the Trickster's heart.

As the voices in the Hollow became still, the Tales Teller turned the page. She felt the Apothecary's eyes on her from above and knew he wanted her to continue, but she did not know how. She had committed an act against neutrality and concealed Iona's truth from the Hollow. She had done so, like Buck all those Eden years ago, because for the Squabbles to connect Iona with the Golden Faun could have disastrous consequences and force the neutral beings to rule in favor of the Fates themselves instead of a proper reprieve. So maybe it was better the Breedling knew none of this, that he was unable to bring this truth to light.

Her ears twitched as the Apothecary addressed her, and she felt a sharp twist in her chest. She took a deep breath, her skin shifting to a neutral white, and knew she was not going to be able to lie a second time.

"Nearly two decades later," she began, "after several accounts of trickery and villainy, Stingy Jack met his match in the fabled shepherdess, Iona Covington, who sought to bring about the reformation of the cursed soul." She paused as her transparent skin shimmered pink and lifted her catlike eyes to the witness stand.

It was clear Jack remembered his part of his story, his hands gripping the rail as his demeanor shifted. The Tales Teller watched the Breedling reach for his wrist and wondered if the gesture was to comfort or restrain. Jack looked at her, meeting her gaze in a way that begged her to be quick. She gave him a somber smile as though to say *I will do the best I can*, before returning to her pages. Her voice once again transcended the Hollow, the room fading to black before opening upon the Irish countryside.

The Tales Teller's voice described every inch of the sprawling scene, bringing to life each blade of grass, toadstool, and moss-laden stone. It was the field Jack and Iona had frequented while the sheep grazed. Iona sat out in the scene, her soft, creamy skin, kissed with freckles, glowing and her cherry-colored hair wafting in the breeze. In her lap, she held a small lamb and stroked its wool, its pink little nose covered by its tiny legs crossed in front of it. The Tales Teller recounted how Jack had fallen for Iona and how she had fallen for him. How her pity broke through the decades of evil deeds, inspiring him to be better than a game piece for Hades to play. She brought out his humanity.

"It must be remembered," said the Tales Teller, "that Iona Covington was first and foremost a free spirit. She possessed a hearty will, not given to many women in her Eden time. She was strong and fierce but, above all, gentle. Her physical appearance is of no importance to this court; however, it is what charmed those around her, for many traveled far and near to seek her hand, but none of them won her heart. None save for one: the wandering soul who bears her witness. Each amid soul's story is different, their lives a unique set of circumstances. But in the case of Iona Covington, the combination of her love for Stingy Jack and his rivalry with Hades was the most unnatural of storms."

The Tales Teller snapped her fingers and all the torches in the Hollow extinguished. The darkness gave way to faint light, the dreamlike projection showing Iona standing on the porch to her father's cottage, her gaze staring out at a deluge. This was a scene of the Shepherdess she knew Jack did not know about. She heard him gasp, no doubt realizing it was only mere moments before he had arrived. The night she died.

"Iona took a sip of her warm tea, the peppermint calming her nerves. She was still on edge from the previous day's event, when Jack's rival, Hades, had made his presence known. The storm clouds had gathered at that time, feeding off their supernatural energy, and it began to rain sometime after. Iona had been aware of her love's condition the moment they had met. She had never admitted to knowing and never revealed they had met once before. Instead, she had listened to his confession as he admitted to knowing the Devil. This part she knew as well, but she did her best to appear shocked, for it was clear he had not admitted intimate details about himself in quite some time."

"What are you saying?" objected Jack's voice in the dark. "What ye say is a lie. Iona and I never met previous to our first meeting."

"Master Jack," boomed the Apothecary. "What Madam Teller reads is not hearsay, it is the inner thoughts of the soul. You will be wise to still your tongue."

The Tales Teller looked out from the top of her vision, just enough to see the Trickster's reaction without directly catching his eye. He was shaking his head, Buck trying to keep him calm. She then stole a sharp glace at Hades, the fiery deity waiting on her. She flushed beet red and withdrew as a smirk broke upon his face—he was clearly beginning to realize that there was more to the story of the Shepherdess. The Tales Teller cemented her eyes on the pages before her, the scene overhead continuing to tell Iona's story without her narrative.

Iona stepped back into the cottage and closed the door, shaking off the droplets of rain that managed to kiss her face and hair. She headed over to the fireplace and planted herself in front of it, drying her clothes. To pass the time, she began to hum, trying her best to keep her mind from thinking ill thoughts of her love. Jack had been gone far too long, and she was beginning to worry something awful had happened. Maybe he was stuck in the village because of the storm, but even this only made her worry more. None of the villagers liked Jack; in fact, deviously wicked rumors had spread about the outsider, and she herself had become a target of their scrutiny.

The Tales Teller blew on the open page, giving volume to the moving illustration as the voices in Iona's head resonated in the chamber of the Hollow.

"*I heard he is the son of a whore,*" she had heard one villager say.

"*Well, I heard he was the son of the devil.*"

"*No, no, no,*" another had argued. "*It is not the penny-pinching we must fear. It is the bewitchment of the Lady Iona."*

Crouching to set the teacup on the floor, Iona then stoked the fire. She sucked in a soft gasp as the hair on her neck prickled.

"Ye shouldn't play with sharp things," came a familiar voice from behind her.

Iona smiled. She looked over her shoulder and found an elegant woman standing in the middle of the room.

"Who is that?" asked Jack aloud, his eyes fixated on the woman's face. In the image, her features were not well-defined, but he seemed to register a familiarity with her.

"Ivy," greeted Iona. *"What are ye doin' here?"*

"Nice to see ye too," said Ivy, her expression taken aback, but only in jest—a moment later, she smiled.

Iona laughed. *"Apologies,"* she said, forgetting her worries for a moment, the presence of her oldest and dearest friend having a calming effect on her.

"Oh, no need fer that, love," said Ivy with a wave of her hand. *"I know I have come unannounced, but in the last few days I've grown concerned about yer well-being."*

"The rumors have already spread that far?"

"Not rumors." Ivy placed a hand over her heart, embracing the Shepherdess. *"It's time."*

Iona backed away. *"What? No, not now, I . . ."* She paused, her thoughts returning to Jack. She could not leave. Not now, not without saying goodbye. Not without doing something. *"How much time do I have?"*

"Not long," said Ivy, the woman's expression sympathetic. *"The height of the storm will cover yer leave."*

"Ye mean death," said Iona bitterly, her voice ringing with certainty in the Hollow as it settled an uneasiness amongst those in attendance.

"She knew?" spoke Everlyse.

The interjection from the Mistress of Heaven was not something the Tales Teller had expected. She had been certain the Trickster would have done the honors. Even so, Everlyse had done spoken in almost a timid whisper, as though she had not meant to speak aloud. A sense of hopefulness was tucked in the back of her voice.

"*I would never say that. Especially not in yer case,*" continued Ivy. "*Death is too final, and fer ye, me love, this painful moment is not yer end.*"

"Stop, stop it now," shouted Jack.

"The tale is not yet finished, Master Jack," spoke the Tales Teller, and added her voice once again to the narration of the story. "It was here Iona felt the tears well in her eyes. Even after years of trying to prepare for this moment, it appeared her efforts had been in vain. Her body went numb, every nerve ending conserving as much energy as possible, for she still needed to find Jack, or if not him, Hades. She would have to run to the village, and mentally began to plot her route. Her thoughts became frantic, making the beat of her heart race. Iona made her way toward the door, poker still in hand." The Tales Teller's voice dropped out, allowing Ivy and Iona's voice to speak.

"*Iona, wait!*"

"*I have to go,*" said Iona.

"*Don't,*" said Ivy, positioning herself in the doorway. Her blue eyes pleaded with her. "*Stay here where I can take care of ye until it is done. Ye don't deserve to be alone.*"

Iona lifted her gaze.

"Iona knew Ivy meant well," said the Tales Teller, "because for the past twenty-one years of her life the woman had been like an older sister, a mother figure, her best friend. There was nothing more Ivy wanted in the world than for her to be safe, for what was about to happen to somehow never come to pass. There was no stopping it, however—she would die as predetermined. But she could not leave without doing one last good thing. Her poor Jack, he would not understand, and she feared this heartache would break him."

"Please, no more," cried the Trickster, shrinking to the floor of the witness stand.

The Tales Teller did not let up and continued. "Iona was hopeful that if she could just explain, the truth would help with the pain of losing her. She had held her love to an ironclad standard, and yet she had not shared her secret, the real reason she had fallen for him. She had loved him for nearly all her life. She had not meant it to happen, but she had fallen for Stingy Jack."

"Thank ye fer coming, my dear friend," Iona said at last. *"But I must go. I must find Jack before it's too late."*

"But . . ." Ivy tried to object.

"If it be me fate to be alone at the end, then so be it."

"Don't be foolish, child," said Ivy. *"Ye'll never make it to the village in this deluge."*

"Ye will not dissuade me from me course. It is me time and I will do whatever I wish with whatever breath I have left."

"Iona snuck past her friend's blockade and began to run," narrated the Tales Teller. "She did not bother to say farewell, but under her breath she said she was sorry."

The scene of the cottage faded, shifting to a raining stretch of road.

"Iona's feet splashed in the mud as the sky darkened even more, the sun setting unseen behind the stormy clouds. The wind blew eastward as thunder rolled and lightning slithered through the black. Her heart beat faster, its rhythm keeping time with the irregular pace of the rain. Her arms and legs began to burn, her nerves catching fire, but she pushed through the growing pain. She threw the iron poker into the ditch to alleviate the stress on her arm, but the respite was short-lived. She kept her stride just short of the bridge, but her body crumpled and she slowed. Her sides hurt and her breaths were laborious. She felt her pulse pounding in her head, robbing her of rational thought and began to spiral and shout into the night."

"Hades!" she cried. *"Hades!"*

"Iona reached the wagon bridge and stopped in the center. She spun around, her action mimicking the dizziness in her head. The rest of her body was on fire now, but the rain did very little to temper her rising fever. She continued to twirl, stretching her arms, the rain kissing her bare skin. The skirt of her dress was unable to dance with her, the fabric too weighted. She began to hum, the melody soothing the firestorm in her brain. She spun and spun and spun, until at last she collapsed to her knees. She pulled her arms into her chest and pressed her forehead against the ground."

"Come fer me," she mumbled to the stones and muck. *"I said, come fer me!"* she shouted, throwing her head upward. *"I'm here, ye spineless Devil! Come out and collect yer prize! Take me and leave him be!"*

"Her demand was lifted away by the wind, her offer an empty one. It was not that she wanted Hades to come and collect her— he would not be able to even if he came—but in that moment of panicked weakness, she wished for someone to be with her, even if it were her enemy.

Iona quickly looked around, but she found no sign of Hades. She squeezed her arms around her chest, the chill of the storm finally penetrating her skin. Her teeth began to chatter as her body battled between fire and ice; she felt herself breaking apart and she collapsed, her body curled tight in a fetal position. She started to cry then, her tears falling not for the pain but rather for the love she was leaving behind. Thunder crashed directly overhead and lightning brightened the space around her. A scream built within her chest, ready to trumpet her farewell."

"I'm sorry, me love," she sobbed.

"And with those final words, she released her cry into the storm and vanished from Eden."

"Why didn't ye go to her, ye spineless serpent!" shouted Jack as the torches in the Hollow reignited. There was a level of anguish in his cry, his sobs audible.

All eyes shifted to Hades, whose cocky position resembled a hint of unease.

"Yes, brother," added Everlyse. "Why did you not go to the Shepherdess when she called? Clearly, the mortal was willing to make a trade. Was it the level of sacrifice you could not accept? Or are you yourself in love with Stingy Jack?"

At this, Hades rose from his throne and made strides across the Hollow floor.

The Tales Teller took a step away from the podium as a precaution to remain out of reach. She had tried to keep the hardest parts of the truth unknown, but she had not the strength to do it twice. She had hoped to spare Jack this pain, for despite his detestable nature, she still pitied him in a way. But now the mark was set, and it would be up to the Trickster to trigger it.

Wind & Flame

"Creator Hades," boomed the Apothecary's voice, accompanied by the pound of his staff.

Jack stared down at the Master of Hell, who had paused in the middle of the Hollow floor, flames licking his fingers. The Tales Teller was blurry because of the tears—the realization of Iona knowing about her own death was something he could hardly bear. He felt like he was drowning, his silent heart breaking. Why did she not tell him? He would never have gone into the village that night. Never have gotten into that stupid fight. He could have been there for her in her last moments. But no, he had foolishly gotten himself thrown in the clink.

"Master Apothecary," spoke Hades, the hiss in his voice smooth and even, contradicting his body language. "I wish to bring grievance to the Hollow."

"Your time will come," replied the Apothecary.

"Then it is of no consequence, for it is not with you." Hades snapped his fingers and the jaguar, Tezcat, swiftly left his post and assumed attacking position against the Tales Teller. "But if you interfere with my intentions, I will strike against you."

The tension in the Hollow stirred as Hades continued to stare daggers at his sister, the scent of sulfur building in the room.

Everlyse changed her posture, her dark blue eyes actively alert, her expression no longer indifferent.

"Strike me, bother," taunted Everlyse.

"Don't flatter yourself, sister," snarled Hades. "My grievance is not with you either."

"Finally," she smiled. "Something we can agree upon."

What happened next came in a whirlwind as Jack watched the mute swan fly to the witness stand and pull Buck away from him by the collar of his robe. He tried grabbing the Breedling, but the Valkyrie general slapped him across the face with her wing. The force knocked him down, but not enough to keep him there.

"Let go of me," Buck shouted, his heels dragging backward.

Jack scrambled to his feet as the Breedling locked his ankles around the posts of the rail, preventing Mist from lifting him to the floor below. He hugged the Breedling's waist and leveraged himself so that Buck became a piece of rope in a game of tug-of-war.

"What is the meaning of this?" boomed the Apothecary. "How dare you attack a member of this house?"

"Ahh, but Master Buck is no longer a member of your house," said Everlyse, still seated in her chair. "He is not under the protection of the Fates, so we have every right to question him."

"Not in the Hollow."

"Then where might you suggest other than this neutral sanctuary?"

The Apothecary opened his mouth, but had no words to refute the question.

"Let him go," growled Jack, as he lifted his arm high enough to pluck a feather from the swan's wing.

Opening her beak, Mist gave a snorted hiss, releasing the Breedling. Jack felt the tension give way and lost his balance, his legs going out from underneath him as Buck propelled into his chest and forced him onto his back. They hit the floor with an audible thud, but neither of them stayed down long. Jack pushed Buck behind him as the swan collected herself to reposition on the rail. He held out his hand, prepared to fight, but instead of an attack, laughter broke out.

All eyes shifted to Hades, the fiery deity beside himself in hysterics. "This I thought I'd never see," he said in between breathy fits. "I was sure the only thing Stingy Jack cared about was himself. And yet, here he is," he snorted. Hades lifted his arms in a gesture of grand fanfare. "Behold, the mighty Trickster! Watch as he battles against the angelic general."

"Creator Hades, that will be enough," said the Apothecary.

Jack kept his left eye on the angel, but his right shifted enough to see the Retrievers unfurl their wings and stand ready for a fight, their black eyes keeping close watch for any sign of further provocation. The Chameleon morphed into a creature much like the Retrievers, except its hardened skin was made of charcoal scales and its wings were silver. Its face resembled the might of a dragon, but its slit nostrils did not produce smoke. The Herald screeched and took flight, its magnificent wingspan revealing the underside of black, white, and gray feathers. Jack broke his gaze to follow the winged wolf's path as it perched at the top of the staircase, standing like a gargoyle in front of the grand arch.

The Apothecary was the last to rise, his motion slow and calm as if to promote order, but no one other than Jack seemed to notice. The eldest Euxian stood with authority, but there would be no deterring Hades or Everlyse—a fight between them was imminent. It was dangerous to allow the two deities to fight in such a confined space, but this was their last hope to expedite a dismissal for Iona's trial. Jack did not think about the consequences of such a fight, only that it needed starting.

"Tell me," he spoke out of turn, taking command of the silence. "Tell me, Madam Teller. Is it true Iona knew of her death?"

"Jack, you heard her testimony," came Buck's voice behind him.

"Yes, yes, we are all aware of the Shepherdess's seeing knowledge," said Everlyse. "What is your point, Trickster?"

"If she knew, if what she did to me is the reason I am the way I am . . ." Jack paused, his thoughts incomplete. He was not certain he knew the answer, but he had said with his own lips that he had felt there was purpose behind his immortality. That if the Black Tortoise could grant free will, Hades a soul, and Everlyse the breath of life, then it stood to reason the Golden Faun could grant immortality. To think of Iona as anything but herself was hard, but the more he thought about it, the more the connection felt real. It was why the Eden Wanderer was important, why he was important. And if a young Iona visiting him the day before his mortal death made him the way he was, then it was why Iona was important. And why together they fit into the grander story.

"Stingy Jack, what are you going on about?" said Hades.

"Iona called fer ye," said Jack, staring down at Hades.

"So?"

"So, how could ye not recognize yer own sister?"

At the sound of his accusation, Everlyse rose to her feet. She did not leave her throne, but her expression was beyond flustered.

"Is this true?" she asked.

Jack lifted the corner of his mouth, his smirk twisting his demeanor as the Trickster came forth. He watched Hades squirm, uncertain whether to feed into his statement or completely negate it. He wanted to taunt the Devil more, dangle the knowledge he had discovered, but the Master of Hell was quick on recovery and answered his sister.

"Speculating a thing and knowing the truth are two different things," said Hades.

"Do not play word games with me," said Everlyse, taking a step and shifting her weight forward.

"You do not have to play, for it is not I who is playing," snarled Hades.

"Do not blame this on the Trickster," snapped Everlyse. "You hide too much behind him. Pitiful, really."

Hades squared his stance, flames returning to his fingers.

"There it is," baited Everlyse. "The true nature of flame—hot-headed anger."

"At least I feel." Hades flicked away his fire as though to prove a point. "At least I do not hide behind the hides of my generals. You accuse me of knowing truths. Then what about you, dear sister, and your willful blindness? Of your inability to control your own creations? What is it you think your Beloved Twins hide from you?"

"Alyce and Lyes are of no concern to you," Everlyse replied, leaving the platform of her seat.

"They are when they conspire with a Prince Animawalker and a Master of Eden to steal the loyalty of one of my generals."

"Do not put dark thoughts in my head to provoke me to use action!"

"I would hardly have to lift a finger in this matter," teased Hades. "There has not been action in you since you fought to claim Nova's soul."

"Hades, you had best silence your tongue," threatened Everlyse.

"Make me."

The wordplay happened so fast that no one seemed to hone in on Hades' words, but behind him, Jack heard Buck gasp at the mention of the Eden Master. He felt his fingers grip the cloth of his robe, his forehead pressed against his back. Surely the mortal was all right, otherwise Hades would have gloated.

Jack tried to whisper to the Breedling, but a brush of wind on the back of his neck stole his attention. He watched the gust shrink, producing the ring of a tornado just above Everlyse's head. It was a show of her strength, and he was certain she would strike fast and unpredicted, but he had miscalculated her intended target. Or, in this instance, targets. Everlyse shot up her hand to grip the wind, and instantly three airy tentacles shot across the Hollow. One gripped the Tales Teller by her wrists, the other bound the Retrievers together in coiled chains, and the third snuck past Jack like a phantom and latched itself around Buck's throat.

"Creator Everlyse," boomed the Apothecary as the Chameleon jumped from the balcony to take up a protective post between the Tales Teller and Tezcat.

"As my brother said, our quarrel is not with you," said Everlyse, her tone chillingly even. "But, if you interfere, I have no qualms with striking you. There is a prize to be had here, and if there is anyone who deserves to know the whereabouts of our siblings, it is me. So whether I have to wring the truth out of the historian, the Trickster, or the Breedling, I will, for I intend to collect before I leave this infernal chamber."

In response to the grandstanding threat, Hades began to laugh. "My dear sister, how I have missed this side of you." Motioning toward the witness stand, he continued, "Now, shall we learn once and for all what the Breedling knows?"

A gust of wind whipped at his feet, making him halt.

"Make no mistake, brother, I agree with you there is more at stake here than the prize of a mortal soul," said Everlyse. "But I still have not forgotten that it was your recklessness that tore us apart and that you are the reason our siblings remain lost."

Hades' smile vanished, his eyes igniting with fire.

"That's right, get angry. It is what you do best. You have underestimated me long enough. I will fight you in order to know the truth." Everlyse tugged on the airy ropes, pulling the Tales Teller and Buck to their knees. She tightened her fist and in turn it strengthened her hold around the Euxian's body, the Tales Teller's skin shifting to a shade of blue. Everlyse's robed angels filed in ranks behind their creator, ready for her command. They removed their black robes to reveal their true forms, but as they were in Euxinus, their images could not take proper shape—therefore all signs of them vanished. General Mist remained at her post on the rail.

Hades' pallid face burned in response, and with a snap of his fingers, the demons behind him unrobed, their bodies now invisible to the Hollow. The black jaguar crouched, ready to pounce on the Chameleon.

The air in the Hollow began to shift, the force of wind lifting to the dome of the chamber, dispersing the warmth provided by the flames and most of the light.

"Now tell me the truth," spoke Everlyse. "Is the Shepherdess my sister?"

Jack lifted his eyes from the lethal scene below and turned to Buck, keeping close watch on Mist in his peripheral vision. He retrieved his cross and attempted to burn the bondage off the Breedling's neck.

"It will not work," said Mist. "Sea does not affect Wind in the same manner as Flame."

Jack sighed, realizing the stupidity of his action. He wanted to ask Buck what he should do, but his voice would noticeably carry. He gripped the heirloom in his hand and felt the Trickster stirring. *Start the fight*, the whisper hissed in the back of his mind, its volume low and mischievous. There was only one way in which Jack knew how to start a fight; his days as Irish Fists Jack had conditioned him to the sound of the bell. He looked at the cross, recalling the sound it had made when it hit the lava stone. He raised his hand above his head, and without haste he let the heirloom slip from his fingers. It landed with a resonating chime, the bell signaling the start of a fight.

"Master Jack . . ."

The warning traveled faintly through the screaming clamor, but Jack was able to hear it. He lifted his eyes for a brief moment to the high stage where the Apothecary stood vigilant. He caught the gleam in the Euxian's eyes and knew he was giving them permission to leave the Hollow. Jack nodded in reply, and acted as the Apothecary's stare grew more adamant. He bent down and seized the cross, placing it in his pants pocket, then reached for Buck's arm. And luckily he did, for the leash around his neck yanked on him. Jack shifted his body to prevent him from moving, but in doing so it meant Buck was choking.

"Buck, how do I get it off?" he said with a shout as Everlyse threw the Retrievers over the balcony, both crashing down on the podium, their combined weight crushing it into rubble.

"Use your breath," Buck managed with a hoarse voice, his eyes fluttering.

Grabbing his cheeks as wailing cries and the clashing of angels and demons began, Jack pressed. "Buck, I don't understand, ye need to . . ."

"Disrupt the flow of air."

Jack scrunched his brow, still not registering his meaning.

The Hollow filled with a flash of radiant purple light, smoldering with the glow of scarlet flames. A tremendous shockwave followed, bounding against the walls of the Hollow.

Jack lifted his eyes to the ceiling as fissures appeared in the dome. Another flash of purple appeared, followed by another shock, this time shaking a few pieces of the loose stone from the cracks. Jack lowered his gaze, noticing the change in brightness—several of the basins had lost their flames. He watched as the Squabbles fled from the high balcony before another flash of purple appeared. As he looked down directly at the podium, the Retrievers and the Chameleon engaged in fierce combat with Mist and Tezcat to protect the still-subdued Tales Teller. Jack glanced over his shoulder, not realizing they had lost their angelic gargoyle.

"Jack, get this thing off me," said Buck, recapturing his attention.

Jack stared at the airy leash. Buck had said to use his breath—he leaned forward and blew on the Breedling's neck. The wind twitched but did not relinquish its hold. Jack tried again with a stronger breath, but it still did not work. He sighed, hot air wafting against the airy collar. He heard Buck gasp as the element released him.

In response to the severed connection, Everlyse screamed and pulled on the remaining thread of wind, forcing the Tales Teller into her grasp.

Jack looked through the rail as the Mistress of Heaven grabbed the Euxian by her scruff.

"Tell me the truth," she cried.

An immediate stillness fell over the chamber, every combatant frozen in place waiting on the answer. Jack glanced at Hades, the fiery deity still standing in the center of the floor. Jack scrunched his forehead. Had the two deities not engaged each other?

"Buck," he whispered. "Have we accomplished our mission?"

"Are Everlyse and Hades fighting?"

"I don't think so. Hades is still standing in the same spot. I think only the angels and demons are fighting."

"Then no," coughed Buck. "It is not enough. Hades and Everlyse must come to blows."

"What is the truth you wish to know?" came the Tales Teller.

"Is the Shepherdess my sister?"

Jack felt the anticipation build in his chest. It was the answer he wanted to know as well, but that would have to wait. He sprang to his feet, gripping the rail as the Tales Teller opened her mouth.

"Creator Everlyse," he spoke. "Why do ye leave such truth-telling to the Euxian? She has deceived us once already, who's to say she will not lie again?"

"Her tongue rings more true than yours, Trickster."

"Ah, a valiant point," teased Jack. "But I don't know the truth. Not for certain, not really, but Hades does. He figured it out long ago. He thought I didn't know, but I know him better than he knows himself. How else was I able to trick him and continue to best him at every turn?" At this, the heavenly deity gave him her attention. He grinned wickedly. "I understand now why he was stalling me that fateful night. Why he came to taunt me at Iona's cottage moments after she had left. It wasn't to punish me, it was to punish her."

Everlyse immediately tossed the Tales Teller aside and stepped forward. She made herself taller with every step, her wind rising to the strength of a hurricane, and stood in front of her brother, who for once looked calm. Jack bit his lower lip, hoping his manipulative words would be enough. Everlyse was desperate, her apathetic façade crumbling. She loved her sister, he could feel that, and she would do anything to get her back. So for Hades to have harmed her in any way—Jack held his breath as Hades spoke.

"Yes."

The confirmation sent Everlyse over the edge, blasting a gale-force wind that shook the entire Hollow, the cracks in the stone expanding as fighting resumed. Wisps of wind and shadows darted in and out of sight; the sounds echoed and resonated in the Hollow as flashes of purple light swirled more frequently. The smells of burning feathers and flesh polluted the once-neutral chamber as the black stone glistened with splatters of scarlet and azure, the marks of blood.

Everlyse and Hades fought hand to hand, dancing amongst swirls of wind and flame. The spectacle was unlike anything Jack had ever seen. He had anticipated carnage, but this was a simple strength. There was elegance to their fight. A mutual understanding of love and hate. Every time Hades would come with fire, Everlyse would wave it away. And every time she came at him with a lash of wind, he would embrace it into his flame and extinguish them both.

"Jack, we need to leave," he heard Buck say, the Breedling taking him by the wrist. "The Hollow is no longer safe for us."

Jack did not acknowledge the Breedling, but he did not resist his pull either. He kept his eyes fixed on the sibling deities as they made their way up the stairs. He felt an awed sort of satisfaction as a mighty grin broke across his face. He had done it. Somehow, he had been able to play off the charged emotions of the two deities, had said just the right words, and for the first time he appreciated the darker side of himself. Iona was safe. It was the last thing to come to mind before he toppled over, his ribs ramming against the edge of the next step. He groaned as he cradled his side, realizing Buck was no longer holding onto him.

Turning his head, he saw Buck sprawled out on his stomach at the top of the stairs. Mist stood on his back, pinning him to the floor, snapping at his body with her beak. The blatant attacks must have had some strength behind them, because every time she struck, Buck cried out in pain. Jack motioned to assist the Breedling, but his eyes caught the pale yellow spheres of the melanistic jaguar, its long tail whipping maliciously as it prowled up the stairs. It crouched at the ready to pounce on its prey.

"You shall not leave this Hollow in one piece, Trickster," said Tezcat as the jaguar leapt toward him.

Jack frantically stuffed his hand into his pocket and recovered his cross. The jaguar landed on all fours over him—without thinking about the consequence, he thrust the heirloom against Tezcat's chest. The jaguar roared loudly as the cool silver seared its fur, the blessed relic of the Black Tortoise pilfering the demon of volition.

Tezcat reared back and took a swipe at Jack, cutting through the sleeve of his robe and the bandage on his arm. Dark blood instantly soiled the white fabric as Jack screamed. Using every ounce of strength in his leg, he kicked Tezcat off him, forcing the demon to tumble down the stairs.

Jack huffed a few labored breaths, stuffed the relic back in his pocket, and pressed his arm against his chest. Changing positions, he began to ascend the last few steps to assist Buck, but out of nowhere, the Herald swooped in and captured Mist with its talons, lifting the swan away.

"Buck," he shouted over the chaos as he rolled the Breedling over on his back. There was glistening gold blood gushing from a wound on his neck. Buck was breathing rather heavily, his eyes fluttering in and out of consciousness. "Buck." Jack patted the Breedling's cheek. "Oi, wake up."

Buck shook his head and fluttered his eyes open. "Jack," he managed, his expression twisting in pain. He reached his hand up to his neck and winced.

"Ye need to put some pressure on that," Jack said.

"So do you," said Buck, removing the gold and black tassels from his neck. "Here, wrap them around your arm and tie them off."

Jack took them and tied the new bandage with the help of his teeth.

"There, now help me up," Buck grumbled.

Jack locked elbows with Buck's free arm to hoist him up. The Breedling managed to stand, but barely.

"Oi, don't ye pass out on me now, Breedling—ye've still got a lot of explaining to do when we get back to the Apothecary's coffin." He threw Buck's left arm over his shoulders and together, relying equally on each other for support, they exited the Hollow as another gale of wind rocked the chamber.

Their ascent was troublesome, each trying not to trip over the other. Jack felt the heat radiating from Buck's body as the pain in his neck seemed to magnify. He tried to keep talking to him, but halfway down the mountain the smell of sulfur began to wreak havoc on his breathing and his fever returned, the strain of the Wicker's Curse pulsating in his arm. He focused on Iona, the hope of seeing her again, but the mounting pain caused him to falter and force more of his weight onto Buck.

Buck readjusted himself accordingly to gain better balance, but he could tell he was having a rough go of it.

"Buck, we should stop," he huffed. "Just for a tick."

"No, Jack," groaned Buck. "We are almost there. We cannot stop now. We both might bleed out into unconsciousness. We are not safe here, we have to"—his voice faltered—"we, we need to get to the bottom."

Jack did not say anything, but kept going, the torchlight of the Equadria getting closer, until they were about a block away.

He felt the light tremor in the soles of his feet before the sound of the explosion happened and the night sky brightened with purple light. The blast rocked the entire mountain, the force cascading like an avalanche. It knocked them both off their feet, sending them tumbling down the remaining stairs. Jack felt the impact of the street against his shoulder, his head bouncing off the ground. He tried to move, rolling slowly to his other side, his eyes catching the horrific sight of purple flames burning in the place where Squabbles Hollow once stood. He turned his head, managing to find Buck, the Breedling facedown and unconscious. He tried to crawl over to him, but the effort was too much, and as he began to lose consciousness, he heard the distinct sound of Miriam's voice yelling Buck's name.

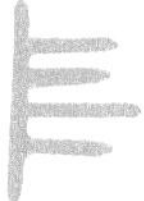

The War Room

Miriam leaned against the doorframe of the healing room, her attention focused more on her sleeping brother and the Trickster than the heated debate going on in the Apothecary's tea kitchen. They had all gathered in the coffin after the Hollow exploded, with the exception of the Herald and the Chameleon, both of whom were biding some time before the rest of them had to make an appearance in the palace.

"You really did it this time," shouted Serkan, a superficial red lash visible on his cheek. His robe was a tattered mess, revealing the silk of his shirt and the leather of his black pants. Miriam watched the Retriever's wings unfurl slightly, mirroring his temper—his whole body was ready to spring, his black eyes staring intently.

"My love, calm yourself," said Jardina. The female Retriever looked no better than her counterpart. Her pale facial features tattooed with bursts of black, blue, and purple.

"I will not! We could have died," shouted Serkan. "We all could have died. And what would have become of your masterful plan then, my Eldest? None of us would have lived to reap any benefit from it."

"Serkan, that is enough," said the Tales Teller, her white gown in ruins, torn nearly to the point of leaving her naked.

"No," interjected the Apothecary. "Let him speak. He has a right to it."

At the sound of this, Miriam heard the male Retriever groan in frustration, the eldest Euxian's calm exterior no doubt dosing the heat of his temper. She heard Annaliese snort over her shoulder, the Scar Healer hiding from the argument on the stairs.

She was grateful the Scar Healer had shown when she did, for she would never have been able to get both Jack and Buck inside on her own. There had been so much blood, and none of the council had yet returned from the Hollow. In fact, at the time she had thought they were all dead, but she did not let fear take hold of her. She prepared simple remedies and cleaned the wounds before Annaliese used catgut to patch the skin. The wounds would have undoubtedly healed on their own, but they could not risk it, even if both Jack and Buck were seemingly immortal. Besides, they did not have the luxury of time to find out.

Miriam had made little conversation with the Scar Healer since her arrival, but she had sensed the difference in her right away. She knew well of her cousin's character, having witnessed her in action as she dispatched the Wickers. Miriam had once compared it to the fighting tenacity of Lady Vala, a uniqueness brought on by her first charge to Eden and the bond she had forged with the Animawalker that never seemed to separate from her. Annaliese's transformation was not the same as Buck's metamorphosis, but the marks on her aura were similar to that of the Black Tortoise. And Miriam was certain the freedom she now enjoyed was as a result of the Eden Wanderer's influence.

"Argh," groaned Annaliese, hopping up from the stairs. "What in the name of fate is the matter with all of you?"

Miriam did not move from her spot, but her full attention nevertheless fell on her cousin. Annaliese stood with her hands posted at her sides, her stance a warrior's pose. Her fluorescent hair shimmered, the butterfly hidden from sight. Miriam studied her aura again, the coal dust more prevalent now that she was standing still. She was free, no trace of the Fates' shackling grace left upon her. Miriam felt a twinge of something that made her upset, but she could not name the emotion. She shifted her weight to try to shake the feeling.

"You are one to talk, Breedling," spat Serkan. "Why are you even still here? Go enjoy your freedom."

"Do not shout at her," spoke the butterfly as it fluttered from the Scar Healer's hair.

"Zarna, stop," said Annaliese, her voice pinched with a hint of terror, the fierce warrior vanishing. She reached out her arms swiftly and captured the Animawalker in her hands, pulling it toward her chest.

Miriam found the motion incredibly intimate, a means of protection. She would not have put it past Serkan to have attacked the Animawalker after the minor provocation, and she shuddered to think what type of display might have unfolded. Instead, she thought about the Retriever's question, one she had had herself but had stifled the urge to ask. She gauged the uneasy expression on her cousin's face, realizing Serkan had struck a vital nerve. "You cannot," she said, her voice soft. Everyone looked at her, except for Annaliese, who failed to mask her secret. Miriam pushed away from the doorframe. "That is why you are here: you cannot leave."

"Annaliese," spoke the Apothecary. "Is this true?"

"I tried," the Scar Healer said in an uncharacteristically timid voice. "We tried." She opened her hands to release the butterfly, which fluttered its wings and took a post on her shoulder. "Every Eden Scar is blocked. I asked Zarna to try, but she would not do it for fear we might be separated. The only way out is . . ."

"No," objected Miriam, swinging her arms to her sides. "You cannot honestly be thinking of trying to convince the Fates to send you. They will have you branded a traitor the moment you set foot in the palace."

"Calm yourself, Miriam," said the Apothecary. "Annaliese knows she cannot go to the Fates."

"Then . . ." Her eyes widened as the recognition of her cousin's intentions dawned on her. She glanced over her shoulder at her sleeping brother. "Buck knows the way out." Whipping her attention back to her cousin, she said, "I am certain he will tell you when he wakes."

Annaliese smiled, but it did not reach her eyes. "My escape is not dependent on him, at least not in that way, for I cannot make the same fall as him. I am not broken enough, nor do I need to break my shackles, for as you know, they are already gone. What I do need is his means of escape this time."

"The mortal," said the Tales Teller, her voice slightly dreamy.

"What about him?" asked Jardina.

"The bond that Charles Reese shares with Buck is what tethers him to Eden," said the Apothecary.

"And as such, it is only Charles's voice that can call him back," said the Tales Teller.

An anxious silence fell upon them after that, each one left to their own thoughts.

Looking over her shoulder again, Miriam recalled the earlier conversation Buck and the Apothecary had had about his mortal master. She had been standing just outside the door, ear pressed to it, before seeking the Tales Teller's assistance. What little she had gleaned was that Charles Reese did not accept his mantle, that the mortal really had no idea of the power he now wielded. So if Charles Reese was unaware of his gift, how could he be of any assistance? He had no reason to call her brother by name.

A sharp whistle ripped her from her reverie and made everyone practically jump out of their skins, including her. Both the Retrievers and Annaliese froze in fighting stances, while the Tales Teller let out a whimper as she clung to the Apothecary's arm, their expressions beset with fear. The Apothecary was the first to move, pulling the kettle off the stove to prevent any further disturbance. Miriam watched the eldest Euxian lift his shoulders in a heavy sigh. He kept his back to them, no doubt trying to see a way out of their predicament.

"My Eldest," rang the Tales Teller's voice, her skin shifting to a shade of midnight.

Miriam gasped at the rare sight. The Tales Teller's flesh only shifted this color when the Fates forcibly summoned her to the palace. Her feet began to move involuntarily toward the door, but the Apothecary reached for her wrist to stop her.

"Please, I must go," she said, her voice tight with a hint of pain.

"Not alone," said the Apothecary. "Serkan and Jardina will escort you to the palace."

"But I am unpresentable."

"Let them see you like this. Let them see the three of you as you are. Make them see that there is still fight in the Elements. Let it instill fear into them."

"And what of you?" asked Jardina.

"I shall remain here," said the Apothecary, "but I will not dwell. Only long enough to make certain Jack and Buck are well enough to make their escape."

Miriam wanted to ask how they were supposed to do that without the summons of Charles Reese, but the Tales Teller whimpered again, the distress on her face expressing how much discomfort the silent command was inflicting upon her.

"Please, my Eldest."

The Apothecary released the Euxian historian; as soon as he did her feet glided across the floor, the Retrievers already at the door.

"Go safely," squeaked Miriam, a fit of panic taking hold of her.

Jardina nodded before the three of them were gone from the room.

Miriam and Annaliese stood in a state of uncertainty as the Apothecary went about fashioning two beakers. He dipped his hand into the bowl of water, submerging the hibiscus flowers and then pulled them out, water dripping from his hand.

"Miriam," he said, gaining her attention. "Take the beakers and come with me. Annaliese," he added, and the Scar Healer looked at him. "Please remain here and keep watch. I do not trust that Hades and Everlyse have fully withdrawn from the realm."

"You do not think they will come here?" asked Annaliese, her eyes widening.

"They may, or at the very least, they may send their angels and demons to attack." The Apothecary sighed. "As long as Buck and Jack are here, this is where they will strike first. They are not strong enough to take the Fates head on, not in their palace. Besides, at this point they care not of them, only the whereabouts of their siblings. Now, let us see to our patients and prepare them for departure."

"But, my Eldest," said Miriam, taking hold of the two beakers, a bitter smell in the steam stinging her nose. She followed the ancient Euxian into the healing room. "Depart where?" she continued. "There is no place in Euxinus they will be able to hide. Not once the Fates give the order for their capture. Not even you will be able to grant them sanctuary."

The Apothecary stood between the two beds, his ancient

features worn and tired. It was only then Miriam realized the fragility of the eldest Euxian. It was an unnerving sight, but one that also provided a rare insight. She had never been able to read any of the council members or their auras, but in this moment, she was able to catch a glimpse of the Apothecary's energy. Unlike Breedlings, who had shackles set around their wrists, the Apothecary had his around his neck, a choker to cut through him in the most savage way. And it was not the only thing that marked him.

Miriam stepped further into the room and stood next to him, beakers still in hand. The scars became visible to her, most of them angry patches of scarlet or sharp, neat cuts of azure. The markings were hardly a shock to her; she knew there had to have been times in which the Apothecary was forced to fight. But what did perplex her was a distinct black marking on his back, coupled with something she could not quite make out. She shifted her weight to get a better angle, but the Apothecary turned toward her, blocking her view of it entirely.

"Your keen sight suits you, Mistress Breedling," he said, a soft smile growing on his face. "But there are some things you are not meant to uncover."

"I—" Miriam shifted her gaze and shook her head. "I did not mean . . ."

"It is quite all right. It was my fault for allowing you to see." He placed his empty hand on her shoulder. "Now let us see to your brother and his charge."

Miriam simply nodded as the Apothecary turned to Buck and placed one of the hibiscus flowers over the wound on his neck. He closed his eyes and spoke in a whispered voice; Miriam could not fully make out the words as she sat down on the bed. The Apothecary snapped his fingers and Buck's eyes fluttered open, the flower petals shriveling before dissolving to dust. She met his gaze with a warm smile, trying her best not to get overemotional and cry. She did not want to admit her fear of losing him forever. She did not want to burden him with that notion.

"Miriam?" Buck said, clearly trying to get his bearings. He attempted to sit up, but the ache prevented him from achieving it.

"Here," she said, setting the other beaker on the nightstand. "Drink this." She held him up with one hand and pressed the beaker to his lips with the other.

Buck coughed the moment the hot liquid entered his mouth. "What is that? It is bitter and foul."

"Coffee," answered the Apothecary, taking hold of the other beaker and assisting Jack. "It will simulate you enough for you both to get to safety. I must warn you, the concentration is quite intense, but it is all I can offer you at the moment. We need you on your feet."

"Bloody hell!" gasped Jack, his voice hoarse.

Shortly afterward, Miriam heard the Trickster cough. She continued to assist Buck, despite his protests to get the infernal drink away from him.

"You know, this reminds me of the moment you came back from your charge to retrieve Alhazan," she said, a sense of nostalgia taking hold of her. It had been the moment she had truly begun to feel the way she did about her brother, although she still could not seem to describe it to herself.

"Miriam, why are you bringing that up now?"

"I—" She felt her cheeks warm and pressed her lips together. "This just reminds me of then, I guess. Me being able to take care of you." She smiled. "You had been unconscious for so long when Serkan and Jardina brought you back, and your body was ice cold. Your condition was beyond care, and the Apothecary said we just needed to wait for you to wake up. While you were here, I stayed with you the whole time. I sang songs, read stories from the Tales Teller's library, I even prayed to the Fates. When you finally woke up it was a great relief to me, for I could not imagine being without you."

"Miriam, I—" started Buck, but she did not allow her brother to finish his words and helped him drink the last sip of coffee. They had never talked about that time, not really. The feeling she had felt had been too new to her, and so she had kept it from him. Only the Apothecary and the other council members had known, and she was not sure how much the eldest Euxian had told her brother when he had awoke.

When the last dregs of coffee were gone, she pulled the beaker away, laughing lightly at Buck's displeased expression.

"There," said the Apothecary, before moving to the foot of Jack's bed. "Miriam, have you finished?"

"Yes," she answered, placing the empty beaker on the nightstand. She then wrapped her arms around her brother's waist and laid her head in his lap. Buck draped his good arm around her and stroked her hair while humming notes she did not recognize. Miriam breathed him in, the remnants of fresh rain still lingering about him. "You will be well," she said, her voiced pinched by the threat of tears. "Annaliese did well on your dressing. She—we . . ."

"Thank you," said Buck.

Miriam squeezed him tighter and burrowed her head against him. "You will be well," she said again.

"I will be, thanks to you. Well enough to know I am still here," said Buck.

Miriam pulled away, confused. "Where else would you be?"

"Oh," said Buck, his face growing sullen and pale. "Never mind," he added. "I am just tired."

"The coffee will see to that momentarily, but for now, there are a few matters to discuss," said the Apothecary.

"Jack," said Buck, turning his head to look at the Trickster sitting in bed.

"I'm fine, mate," said Jack, his eyes softly closed. "Now, I have waited long enough. Ye owe me an explanation."

"I have not forgotten, but if you could give me a moment," said Buck. He tried to push himself up further, but did not have the strength. He huffed as a twinge of distress broke on his face.

"No, Buck," said Jack. "No more waiting."

"All right. Miriam, would you be so kind and lift me up?"

"Are you sure?"

Buck nodded.

Miriam helped her brother rest his back against the wall as he let out a labored breath. He did not look at her or Jack, just kept his eyes fixed on the ceiling as though he were trying to find the right words. She had no idea what he was going to say, but based on the council's earlier conversation, she had pieced together enough of what had transpired and of what her brother was about to confess.

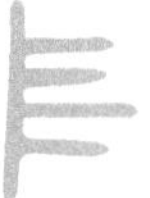

Bartholomew's Confession

The light stung Buck's eyes as he stared up at the black ceiling, his mind conjuring images of what had happened in the Hollow moments before the explosion. He took in a steady stream of air, his throat raw and his mouth dry. There was a lingering throb in the crook of his neck from the bite mark Mist had given him; the softness of the white sheets pressed against his body filled him with a sense of comfort but did not stem the ache of his body. Buck turned to look at Jack, the Trickster waiting on him to speak.

"Before I begin," he said, "you must know what I am about to say may be upsetting to you, but please do not let it be so."

"Dammit, Buck, ye try and weasel yer way out of this again and I swear—"

"I am not trying to weasel out of anything. I just need you to know that in your condition you have to stow your anger. Know that I kept this secret until now with good intentions."

Jack growled in frustration as his skin flushed a little. "I care not of your intentions. Now tell me true, is Iona the Golden Faun or not?"

Buck watched Miriam's eyes widen in recognition, as though she had already come to the same conclusion. He wanted to ask her how she knew, but that was not of great importance. Certainly, the council had been in heated debate before the Apothecary woke him up, and she had pieced together enough to know what had happened. He tried to mask his face with a pensive expression, but he was all nerves.

"You already know the answer."

Jack furled his eyebrows. "That may be, but that does not excuse you from telling me the truth. I want to hear it from your lips."

"Then, yes," said Buck. "That night I found her in the rain, I saw in her the markings of a Creator."

"What do you mean, you found her?"

"I was there as you suspected. I saw Iona dancing in the rain before she collapsed in the middle of the bridge. I listened to her cries, her screams taunting Hades to show himself, but he never did. Because he was with you, Jack—because like you said in the Hollow, it was not to punish you, but to punish her. Punish her for taking you away from him."

"Did he know?"

Buck looked at the Apothecary, his eyes asking for assistance. He had no insight as to whether or not the Master of Hell truly knew his long-lost sister had been right in front of him.

"Had Hades truly realized Iona was the Golden Faun, there is no doubt in my mind that he would have abandoned his quarrel with you for her," said the Apothecary. "But instead, like Master Breedling said, Hades' punishment was brought on by jealousy."

Jack laughed. "I should almost feel flattered."

"As I watched Iona," Buck continued, "she curled into herself, and in that moment I approached her. She grabbed me, mistaking me for Hades. She begged me to let you go and take her instead. I tried explaining to her I was not whom she thought, but all she did was continually plead your case. She was delirious and I tried to calm her down, but she was already too far gone—her soul was breaking and there was nothing I could do. It was in that moment I pitied her, and I had never felt pity for anyone or anything. I was awestruck by her devotion to you, and in the passing flash of lightning, I felt energy surge within her. In her swollen eyes, I saw the Golden Faun."

"And ye just left her there to die like a coward," said Jack through clenched teeth.

"Not exactly," said Buck, lowering his gaze in shame so as not to meet Jack's anger. "It appears that way, yes, but at the time I could not yet resist the pulse of obedience. I had my answer, and it was time to report my findings to the Fates. I pried Iona's fingers from my shirt and ran, leaving her there curled on the ground, her pleading cries following me. I know now what I did was wrong, but in that moment there was nothing I could do to help her."

Jack curled his fingers into the sheet.

"Yes, I ran. Ran as fast as I could, but still her voice echoed in my head, her grief stabbing me like nothing I had ever felt before. It made me slow my pace. Made me question my own feet. And so I stopped. I hesitated, I even brought myself to turn back, but my feet grounded me where I stood. And by then, it was already too late, for her final cry broke through the storm."

Miriam's screech was the first thing Buck was able to register as Jack sprang from the bed and knocked her out of the way. He felt Jack's hands on his shoulders, pushing his back against the mattress—the Trickster's thumb targeted the wound on his neck, the pressure threatening to rip the stitches. Buck latched his hands onto the Trickster's wrists to gain leverage, but he had no strength to fight back.

"BUCK!" screeched Miriam as she made a motion to intervene, but the Apothecary grabbed her by the arm and pulled her away.

"Ye let her die," Jack gritted through his teeth.

"Yes . . . it was . . . my fault," Buck admitted, trying to hold in his own scream.

"Ye let her die," cried Jack, pressing all his body weight down on top of Buck.

"Jack, please."

"That's right, beg," said Jack as saliva dripped from his mouth. "Beg, like she did!"

Buck felt the rise of his voice clawing up his throat. "I had no choice," he huffed. "Not then, not yet. But she helped set me free. She is the reason I could escape, so that I could find you and help you rescue her."

"Tell me the truth," growled Jack. "Is Iona the Golden Faun?"

Buck fixed his gaze upon Jack. There was no madness in his eyes. He was not out of control, nor under any sort of influence. No, in the Trickster's eyes he only saw grief. "Yes," he said, keeping his voice steady. "I believe Iona to be the Golden Faun."

"What do you mean, believe? It is a yes or no."

"Master Jack," interjected the Apothecary. "There is no way for us to know if Iona is the Golden Faun herself or if the Golden Faun was merely a part of the mortal in some way, whether by possession or possibly as Iona's soul. But the how is irrelevant. No matter how, in whole or in part, Iona Covington was or is the Lost Creator—she is the Golden Faun."

"If that were the case, I would have known," said Jack, his voice dripping his denial. "I would have seen her trick. Felt her presence, something."

"Says the man blindly in love," countered the Apothecary.

A moment of stillness fell in the room, and Buck released a

whimper from the pressure mounting in his shoulder.

"Master Apothecary."

It was Annaliese who broke the intensity in the room, but Jack would still not give. Buck risked a glance at his cousin, her expression cold and unreadable, even as she tilted her chin to address the Animawalker on her shoulder. The butterfly's wings shuttered as it lifted and flew across the room, landing upon the Trickster's injured arm. It drew attention to the injury previously brought about by Annaliese's Wicker blade, but the bandage was no longer around his forearm, the skin no longer charred and black. In its place were four claw marks, two of which were stitched together, Jack's pale skin pulled tight. The butterfly lowered its proboscis and kissed the largest wound.

"There is no need to be angry anymore, Jack," said Zarna, her strong voice rather hypnotizing. "The Trickster within you has served his purpose and the curse upon you has been lifted, thanks to Tezcat's foolish bloodletting. You do not have to be the uncontrollable character life forced upon you and that Hades exacerbated for his own amusement. You do not have to be Stingy Jack."

Buck lifted his eyes to gauge Jack's expression after hearing this revelation—to his surprise, there was regret present in the Trickster's eyes. Jack slowly began to release the pressure on his body, the butterfly lifting itself off his arm. Buck felt an overwhelming sense of relief that made him begin to cry. He watched Jack stumble backward in a daze and fall onto his bed, his hands landing in his lap. Buck tried to sit up, the boost granted by the coffee finally giving him some energy, but his strength was still not there.

Ripping her arm away from the Apothecary, Miriam rushed to the other side of his bed, lifting him up and pulling him toward her in order to put more distance between him and his attacker. Miriam propped him against her chest, his breaths heavy, mixed with a few whimpers from the stinging pain in his neck and shoulder. He felt a few tears hit his cheeks and knew she was crying. She kissed his head ever so gently and stroked his hair.

"I have you Buck, just breathe," she said, her voice smooth and caring. "Shhh, all will be well."

Buck glanced over at Jack, then at the Apothecary as he moved toward the Trickster and placed a hand on his shoulder.

"Is it true?" Jack asked, his voice small and childlike, his eyes pointed down at his hands. "Is what the butterfly said true?"

"It is, Master Jack," said Apothecary. "Your fever has broken, and the Wicker's Curse no longer holds any power over your body."

"And the Trickster?"

"As Zarna said, the Trickster has served its purpose, but your reliance upon him is not so easily changed. Only you can fully separate yourself from your duality; in time this will come to be, but know that Hades can still influence your actions, though only if you truly let him."

"Jack," said Buck.

The Trickster bit his lower lip, his fingers curling into fists. "I'm sorry, Buck."

"It is all right, Jack," said Buck, giving him a reassuring smile. "I was prepared for your impulse to lash out at me. Not that I am excusing your behavior, but I knew holding this back from you as long as I have would not serve me well, I am partly to blame for it."

"Spoken like a true martyr," said Jack, a hint of teasing in his voice.

Buck chuckled in response as a smile broke across Jack's face, the tension between them finally broken. There would be no more secrets between them now, and Buck was grateful for that. But there was still one more he would have to tell, and it would be the harder of the two. Buck reached for Miriam's arm and pushed her into him as the Apothecary came to check on his wound. He felt the eldest Euxian press against his skin, and each time he responded with a distressed whimper.

"Many pardons, Master Buck," said the Apothecary as he withdrew his hand and stared patiently at him, a sense of pride brightening his ancient face. "You have shown bravery far beyond my expectations, young one. And when the time comes, when this is all over . . ."

"Master Apothecary," came Annaliese's voice, a hint of urgency lacing her words. "The Chameleon has arrived."

The Apothecary sighed.

Buck wondered what more his former mentor had to say, but whatever it was, the Apothecary left it at that before leaving the room and joining the Scar Healer in the tea kitchen.

"Miriam, why is Annaliese here?"

"Hmm? Oh, she is here to see you."

"Me?" Buck shifted his body, forcing Miriam to relinquish her hold and take a seat on the bed.

"Yes, she said she cannot leave and she needs your help. Which reminds me, I know you—" Miriam bit her lip. "I know you are not at your best, but you also made a promise to tell me of your escape. You said you would help me break my chains."

"And I will, I—" Buck swallowed back his words. He shifted slowly and removed the bedding, realizing he was only half-naked. A pair of white pants covered his legs. He maneuvered to a sitting position and reached for the downy robe draped over the nightstand. He nestled into the cool caress of the silk, breathing in its perfume of fresh rain, lilacs, and earth. The smell was intoxicating, familiar, and calming. Patches of color caught his eye, each marking his new station with the insignias of a Golden Faun and the Black Tortoise. His fingers lightly outlined each, grateful for their presence. Buck did all this without answering Miriam's question, but his silence did not seem to bother her, at least not at first. He attempted to stand and felt the brush of lightheadedness follow, but it passed. He looked down at Jack, who was staring at him with a questioning expression.

"Buck, aren't ye gonna answer yer sister?" he asked.

Buck moved to the foot of the bed, his legs shaking.

"Buck, you promised," shouted Miriam, springing to her feet.

Buck turned around to look at her, his left hand pressing against the mattress to steady himself. "I did, and I will. But what you ask is difficult to say aloud, for like Jack, this is not something you want to hear."

"But I do," objected Miriam. "I want to hear your words. How did you escape?"

"I died," Buck blurted out as he watched the eagerness evaporate from his sister's eyes.

"Oh, Buck," came Annaliese's voice, her presence in the doorway once again, the Chameleon in front of her at her feet, the Apothecary behind her.

Buck did not know why, but for some reason he felt ashamed and vulnerable, like his audience was judging him, or maybe pitying him. "At first," he continued, keeping his eyes down, "I made the choice to try not merely to escape but to end. To end my suffering. To make the pain stop, the loneliness, the confusion. My heart hurt and I could not figure out why. I had not the right words to put toward what I was feeling, but somehow I knew I was wrong, tainted somehow, unworthy of the Fates' grace. Or maybe it was that they were unworthy of me."

Miriam let out a stifled breath, and he knew she was crying.

"I took my existence into my own hands and chose to suffer, to sacrifice myself for a chance at freedom—or, if not freedom, at least peace. And there was no guarantee of that either. But it is the only way to be free of my shackles, my dear sister, and it is the only way you will be able to truly escape."

Buck lifted his gaze and found Miriam staring at him in dismay, her russet skin paling in shade. He took a few steps and rounded the bed, taking hold of his sister's hand.

Miriam shut her eyes tight and shook her head. "What you say cannot be done."

"As I said to you before, when you asked me for Sea's relic, our obedience is rooted deep within us—the only way to get rid of that is to rip it out. You must use your pain and let it eat away at you until there is nothing left. Only then can you let go."

"What," Miriam mumbled, the words sticking in her throat, "does it feel like?"

"First, you will fall into an abyss, but do not fight against it. Know that on the other side, something awful will happen to you. It may not be a raging inferno, but you will be trapped, unable to move. Do not let this fear take hold of you, and know . . ." He took hold of her face and wiped her tears away with his thumbs. She looked at him. "Know that someone will find you, someone truly special. Someone like Charlie. And whatever you do, Miriam, do not turn your back on her. Do you understand? Do not make the same mistake I did. She will be your anchor to Eden, and you will be hers."

"Another Eden Master?" said Jack.

"Judging from the outcome of Buck's escape, it would stand to reason that if Miriam is successful in the same attempt, the result will be the same and she too will be drawn to a mortal in peril. Whether or not the bond is the same remains to be seen, but your sister's fall from grace is not our priority," said the Apothecary.

"What are you saying?" asked Buck, lowering his hands.

"We need to leave," said Annaliese.

"Leave?" said Jack. "How? Buck just said the only way to do that is to die."

"That is only to fall, Master Jack," said the Chameleon.

"But Annaliese said the Scars are closed and there is no way to get to Charles Reese in time to summon him," said Miriam.

"Charlie?" Buck looked back at his sister. It took him a moment to remember the words, but he heard the familiar voice of Father Van Lewen as he spoke the clause of his charge. *No matter where you are, whether here in the land to which you call Eden, or among the lands from whence you came—if Charlie is to ever call on you by name, the name which he gave you . . . you are to be at his side.* Considering their parting, Buck did not foresee Charlie summoning him in time to rescue them from their current plight. He had wounded his heart too deeply to receive a pardon so willingly.

"While all that is true," said Annaliese, her voice capturing his attention, "there is another way."

Huisæng

Annaliese managed to catch everyone off guard, turning first toward the Apothecary and, using only two fingers, striking him in the temple. The eldest Euxian fell dead away onto the floor as she spun and reached down to the Chameleon. With two small fingers she tapped the feline on the neck and froze in her attack pose as the cat flopped onto its side. She hoped her sleeping technique would keep both her targets incapacitated, at least until she was able to see them all to safer quarters. She collected herself, looking back up at the three bewildered faces staring at her.

"Annaliese, what have you done?" asked Buck.

"I have guaranteed us some secrecy to make our escape," she said, motioning toward the tea kitchen.

"Wait," shouted Miriam.

Annaliese sighed. She had no time to baby them, not with the Coymorphs coming. She turned back into the healing room and stepped inside. "We have no luxury for this nonsense. Now you will either come with me, or we will all be bait for the Coymorphs."

"Coymorphs?" said Jack, finally getting to his feet. "Buck said the watchdogs don't patrol the Equadria."

"True, but the Creators have not attacked Euxinus since their collective exiles. That little stunt they pulled by blowing up the Hollow is tantamount to a declaration of war—not to mention it has put the Fates in a state of paranoia, and they are taking every precaution, even as far as sending their mutts to guard the main artery to the palace. The Chameleon can corroborate this news, as it was the spy who reported it, but as you can see our council members are indisposed at the moment. And I assure you they are not dead, merely sleeping."

"Well, ye don't need telling me twice," said Jack. He stripped off his robe and dressed himself with the fresh clothes piled on the nightstand, throwing a blue, long-sleeved shirt over his head and pulling up a pair of black trousers. He sat back on the mattress to fasten his feet with shoes and laced them sloppily, his fingers trembling, then he grabbed his pouch, secured his silver cross inside it with his turnip lantern, and tied it to his side belt loop.

The Eden Wanderer was by Annaliese's side without so much as an objection, and she was fairly certain it had something to do with his previous encounter with the Euxian watchdogs and the fact that he refused to have a repeat visit to the Reformatory—or, worse, a full encounter with the Fates. It was her cousins she found herself concerned with, for they had not moved. Miriam still stared in horror at the silenced bodies of the Apothecary and the Chameleon, and Buck—well, he had his gaze fixed on her, his expression unreadable.

"Cousin," was the only word Buck was able to speak as blood-curdling screams shook the coffin.

Annaliese pressed the heels of her palms over her ears and made her way into the tea kitchen. She looked out the front window as the chorus of Coymorphs blasted another call. She counted six in the Euxian Square, each one posted outside the front door of each coffin.

"*Annaliese*," chirped Zarna—but it was not her ears that caught the sound of her mate's call. The Animawalker's voice rang in her head, such was the bond that they shared.

"*What?*" thought Annaliese.

"*Do not be a hero,*" Zarna scolded, her antenna twitching. "*You cannot take on six Coymorphs at once. We cannot afford capture. Not now, not after what you have done. The Fates could forgive the witchcraft of the Eden Wanderer, but not blatant attacks on the council.*"

"*Then what do you propose we do?*" thought Annaliese, shifting her stance to determine if there were more Coymorphs outside the square, but she could not get a good enough angle.

"*We need a distraction.*"

Annaliese pulled away from the window as another cry rang out from the chorus of Coymorphs, pressing her hands against her ears. She meant to return to the healing room, but Jack, Buck, and Miriam were already standing in the tea kitchen, their expressions hinting at a tinge of uncertainty. It was then, looking at the three, that Annaliese realized Zarna's meaning.

"*Buck will not hear of it,*" she thought. "*He just got Miriam back, he will not send her out as a sacrifice.*"

"*Then we will have to let her be the one to make the choice. For her to make that sacrifice for him. It is the only way we survive and she gains the means to escape. The torture alone will send her to her end.*"

"*Zarna, you should not think of such dark things,*" thought Annaliese, lowering her arms once more.

"*I try not to, love, but the moment calls for dark if we are to remain in the light.*"

"Annaliese, what is going on?" asked Buck.

Her ears registered his voice, although it seemed slightly far away due to the lingering ring in her ears. "The Coymorphs are already here," she said.

Miriam and Buck both moved toward the far window near the front door, their eyes growing wider as they stared.

"How many?" asked Jack, keeping his distance.

"Six for sure, maybe more," said Buck, his voice despondent. He lowered his head, a flash of hopelessness creeping across his face. He signed before looking at Annaliese. "We are trapped."

"At the moment," said Annaliese. "Where we must go is out across the square."

"And despite what you might be thinking," interjected Zarna, "Annaliese cannot take on six watchdogs alone."

"What about ye?" asked Jack.

Annaliese glared at him.

"What? From what I heard, Animawalkers are able to transform into mortals."

"Yes, Jack, but you have to remember that in mortal form Zarna will become vulnerable," said Buck, moving back into the center of the room. "Euxinus is not kind to the Children of Sea."

"Then what are we supposed to do? Neither of us have weapons, nor am I about to allow myself to be turned into a ragdoll again."

"We could—" started Buck.

"I could distract them," said Miriam, her voice clear and unwavering.

"Absolutely not," declared her brother.

It was as Zarna had predicted, although she had thought it would take a little more manipulating on her part to get Miriam to have such a revelation; that was her mistake in underestimating her cousin. Buck, on the other hand, acted as she had known he would. Miriam tried to protest, citing all the reasons it had to be her—she even pointed out that Annaliese had yet to mention the location of their escape. At this, Annaliese flushed, her black skin sparkling with fluorescent freckles. It had not been her intention to keep their escape route a secret, but with Miriam present, her instincts must have known before she did to withhold the information from her cousin.

"Ye know, she's right," added Jack, a hint of suspicion in his tone. "Ye still haven't said where we're going."

"And I will not," said Annaliese. "Not if Miriam is planning to give herself away. We cannot afford our route to be compromised."

"Well, you can say it, because Miriam's coming with us," said Buck as his sister reached for his face. "No," he refused her advance. "You are not going to . . ."

Miriam fought her way through her brother's defense and took hold of his warm golden warm cheeks. "Let me do this," she said. "I can give you enough time to get away, to be safe." Pressing her forehead against her brother's brow and lowering her hands to his shoulders, Miriam taking care not to cause him pain, she trailed her fingers down his arm until they found security in his hands.

Buck tried to respond to the touch by gripping firmly.

"Brother, please, do not make this harder for me," said Miriam.

"Buck, you have to let her go," said Annaliese. She acted as though to take Buck on with force, but the Eden Wanderer surprisingly stepped in her path. It was hard to decipher his motive, but she seemed to get the sense he was allowing them the opportunity to say their goodbyes.

Buck closed his eyes, a tear falling down his cheek and landing on their jointed hands. Annaliese's stomach twisted as she read his expression, every thought and emotion visible on his face. He wanted to spare his sister from this even though he knew what her sacrifice meant, that it would be enough to break her and allow her the means to escape. The tears multiplied as his breath hitched.

"I understand," he conceded as he nestled against her forehead.

A sob caught in Miriam's throat, her body beginning to tremble. A few tears rolled down her opal face. "I am scared," she admitted, her streak of confidence faltering the longer she stayed.

"I know," said Buck, bringing their hands up to his lips and kissing hers. "Just remember, in the end, the pain will pass when you will it to."

Miriam closed her eyes and breathed in deeply.

Annaliese watched her cousins, enraptured by their devotion for each other. It was the same commitment she shared with Zarna, except in her case, it was a feeling between lovers, not siblings. Buck pulled back, sliding his hands away from his sister's fingers. Annaliese watched as the grace in Miriam flickered, a light that once shone so brightly fading with every thought of defiance. She admired her cousin, more than she would admit in words, and she was in awe at how sure she was in accepting her fate. Miriam gazed at her brother, memorizing every line of his face. She leaned in and kissed his cheek as he closed his eyes, neither one knowing if they would ever meet again. Miriam withdrew and walked to the door, doing her best to hold back sobs.

"Wait." His voice rang with desperation as he reached for her arm. "Miriam, if I could take your place . . ."

"Shh," Miriam pressed her fingers to his lips, stopping him from senseless rambling. "Rest easy, dearest brother—you have already once taken my place, the place of us all. I understand that now, as hard as it may seem. I know what you did was right, though I cannot be sure why."

"But—" insisted Buck.

"Tell me, brother, what can I do to put you at ease?"

"Absolve me," Buck replied. "You know my secret; you know what I have done. More importantly, what my actions have done to you."

Miriam flicked her head in shock.

"Buck, you know that is not in her power to give," scolded Annaliese, the plea shaking her from her reverie. "No Breedling can grant absolution."

Buck lowered his gaze.

"But there is something I can do," said Miriam, cheer in her voice. "A promise I can make to you, the one that I care most for above all others. When I finally break my chains, and meet my special mortal, I will go out into Eden and find the one who you call master, the one who can absolve you. All you have to do is speak his name."

"Charlie," said Buck, gulping back a sob. "His name is Charles Reese."

"Then I give you my word, I will find your Charles Reese and ask that he summon you back, as it is the only way for you, your charge, and our cousin to leave this place. I will speak of the deeds you have done here so that he may know the character of his servant. I make this my first promise to you." Miriam leaned in and kissed him on the forehead. "Now," she said, "do not watch me leave. Stay here away from the windows." She lifted her gaze and addressed the Eden Wanderer. "Take care of him," she said.

Jack merely gave a baffled nod in reply.

"Well, then, till next we meet," she said. "Cousin."

"Journey well," said Annaliese, keeping her distance so as to maintain a strong front, but Zarna was already comforting her through their link.

Miriam walked out of the coffin, closing the door behind her, and Annaliese moved instantly to the window to keep watch for an open path. Out of the corner of her eye, she saw the Eden Wanderer place a hand on Buck's shoulder in what appeared to be comfort, their connection stronger now than the first time she had met them. She watched Miriam as she did well to keep close to the coffin, skirting behind the closest Coymorph, but she only made it past the tea kitchen window before the watchdogs cried and took up chase.

Buck collapsed to his knees. The Eden Wanderer took hold of him in an awkward embrace, but after her cousin began to sob, Jack seemed equipped with reassurance.

Annaliese observed closely as four of the watchdogs darted to block Miriam's escape toward the palace, but she outmaneuvered them by diving through their legs and took off in a fevered run. The four Coymorphs trailed in pursuit, leaving one watchdog outside the front door and the other across the square in front of the Tales Teller's coffin.

"*You may have to use brute force, my love,*" said Zarna, fluttering her wings and perching herself in her hair.

"I know," said Annaliese aloud.

"Know what?" asked Jack.

Annaliese pushed off the windowsill and moved to the middle of the room.

"Time to move," she said.

"Move?" said Jack. "Move where? We can't leave now. Buck's a wreck; he'll give us away fer sure."

Annaliese crouched in order to engage her cousin face-to-face.

Buck lifted his head to look at her, unable to hide the utter defeat in his eyes. "Did I do the right thing?"

"You did what was necessary," said Annaliese, doing her best to be absolute with her words.

"But my own sister," stammered Buck. "How could I knowingly send her to her death?"

"You have not the luxury to second-guess yourself, cousin, and you know better than any of us that you sent her not to her death but to her rebirth. So now you must get up. There is no time to mourn—we must move now or risk the chance of wasting Miriam's sacrifice." She knew it was harsh, but it was the only thing strong enough to bring him to his senses.

Buck did not react with hysterics but, rather, stopped his tears and collected himself enough to get to his feet.

"What do you want us to do?" he asked, his eyes and cheeks swollen.

"Give me a twenty count and then run across the square to the Tales Teller's coffin," she instructed, drawing her blade from its sheath nestled between her shoulder blades.

"What? Why?" protested Jack. "Won't that trap us inside? I thought we wanted to get out of here."

"And we will, but first you need to do as I say."

"On your mark, then," said Buck, his face stern.

"Bloody Hell, why not?" sighed Jack with a roll of his eyes and readied himself beside Buck at the door.

Annaliese did not bother to close the door behind her and sprang from the ground, using the Coymorph's fur to assist her in her climb before slicing the watchdog's throat. It was blood she did not wish to shed, the obedient beasts merely a product of their creation—they were instinctually superior but also innocent. She felt the ache in her chest as the creature fell to the ground. She jumped off its back, landing on her feet as the creature's head hit the stone. The thud alerted the other Coymorph across the way, and Annaliese led it around the fountain, drawing it away from the Tales Teller's coffin.

She leapt onto the outer ring of the fountain, dark water sitting in the pool basin, as she ran around the circle. It forced the watchdog into an unwanted maneuver, unable to keep its stride small enough to make the sharp turn. Once she achieved her slingshot tactic, instead of killing another Coymorph, Annaliese sprinted toward the Tales Teller's coffin. She readied to kick in the door, but Jack had it open enough for her to sneak in, just as the watchdog sped past behind her.

Jack slammed the door with panting breaths and rolled onto his back, leaning against the door.

Annaliese moved directly into the study and walked behind the desk, not wasting a single breath as her hands searched for the book she needed. The Tales Teller had told her where to find it in case the moment arose, but with everything that had happened, the historian's materials were not in well-kept order.

"Annaliese, what are you looking for?" asked Buck.

"The Seventh," she said, pushing a pile of books to the floor to spread them out. "Help me look."

"The seventh what?" asked Buck, turning to the double bookshelves against the wall.

"Buck, are you dense?" asked Annaliese, lifting her head and ceasing her search. "The Keeper."

"I thought the Keeper was dead," said Jack, moving away from the door. "The Tales Teller told us Hades murdered her during the War of Wind and Flame."

"Your memory serves you well, Eden Wanderer," said Annaliese, "but that is only the end of her story."

"But she was not just the Keeper of Death," said Buck. "She . . ." He paused as though there were a block on his thoughts. "Huh, I could have sworn there was something else."

"Wait," said Jack. "If she was the Keeper of Death, who takes care of all the amid souls?"

"They go to the First," said Zarna, reappearing on Annaliese's shoulder.

"The First?" said Buck, his voice questioning the familiarity of the word.

"Who's the First?" asked Jack.

"Of that, I do not know," said Annaliese. "I have only heard of the creature in passing."

"Ye mean spying," said Jack.

"If you want to be blatant about it," said Zarna. "Then, yes, I spied on the Tales Teller to get this knowledge, but I never did learn the creature's identity, only where it resides."

CATACOMBS

Buck wracked his brain as Annaliese and Jack rummaged through the shelves and stacks of materials. He knew the tale of the Keeper—well, he thought he knew the tale. He tried to remember any of the details, but each time he got close to the knowledge in his head, it seemed to evaporate. It was odd, like someone had erased his memories. He scrunched his brow, fighting against his own mind, but the harder he tried, the worse it got.

"The Seventh," he said under his breath.

"Buck, ye all right?" asked Jack as he pulled a book loose from the shelf.

"The Keeper was the seventh member of the council," he said aloud. "She was the Keeper of Death, created by the Fates with the sole purpose to dispose of the slain."

"But she didn't," said Jack. "We saw the mass grave in the cavern."

"Yes, you are right." Buck lifted his head. "Annaliese, what is so important about the Keeper?"

"This," his cousin replied, as a smile broke across her face. She lifted a tablet out from underneath a pile of scrolls, then turned to the back corner and stuck it into the wall.

The loud *pop* followed, she pulled on the back shelf, opening a secret door.

"Bloody brilliant," said Jack, enamored by the trick. "Where does it lead?"

"After you," said Annaliese, allowing Jack to step through the passageway. "Your turn, Buck."

Buck made his way across the study, not bothering to avoid stepping on any of the scrolls littered on the floor. He did not hesitate to follow at his cousin's request, but he felt wary about what lay beyond the door. There was a tug from his subconscious, giving him a sense of déjà vu; the dark space seemed familiar as he passed through, Annaliese resetting the bookshelf behind them. The passage was brief opening on the other side into a dimly lit parlor.

There was only one candle set in the hanging dark crystal chandelier, the flame barely alive. Its glow only managed to dazzle part of the ceiling, spotlighting the center of the room; Buck noticed Jack had already begun to reach for his lighter. Once the Trickster brought his flame to life, it magnified the light in the room. They both let out surprised gasps as their eyes gazed upon hundreds of orange hibiscus flowers strewn about the empty room. There was something peaceful yet somber about the arrangement.

Buck felt a sudden chill creep across his neck and had a sinking ache in his chest.

"Whose tomb is this?" asked Jack.

"Tomb?" said Buck. He looked at Jack sideways, his spoken question making sense the more he thought about it. "We are in the Keeper's Coffin," he said, looking back at Annaliese. "But why here? How do we make our escape from here?"

"We are standing on it," said Annaliese.

Buck glanced down, and through the dance of shadow and light, he saw the outline of the trapdoor—similar to the one in the

Tortoise Shell. Jack cast his lighter overhead, revealing the image of a serpent apparently etched into the handle.

"Annaliese, how is this possible?" asked Buck. His thoughts were in a mass panic, trying to piece together anything he could remember about this particular symbol.

"What?" asked Jack.

"The Catacombs are real," said Annaliese as she crouched down and took the handle. "Before the Collapse of the Elements, the Dowel of Sea, said to be the water deity's first creation, dug tunnels underneath the bed of its creator's vast sea. The intent was to provide Sea and his siblings with a place to hide if at any point the occasion should arise." She paused to pull the trapdoor open, but it would not budge. Annaliese asked Zarna to continue while she tried accessing their escape route.

"As you know, when the Fates stripped Genesis Peak of Earth's beauty and tossed her into the sea, the Golden Faun emerged. She was not, however, an excellent swimmer and could barely remain afloat. Frightened she might die, the Golden Faun called out to her brother for help. She drifted until the Fates hurled the last bit of her body into the water, and then she began to drown. When Sea finally reached the naked mountain, he dove into his depths and found his sister resting on his bed, half-dead and unable to breathe. The Animawalkers believe, although our Father never spoke of it, that in his desperation, he pressed his lips to his dying sister and breathed into her. This, however required a great deal of strength, and, unable to return her to the surface, Sea stole her away to the entrance of the Catacombs and ordered his Dowel to take her to the end."

"Wait," said Buck, his mind spinning. "Then if Sea knew where Earth was, why did he not go back for her before he left? If the Golden Faun has been trapped in the Catacombs all this time and you knew of it, why did you not rescue her—how could she be lost if you knew where she was?"

"Remember, Buck," replied Annaliese, lifting her head, "the Fates had already destroyed Sea's physical form, no doubt diminishing his strength. It is not even known how he managed to escape Euxinus."

"Maybe he died, um—like Buck, I mean," said Jack.

The comment should have made him upset, but Buck found the sound logic in Jack's observation. For if Sea had actually taken his own life, then it was possible he had emerged in Eden as the Black Tortoise in a similar manner. Maybe that was even one of the reasons he had been able to perform the task himself—the Black Tortoise had created the way out.

"An astute theory, Master Jack," said Zarna.

"I'm known for a brilliant idea every now and again," Jack said, laughing. "But that doesn't answer Buck's question. If ye knew the Golden Faun was down there this whole time, then why the bloody hell didn't ye just go and get her?"

"Because," said Annaliese, pitching the handle aside in frustration, "we have never been able to get the blasted thing open."

Jack lowered his arm in response, the light honing in on the door.

They fell quiet after that as Buck tried once again to recall anything that might help them, but a mournful cry broke through his thoughts. It was unlike anything he had ever heard come out of the Euxian watchdogs. Buck watched Annaliese tiptoe toward the cracked, blackened window to peer outside.

"How does it look?" asked Jack.

"By the devastation of the Fates," swore Annaliese, moving away from the window. "The Retrievers are in the square."

"That does not leave us with much time," said Buck, fixing his eyes on the latch. "Tell me, cousin," he began, fishing for the right words. "If this is all true and the Golden Faun has been hiding deep in the catacombs, how did she orchestrate her escape?" He lifted his gaze to meet a large smile on Annaliese's face.

"Finally, the right question," she said. "The First."

"The First what?" asked Buck.

"The First Keeper of Souls," said Annaliese.

"The Seventh," gasped Buck, the dam in his brain finally letting loose. "The Keeper. The promise."

"Buck, what are ye on about?" asked Jack.

"That is why you cannot open it," said Buck, his voice spiking with a hint of giddiness.

"Buck, keep your voice down," snapped Annaliese.

"The Apothecary, he told me about the Keeper," he rambled, the thoughts coming to him in no particular order. "He said the Coffins of Seven are a true reflection of the Original Seven—three Fates and four Elements. He said that when she was captured, the Keeper told Hades he would never control Eden, not really. She promised that one day a creature would wander Eden, unclaimable by the forces of Wind and Flame, and with the coming of this creature, Earth and Sea would take their mantles as rulers of the realm."

"Wait, are ye telling me I was prophesized?" said Jack, raising his voice. "Why didn't ye tell me this before? Sure, I probably wouldn't have believed ye, but had ye explained it that way, all this could have made more sense instead of making me piece it all together."

"But that is the thing—I could not tell you, because I forgot," said Buck. "The Apothecary made me forget everything about our conversation before I left on my charge to find you and the Lost

Creators. The thought has been nagging at me since we passed through the Scar. But now it makes sense. You are the only one who can open the door, Jack."

"How do you figure that?" asked Annaliese.

"It's fairly simple, love," teased Jack as he reached into his pouch. "As the Eden Wanderer, I represent the return of Earth and Sea." He paused to assemble his lantern. "It's like Buck said—he was meant to leave Iona, so that he could find me and together we could save her. He has led me this far, so there is no reason that a door created by the Black Tortoise should be able to keep me out."

"Your bold confidence is astounding," said Zarna, her tone incredibly sarcastic.

Jack let out a throaty laugh as a stronger Coymorph blast trumpeted just outside the Tales Teller's coffin. "Here," he said, shoving the lantern into Buck's hands. "Hold this."

The Trickster reached for the serpent handle and gripped it with his hands. He took a deep breath before pulling and sprang the trap with unexpected ease; this caused him to lose his balance, but he secured his stance with the help of the vertical door.

As Buck held the lantern over the entrance, the sight of a slanted chute coming into focus.

"All right, down ye go," said Jack.

Annaliese crouched down first, and without so much as an acknowledgment, she disappeared from sight.

Buck insisted Jack go next, handing back the lantern, asking for his lighter. He held the trap open for him as he took the plunge and vanished into the darkness below. Rounding the door, Buck flicked his wrist to spark the flame to life. He looked out at the tomb one last time, his memory recalling the image of his mentor staring out the window of his tea kitchen, his expression set with a sense of longing. He had not known it then, but looking at the dazzling decoration of orange he understood. The Apothecary had loved the Keeper. He felt a pang of sadness for the eldest Euxian and hoped when they met again he could give his condolences properly.

Buck extinguished the light with another flick of his wrist. He took a deep breath as darkness consumed the coffin once again. He lowered himself into the mouth of the chute and, without hesitation, he slid into the unknown beneath him, the trapdoor slamming shut overhead.

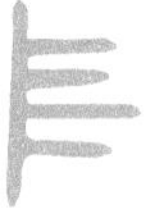

From the Library of the Tales Teller

The Seventh

The Apothecary finished his preparations for a fresh brew of tea. As he poured the mixture into two beakers, the ancient Euxian's frail fingers shook a little, although not from age. It was the first time, in most recent memory, that he was nervous, a mortal feeling he only experienced when the Fates' magic was working against his autonomy. He stirred the warm water until the ingredients dissolved and with a steady hand moved away from the iron stove and gave Bartholomew one of the beakers. He pulled up his stool and sat opposite the Breedling, laying his hands amongst the bowls scattered about on the counter. His uneasiness was magnified as his pupil stared absentmindedly at him.

They sat that way for an ungodly span of time, as though frozen, until Bartholomew spoke.

"Master Apothecary, tell me how the Seventh died," said Bartholomew, reaching for his beaker of tea.

The Apothecary curled his fingers and wrinkled his brow. He did not want to answer, knowing well that the death of the Seventh was not a story meant to be shared, rather to be kept as a secret. It was not the first time the Breedling had broached the question, having inquired several times about the deceased council member after learning of the ill-fated creature in the Tales Teller's library. Often, changing the subject was easy, while at other times, he gave his star pupil random pieces of the tale. All the information was superficial and part fabrication, but he did confirm the Seventh's death occurred during the War of Wind and Flame, killed by an unknown assailant—the latter of which was not true.

Bartholomew continued to wait patiently and took a sip of his tea.

The Apothecary felt the words build in his throat, unable to keep them down. He sensed the Fates' decree cutting into him, pulling tightly on his long leash. He kept his gray eyes fixed on the counter, poised to hide the loss bleeding into them, for such emotion would only confuse the Breedling.

"As you wish," spoke the Apothecary. His deep voice purred in his throat. "I will tell you of the Seventh."

Bartholomew's face beamed with excitement, unaware of how insensitive it made him look.

"But I will tell you on one condition," added the Apothecary.

Bartholomew's expression softened into a frown.

"You must promise me you will not share this with anyone. Not your sister, members of your kin, or any other Euxian creature, not even the Fates. When I am done telling you of the Seventh, you will forget I ever said it and not ask me of it again."

Bartholomew nodded. "Yes, my Eldest. I swear I shall not ask this of you again, nor shall I ever admit to knowing it."

The Apothecary raised his beaker, and Bartholomew did the same. They clashed them together and took a sip, sealing their promise.

"As I have already told you once before, the Coffins of Seven were created by the Fates in response to the war between Wind

and Flame. Myself, along with the Tales Teller, the Retrievers, the Chameleon, and the Herald, were charged with the command of their army. As the war persisted, many of the Fates' warriors began to defect, convinced by Wind or Flame to abandon their masters. The Retrievers were charged with the capture of these renegades to hand them over to the Fates. The death toll was catastrophic, and soon the Fates realized they needed a caretaker for their dead. And so created their seventh, the Keeper."

The Apothecary paused to take another sip of his tea. The bountiful flavors of rosemary, lemon, and honey could not soothe his uneasiness. He bit the inside of his lower lip, determined to say no more, for he could not yet trust his young friend with such knowledge. Not while he still called the Fates his masters.

"The Keeper," whispered Bartholomew, as though committing the fallen creature's name to memory despite his promise.

"Yes, Bartholomew, the Keeper," continued the Apothecary, unsettled. "The Fates blessed her with the ability to care for and give last rites to the slain. She was uncharacteristically gentle for an Euxian. She was the best of us, the most neutral, even more so than the Fates. Her words made one listen, even those creatures of limited feeling or will. Across the battlefields of Eden, she gathered the dead, both from our world and from the armies of Wind and Flame. She took them into herself, removing them from the world and moving them onto the next, if there is a next for creatures such as us."

Removing himself from his stool, the Apothecary walked across the tea kitchen. He stood near the far window gazing out into the square, staring at the vacant, two-story structure beyond the fountain, a ghostly memorial—a true coffin.

Bartholomew swiveled to continue their conversation. "Please, Master Apothecary, tell me what happened."

The Apothecary hesitated, but again his lips would not listen. "The Keeper was captured by a band of demons and taken before the Scarlet Phoenix."

"How?" Bartholomew asked, stunned. "Certainly, her detail would not let her . . ." He gasped.

The Apothecary sighed as he rolled his hunched shoulders and clasped his hands behind his back. "Your instincts are true, Bartholomew—there was no guard to keep her safe. And even if she had had one, it is hard to say if it would have made a difference."

"But what could the Scarlet Phoenix want with the caretaker of death? Surely, the Master of Hell did not think she would betray her masters."

The Apothecary smiled and turned toward Bartholomew. He had taught the Breedling well and hoped that soon his inquisitiveness would bring him to question the very core of his being one day.

"Flame sought to return to Euxinus and reclaim his home, but in order to gain any foothold he would have to break the power of seven governing the realm. The Keeper was the most venerable of our council, but what the Master of Hell had not anticipated was the strength of her resolve," said the Apothecary.

"Seven," said Bartholomew, dropping his gaze to the floor, lost in a moment of thought before reengaging his mentor.

"Yes, Bartholomew," said the Apothecary. "The Coffins of Seven are a true reflection of the Original Seven—three Fates and four Elements." The Apothecary turned away from the Breedling to look out the window once more and released a longing breath. "I do not know what the Scarlet Phoenix tried to offer her or how many threats he made, but what I do know is she remained loyal to the end."

"How do you know?" asked Bartholomew.

"The Chameleon managed to infiltrate the Scarlet Phoenix's higher ranks. Not the Octet, mind you, but high enough. Upon the spy's return, the Chameleon reported the Keeper had held her tongue as Flame burned her repeatedly, each time her voice fading until it was raw and nothing more than a whisper. In her final moments, she laughed hauntingly at the Master of Hell and spoke a warning."

Bartholomew choked on his tea, caught off guard by the news. In all his studies he had not once come across any mention of an Euxian possessing a divine tongue, words spoken in promise. But then, the Keeper was a member of the council, and still a complete mystery to him. He set his beaker on the counter and crossed the room, taking his place at his mentor's side. He looked out the window at the dark coffin across the square, and without an ounce of sympathy in his voice asked the question.

"What did the Keeper promise?"

"'You may do away with me, but know this, Spirit of Flame,' she said. 'From my ashes, another will take my place, touched by your fire and innocent like me. The Coffins of Seven will be whole again, of this I swear. Euxinus shall never be yours again.'"

"But, Master Apothecary, the Fates have never created another caretaker," said Bartholomew. "Her coffin remains empty."

"As it always shall," affirmed the Apothecary somberly. He felt his eyes glisten and blinked away the threat of tears.

"So she died then?"

"Yes, but not before she made one final proclamation," said the Apothecary, a hint of pride in his voice. "She told Hades that though he had control over Eden, it would not last forever. In her promise, she spoke of a creature that would one day wander Eden, unclaimable by the forces of Wind and Flame—with the

coming of this creature, Earth and Sea would take their yokes as rulers of the realm."

"The Eden Wanderer," breathed Bartholomew.

The Apothecary hardened his expression and lowered his chin. "Master Breedling, where did you hear that?"

Bartholomew looked up, his expression unsure, as though fighting the urge to answer. "The Fates told me," he professed. "I have been charged to find this creature if it indeed exists, as well as the whereabouts of the Lost Creators."

The Apothecary felt his face warm, though it did not blush.

"My Eldest," said Bartholomew, ill-equipped to understand his mentor's fright.

"When are you to leave?"

"As the Fates command, now will suffice," answered Bartholomew with a smile. "You have told me all I need, as they knew you would."

The Apothecary swallowed back a flash of anger. No wonder he was all out of sorts, his nerves frazzled. Naturally, the magic binding the Breedling to his charge would force him to speak of the Seventh. The Apothecary curled his fingers into his palms. How he detested the Fates and their hold over him. He took stock of their conversation and after a moment realized he had managed to tell Bartholomew only what the Breedling needed in order to carry on with his mission.

"Then safe journey to you, Master Breedling," said the Apothecary and bowed his head, his expression somewhat relieved.

Bartholomew bowed low in return and responded, "Till next we meet, my Eldest."

The Apothecary watched the Breedling as he rounded the fountain in the quiet square and walked along the Equadria toward the palace.

"The moment has arrived, my sweet," he whispered, speaking out toward the dark coffin. "As we promised."

The Apothecary sighed, still feeling guilty for what had happened to her. She was the one who had said the words, the one who gave her last breath to bind weight to the promise, but the words she had spoken were his, not hers. He had said them to comfort her and reassure her that there would be a place for them. He never meant for her to use them. Or to give her life to his cause, his master plan that he had begun all the way back then. She was the start, for her death set everything in motion.

The Apothecary's eyes glistened as he felt the lingering ghost of her presence in the tea kitchen, her soft voice whispering to him.

"With the coming of the Eden Wanderer, it shall herald the return of Earth and Sea, but centuries shall it be until second chance for Lovers meet. Eden's champions will be crowned, some masters, some warriors, some merely breadcrumbs, but each are equally measured and entrusted with the protection of the Eden Wanderer's journey, though unawares they may be. And in turn, ultimately, the fates of Tortoise and Faun."

Acknowledgments

It takes a fan base to raise an artist, and I am grateful to the ones I have. It's taken almost a decade to get to this point, so to those of you who were with me in the beginning and to those who have recently come on this journey with me, thank you. Your support is beyond measure, and you help me realize my dream more and more.

To my publishing team: Laura Zats; my magician Steve Meyer-Rassow; my Jiminy Cricket, Amanda Rutter; my proofreader, Graham Warnken; and the rest of the Wise Ink team. You continue to provide a path to help me find my literary way.

To the creators of The Great Pretend Ears: thank you for creating pink camo cat ears. Without them, my concentration would be a muddled wreck and I would never have been able to graduate from college.

To the Adventurous Year that was 2018, forever immortalized will you be on this page. The Comic Cons, the Concerts, the Cities visited, and all of the new friends/fam made.

Special shout out to my girl Tia and my Bangtan Sorority sisters: Donna, Trish, Jenau, Aidni, Inga, Kathie, Tina, Jess, Rachel, Jennifer.

All her life, Kimberlee knew writing was her passion and that words had power. Inspired by her love for American nostalgia/history and mythology, The Element Odysseys became her first published series with the release of *The Breedling and the City in the Garden* in September 2016. With two decades under her fingertips, Kimberlee continues to expand the series as well as creating unique, and fantastical new stories. When she is not in her writer's room, she's meeting readers at comic cons and book festivals. In her spare time, she enjoys cycling around the bluffs of her Southeastern MN home and catching up on South Korean pop culture.

www.ingramcontent.com/pod-product-compliance
Lightning Source LLC
Chambersburg PA
CBHW050238110726
47898CB00007B/2194